≈

THE LAKE

≈

≈

THE LAKE

≈

R. J. SUNDEAN

RJSUNDEAN.COM

CHAPTER 1

THE CATALYST

Alicia looks at herself in the mirror. She is still unhappy with how her dress fits over her hips and tugs each side down a little. *Better*, she thinks. But the little bump of her belly causes the material of her dress to stretch a small bit at the front.

She wonders if anyone will notice. *And if they do notice, will they think I'm just getting fat?*

She runs her hands over her little belly bump, smiling. Seventeen weeks. That's what the doctor told her when she went for her last checkup. She takes a deep breath and thinks about how the father will react tonight when she finally tells him he's going to be a daddy.

Butterflies flood through her at the thought of his possible reactions.

What if he rejects me? What if he wants nothing to do with me or the baby when he finds out?

She pushes these thoughts from her head. Her nerves are

bad enough right now, between trying to decide how she's going to be able to take care of a baby at eighteen years old and wondering if she's going to have the father by her side while she figures it all out. She looks back into the mirror at her reflection and takes a deep breath. Her shoulder-length brunette hair is done up in a waterfall braid with loose curls, and she's wearing just enough eyeliner and eye shadow to highlight her light-brown eyes.

It will all work out, she tells herself.

Her mother's voice cuts into her thoughts. "Alicia, are you ready yet? Nick should be here any minute."

Alicia tries to steady her nerves and nods at herself in the mirror. *Tonight is going to be one of the most important nights of your life, Alicia, so get yourself ready.*

"Yes, Mom, I'm ready. I'll be down in a second."

She takes one last glance at herself in the mirror, making sure her hair is in place and her now slightly larger than normal breasts are not too obvious. She still hasn't told her parents about the baby. She'll need the father with her when she breaks that news to them, because she knows they'll flip out and only tell her how she's ruined her life and her future by making stupid decisions.

Satisfied, she turns from the mirror, grabs her clutch from the dresser, and heads out of her room toward the stairs. She walks carefully on the carpet, as she's wearing heels just a bit higher than she's used to wearing. She can hear her parents downstairs, fussing over taking pictures and where the best spot in the house would be to take them. Reaching the stairs, she carefully takes the steps one at a time until she's finally at the bottom and standing in front of her overly excited parents.

This feels like some cheesy teen rom-com, she thinks.

"Honey, you look amazing. Red really is the perfect color for that dress," her mom gushes with a huge smile on her face.

"Thanks, Mom," she responds, desperately hoping that the doorbell will suddenly ring, announcing that Nick has arrived and giving her the chance to escape this emotional parental awkwardness. She already has enough of an emotional roller coaster ahead of her tonight.

Her mother interrupts her thoughts once again. "Oh, we need to take photos of you before he gets here!"

She nods, giving in to her mom's wishes, and lets herself be led to a spot in the living room in front of the fireplace. Her father, still smiling but oddly quiet, holds the camera and starts snapping photos. She follows the commands given to her.

"Turn this way, Alicia." "Look that way, could you?" "Smile more, Alicia." "What if you turned this direction?" "How about looking right at the camera for this one?" Her mother spews a constant stream of requests, each one requiring a head to be tilted this far or angled in this direction, or a shoulder to be turned this way. Just when Alicia almost has enough of the forced photo shoot, the doorbell thankfully rings.

Both her parents turn toward the sound, and she can see their smiles get even bigger. She hopes those smiles will still be there when she tells them they're going to be grandparents.

3

"Nick's here!" her mother exclaims, as though it's a surprise that her date is here.

She shakes her head and heads toward the door, opening it. On the other side stands her date, Nick, dressed nicely in a tuxedo. The two front buttons of his jacket strain against the size of his midsection, and his slightly heavyset face is flushed. She wonders how he'll take the news of the baby.

"Wow. Alicia. You look amazing," he stammers. She smiles at him. Nick has always been really nice to her and is one of her few friends she considers a best friend. He awkwardly extends a plastic container he was holding behind his back. "This is for you."

She reaches out and takes the container from him. A corsage, made of roses and sunflowers, is nestled inside. "It's beautiful. Thank you, Nick," she says. "Can you help me put it on?" She hands him back the container and extends her left arm.

She can hear the shutter clicks going off repeatedly behind her while Nick fumbles to open the plastic container. He finally gets the container open and for a moment almost drops both the container and the corsage to the ground. Alicia giggles a bit and jokes, "Will you hurry up already?" She sees a jolt of panic flash on Nick's face, and Alicia immediately regrets saying anything. *Why is he so nervous?* she wonders. "Nick, it's OK, I'm kidding," she says, hoping to calm him down a bit. He glances up at her, nods, and takes a deep breath. Corsage in hand at last, he sets the plastic container on the table next to the door and carefully guides the elastic band over her fingers and onto her wrist. He lets the band go and pulls his hands back, leaving the bright-red-and-yellow bouquet to rest on its new home for the remainder of the evening. She looks at the flowers now draped on her wrist and back at Nick, smiling brightly. "I love them," she says. Nick's nervous smile returns.

Her mother's voice interrupts the moment. "Photo time!"

Alicia groans inside and turns toward her mother with a look of exasperation. "We have to get going, so can we please make this quick?" Her mother barely registers the request and resumes her photo-taking journey in an effort to capture all the memories of her little girl's senior prom. Her father remains wordless, snapping away with the camera. She hopes he isn't playing it quiet just to build up to his fatherly speech about what can happen if you're not careful and what will happen to her date if she isn't home by curfew. She wonders how disappointed he'll be when he finds out his tough but concerned dad speech clearly didn't work. Alicia pushes the thought from her mind and forces herself back to the situation at hand. Nick, being a good sport, is letting her mother pose him like a store-window mannequin modeling the latest in men's clothing. "Nick, let's lower this arm just a bit. Oh no, that doesn't look right at all. Let's raise that arm back up a bit instead."

She smiles. Nick has always been such a good friend to her. She knows he cares about her. Cares about her in a way she'll never be able to reciprocate, because her heart will forever belong to the father of the little peanut currently growing inside her belly. The father who has also been Nick's best friend since as long as either of them can remember. She wonders if telling Nick about the baby will ruin Nick's friendship with him. She wonders if it will ruin her own friendship with Nick. She shakes the thoughts from her head. No, Nick has stuck by her side and his best friend's side, even after finding out that she was dating his best friend. Which was over two years ago. *No,* she reassures herself, *Nick is going to be happy and supportive just like he always has been.* Another thought races through her mind. *Will the soon-to-be daddy act the same way?*

"Alicia, let's go take some photos outside in the natural light."

She groans inside once again. "No, Mom, we need to get going or we're going to be late."

A momentary look of sadness crosses her mother's face, the ever-present smile faltering for just a second. "Fine. You two be safe and have fun."

That must be the cue her dad has been waiting for, because as soon as her mother finishes saying "fun," her dad clears his throat. "Nick, may I speak with you just a moment, son?" Alicia looks from her dad to Nick. Nick's face is now frozen in a state somewhere between a smile and panic. Alicia giggles a bit. Nick's best friend has heard this speech numerous times before. Nick nods and follows her dad into the nearby kitchen, and immediately her father's voice can be heard, steady and stern, covering what's expected of a gentleman and what time she'd better be home by. Alicia glances at her mom, who shares a quiet laugh with her. They both know this speech and both know very well that if Alicia is late, it's her own fault and not that of whom she's hanging out with.

"Dad, you do realize I am eighteen years old now, right?" Alicia yells toward the kitchen, hopefully reaching the ears of the two men still talking out of view.

Her dad's voice quickly counters, not missing a beat, "And you still live under my roof, young lady!"

She laughs again as both her father and Nick appear from the kitchen. Nick still looks terrified, while her dad's smile is ear to ear. *Mission accomplished, Dad*, she thinks, still smiling as she shakes her head. "Can we go now?" she asks.

So that her parents can't object or, even worse, start taking more photos, she reaches out and grabs Nick's hand, leading him toward the front door. Her father's voice follows them as they rush out the door. "Have her home by midnight, young man."

She shakes her head again. "Dad, I'm eighteen, not fifteen," she states as she steps outside. She releases Nick's hand once the front door is closed behind them. "Sorry, Nick, my dad has been using that speech for years. He really wouldn't do any of the stuff he says he will," she says, hoping to erase the panic from Nick's face. Nick nods, a clear wave of relief washing over him. He picks up his pace and passes her, rushing toward the passenger side of the door of his mother's truck, which he borrowed for tonight. By the time he gets to the truck and opens the door for her, his smile has returned. "So, safe to say your father won't hunt me down and remove my testicles with a rusty butter knife if you're not home in perfect condition and by curfew?" he asks.

She laughs. "No, not at all. And normally he says he'll use kitchen shears, so the rusty butter knife is a new addition to his dad speech," she says as she carefully gets into the passenger side of the truck, taking care not to leave her dress hanging out the door to get caught when he closes it. Nick shakes his head and pushes her door closed, quickly turning and walking around the front of the truck to the driver's side. As he opens the driver's door and gets in, he looks over at her and says, "I honestly thought he was going to take my balls off right there in the kitchen." She laughs harder now, knowing that Nick is actually being sincere and probably did think he was about to be neutered by her father.

Nick, still shaking his head, starts up the truck and begins to back out of the driveway. The school is only a few miles away, but they have plans to meet up and get something to eat before going to the dance.

The trip to the restaurant is quiet, with just the radio on, playing the latest hit from this week's top-ten list. Alicia smiles the entire way, thinking about Nick's reaction to what her father said as well as anticipating the evening. The drive is over almost as fast as it began, and soon Nick is turning off the main road and down the drive leading to the restaurant.

Ellie's is the only actual restaurant in Orchard Lake, the town where she lives, and is the only bar in town in the evenings. It's also where Alicia works on the weekends, and sometimes weekday evenings, as a waitress. *Nothing like having your prom dinner at your place of employment*, she thinks.

Alicia doesn't mind, though, because the best part of Ellie's is that it's owned and operated by Nick's mother, Karen Ellie. Mrs. Ellie has always been like a second mom to Alicia and will be thrilled when she finds out that Alicia is pregnant. She only hopes her own parents will be as thrilled as Mrs. Ellie.

Of course, Alicia and Nick could have opted for dinner in Shelton or Rockville, but it would've been a long drive there and back, and Mrs. Ellie insisted they have dinner in town at the restaurant. The parking lot is full, but Nick drives around the lot to the back, pulling the truck into a well-worn parking space reserved for employees. He turns off the ignition and looks out the front window at the lake. Alicia follows his gaze and looks over the lake. The setting sun reflects across the water, mixing shades of red and orange with the various blues and blacks that normally paint the lake. The surface is completely still, as though it were just one big piece of smooth glass from bank to bank. *The view really is pretty*, she's thinking when she feels a warm hand on top of her own, which are folded neatly in her lap. The unexpected contact startles her and a scream almost escapes her lips. She quickly glances down and sees Nick's right hand on top of hers. She glances over at him. He's looking even more panicked than before and appears like he's about to say something.

As soon as his mouth opens, another voice enters the truck, loud and forceful.

"Hey, you! Get your damn hands off her!"

Nick's mouth immediately shuts and he jerks his hand back

from hers. Alicia watches as a flash of anger distorts Nick's facial features and quickly disappears. Laughter erupts from outside the driver's side, and a very familiar face comes into view through the window.

Colin. Nick's best friend and the father of her little peanut. With his muscular frame covered in the same style tuxedo as Nick's, Colin runs his hands through his short black hair, smiling.

Alicia's own smile returns, her eyes lighting up at the sight of Colin's face, and she laughs. Nick shakes his head and turns to Colin, not missing a beat. "I think you got the wrong car, McFly."

Colin pulls the driver's side door open, gives Nick a big hug, and both guys begin laughing hard. Alicia shakes her head. *Leave it to these two to reenact a scene from* Back to the Future, she thinks. "You two are idiots, you know this, right?" she asks. Both guys look at her and laugh even harder.

"Took you two long enough to get here," Colin states and looks at Nick. "Did her dad give you the dad speech? Tell you he was going to remove your balls with shears?"

Nick nods. "He did, but he said he was going to use a rusty butter knife to remove them, so you better make sure she stays in the exact same condition as she is right now, because I kinda want to keep my balls."

All three erupt in animated laughter at this. Once the laughter starts to die down, Alicia raps the knuckles of her right hand on the passenger side window. "One of you gentlemen going to come open the door for a lady?"

Colin sticks his tongue out at her and jogs around the front of the truck to the passenger side, grabs the door handle, and opens the door. He bows deeply and waves his left hand with a broad flourish. "Forgive me, my lady, for I am but an uncouth man who was never taught any better," he quips, doing his best impression of a British accent.

She shakes her head and tries to match the accent. "You are forgiven for now, sir, but I expect better treatment from this point forward." She steps out of the truck, taking care with her heels on the gravel of the parking lot, and into Colin's open and waiting arms, allowing them to fully envelop her. "Hi, beautiful," he whispers into her ear. "You look absolutely amazing."

Alicia rests her chin on his shoulder, trying not to get any makeup on his black tuxedo jacket and not wanting him to let her go. She closes her eyes and breathes in, happy to have his arms around her.

The sound of the restaurant's back door opening interrupts her moment.

Karen Ellie's voice follows the sound, her full-bodied frame filling the doorway. "Oh my, don't you all look elegant! Colin, let that pretty young woman go and bring her in here so she can get some dinner. Nick, come give your momma a hand."

As Alicia pulls herself from Colin's embrace, Nick closes the driver's side door and heads for the back door of the restaurant. Colin takes her hand and nods toward the building. "C'mon, gorgeous, before Mrs. Ellie brings the food out here and forces it down our throats." Alicia laughs and nods in agreement, carefully making her way across the gravel lot to the back door. The last thing she needs tonight is a twisted ankle.

She steps through the door and into the back hallway as Colin leads the way toward the dining room. The sound of music playing from the jukebox in the dining area reaches her ears, intertwined with laughter and conversation and the clinking of silverware against plates. Mingling with this symphony of noise are the sounds from the kitchen, which is located to the right, just down the hallway she's currently standing in. From the kitchen she can hear a cacophony of sizzling and bubbling, pots and utensils banging into each other, and voices barking out various directions. Shelves filled with pans, large cans of food, and loaves of bread line the left side of the hallway.

She continues down the hallway behind Colin, the merriment from the dining room and the kitchen sounds continuing to grow louder as she approaches both. The bell from the pass-through rings, announcing an order ready to go out to a table. A few more steps and the hallway opens up on the right to reveal the large kitchen, very busy at the moment as the various cooks prepare all the diners' meals. Mrs. Ellie is in the center of it all, checking prepared plates and reading off new tickets that come in. She glances over at Alicia and winks, giving her a huge smile. Alicia smiles back and continues following Colin past a large dual sink on the left and finally through a doorway into the dining room.

The bar, modest in size, with about six bar stools and a full liquor cabinet display behind it, lines the right side of the dining area next to the kitchen pass-through. The dining room proper has five tables with four chairs each. On a normal evening, one or two tables max would be occupied. Tonight all the tables minus just one are completely filled and overflowing with well-dressed teenagers, all getting their fill of food before heading to the prom.

The one empty table in the restaurant is situated at the far front end of the dining room. In its center are three lit candles adorned by a circle of shiny red garland and tinsel. Three chairs are placed at even intervals around the table. Colin leads Alicia past the bar and toward the empty table, stopping along the way to greet and high-five classmates who are already seated and eating. Alicia hears her name and looks over at the other tables, seeing some of her own friends waving at her. She waves back with a big smile, happy to see that none of the other girls in the room is wearing the same kind of dress she is.

Colin breaks away from being a social butterfly and comes back to her, taking her by the hand and leading her the rest of the way to the empty table. He pulls out a chair for her and motions to it. "Your throne, my lady," he remarks, loud enough for her to hear over the music and the other voices in the dining room.

She flips a hand in the air as if to dismiss his presence and sits down, giggling at him. "Please fetch me my beverage, peasant," she states, causing Colin's grin to grow even larger.

"Yes, my lady, at once!" he replies, bowing once more.

Colin heads toward the kitchen to get her requested drink. Alicia shakes her head and laughs. She looks around the dining room for Nick, wondering where he disappeared to. Just as Colin reappears from the kitchen holding two filled glasses, Nick appears, walking down the stairs at the far back of the room next to the pass-through.

Above the restaurant, on the second floor, are a couple bedrooms, a bathroom, and a living room, where Mrs. Ellie and Nick live. Alicia knows Nick can't wait to move out on his own, but Mrs. Ellie isn't very happy about that idea.

Alicia watches as both guys maneuver through the crowded dining room and take their seats at the table. Colin sets one of the colas in front of Alicia and winks at her, setting the other drink in front of himself.

Nick looks around the table at the two drinks and looks at Colin. "Where's mine, dude?"

Colin points toward the kitchen. "Still in there. I'm her boyfriend, not yours."

Nick gives Colin the finger, smiling. "And she's my date tonight, not yours."

Alicia rolls her eyes at both of them.

Dinner is filled with laughter and jokes, and one by one the tables in the restaurant empty out as the guests finish their meals and head off for the main event of the evening. Alicia finishes the last sip of her soda at the same time Mrs. Ellie approaches their table with a big smile on her face. "Did you kids have a good time?"

"Yes, Mrs. Ellie, it was delicious as always," Alicia states.

"Aw, good. 'Bout time for you all to head off to the prom, isn't it? Now shoo, go have a good time," she says.

Three heads nod in unison, and Nick and Colin stand up from the table. Alicia follows their example and stands as well, turning toward the back door of the restaurant. Colin leads the way, taking her hand and pulling her along through the restaurant and out the door to the gravel parking lot. It's dark outside, as the sun set an hour ago, and stars fill the sky. As she reaches the passenger side of the truck with Colin, she hears Nick's mom yell out the door after them. "Nick, make sure you get home on time so you can help clean up the restaurant later."

Nick, walking toward the driver's side door, audibly groans and yells back, "Yes, Mom."

Colin leans in and gives her a quick kiss. "See you there, beautiful," he states as he helps her into the truck and closes the door. "Nick, drive safely, sir, unless you want me to go get a rusty butter knife!" Both guys erupt into laughter and Nick starts the truck, putting it in reverse to take them to their next destination.

The ride to the high school is uneventful. Nick is focused on the road, deep in thought about something, and the radio is turned down low. Alicia listens to the various groans and creaks the truck makes as it hits random bumps in the road. She looks over at Nick, feeling a bit of remorse for him. He's been under his mother's rule for as long as she's known him, and there's little he can do that isn't controlled by his mother.

She hopes that one day he can get away from it all and just live his own life as he wants to. It's also one of the reasons she decided to go to prom with him instead of Colin. She knew Mrs. Ellie would be more willing to let Nick go tonight if he had a date, since Nick has rarely dated at all since Alicia met him. Especially if the date was her. Plus, deep down, she knows she asked him for her own selfish reason. She figured that if Nick was her date, maybe he'd be less likely to freak out when he found out she was pregnant with Colin's baby. Maybe as her date, he'll feel obligated to help her with Colin's reaction when Colin finds out he's going to be a daddy. And maybe everyone will be completely fine with the news and she's panicking for no reason. Alicia sighs. *That's a lot of maybes*, she thinks. She continues running every possible scenario for tonight through her head—both good and bad—until she feels the truck come to a stop and the engine shuts off.

"And here we are!" Nick exclaims. He gets out of the truck, and soon her door opens. "Let's go have some fun," he adds. She nods, carefully getting out. She waits for Nick to close the door and lock the truck, and they both walk up and into the building together, waving and saying hi to friends as they go.

The entrance to the gym is covered in balloons, with a brightly colored streamer archway above welcoming the attendees into the large room. Tables dot the gym floor, candles in the center of each, and overhead disco balls cast little squares of multicolored light all over the floor and walls. Music from the speaker system echoes off the walls, mingling with all the voices of the partygoers. Alicia takes a deep breath, the scent of lavender filling her nose.

Colin appears by her side and gives her a quick kiss on her cheek. "Well hello there, sexy. You here alone?"

Alicia smiles. "No, I am here with this amazing guy right here," she responds as she points at Nick, who's standing to her left.

Nick laughs and turns toward the main room. "Let's find a table and sit down before Colin and I have to fight over the prettiest lady in the room."

Alicia laughs and follows Nick toward an empty table, Colin in tow. Nick finds a table near the front of the room, next to the stage, and takes his jacket off, draping it on the back of the chair. She pulls out her own chair and sits down, looking at the decor on the table. An etched glass holding a candle stands in the center of the table, surrounded by tinsel and glitter. The lavender scent Alicia initially noticed is from the candles making up the centerpieces of each table. She takes a deep breath of the pleasant smell, preparing herself for what's about to happen. Preparing herself for what she is about to tell Colin. Preparing herself for how both he and Nick may react to the news.

Colin's voice interrupts her thoughts. "Who wants a drink?"

Nick raises his left hand and nods. She looks over at Colin and nods as well. Colin steps away from the table and heads toward the far back wall where the punch bowl is.

The next song queues up and begins to play over the speaker

system. She recognizes the tune, "Truly Madly Deeply" by Savage Garden. *Fitting song*, she thinks.

She looks over at Nick, who's gazing around the room and taking in all the details. He must feel her watching him, because he stops surveying the room and stares at her. "You OK, Alicia? You look like you have something on your mind."

She nods and takes a deep breath. "Nick, promise me that no matter what happens tonight, you will be there for me?"

Nick keeps staring, the panicked look from earlier today quickly returning. "Alicia, I will be there for you for the rest of your life. I promise you that," he says, the tinge of questioning in his voice revealing he's clearly wondering why she just asked him that.

She nods at him and looks back toward Colin approaching the table, precariously balancing three plastic cups of punch between his hands. His eyes are focused on the cups, but had they instead been focused on her, he might have seen the panic on her face. The panic that's been building for weeks and is now about to erupt. The panic screaming for her to let the truth out about the baby.

Just as Colin reaches the table and sets down the cups, he loses his grip on the left cup and it begins to fall. Colin quickly reaches out and catches it, saving it from tipping over—but in that same movement his hand hits the glass enclosure holding the candle centerpiece and sends the candle toppling over, splashing hot wax across the table and onto Nick's tuxedo jacket still draped on the back of his chair.

"What the fuck, Colin?" Nick yells. "Are you fucking kidding me? My mom is going to kill me!"

The panic inside Alicia finally reaches a tipping point and erupts. The next words out of her mouth bring both Colin and Nick to a complete and silent standstill.

"I'm pregnant!"

CHAPTER 2

THE PRESENT/PAST

"**M**ommy! Look!"

The voice breaks through her reminiscing and brings her back to present day, where she's currently standing in front of multiple shelves filled with a variety of pasta. Her little girl, Penny, eight years old as of last week, is standing next to her, intently focused on reading the back of a box of shells.

"Look, Mommy, the box says you have to boil these to make them all denty," she says, "Why would you want all denty food? Yuck!"

Penny puts the box back on the shelf and continues down the aisle, picking up the occasional box and looking at it.

Alicia smiles at her little girl and looks down at the shopping list in her hand. Just a few more items and she can head to the checkout line and then back home to get dinner started.

"Stay close, Penny," she says as little Penny almost reaches the end of the aisle. Penny quickly acknowledges her voice and turns back toward her, slowly walking back to Alicia and the shopping cart, meandering from one side of the aisle to the other and still looking at the various brightly colored boxes adorning the shelves. Alicia grabs a couple boxes of the pasta in front of her and adds them to the items already in the cart.

"Are we done yet, Mommy?" says the inquisitive young lady, suddenly standing at her side.

"Almost, sweetie," Alicia says, trying to think of what else she might need for dinner tonight and for the pantry. Her mind draws a blank on her present task, still wanting to take her back to her prom night and how it changed everything. She looks over one more time at her little girl, now hopping from one tile to the next, and smiles. Penny and Colin are the best things to have ever happened to her, and she wouldn't change it for the world. "OK, Penny, let's go," she says.

Penny stops hopping, turns back toward Alicia, and runs to the cart. She stops at Alicia's side and looks up at her. "Can I push the cart?" she asks.

Alicia smiles and relinquishes the cart to her little girl. "Be careful and don't hit anyone, OK?" Penny nods and begins to push the cart toward the front of the store, looking all around her like a nervous new driver taking the car out for the very first time.

After a couple close calls with the end displays of a few aisles and one innocent bystander, Alicia and Penny finally make it to the checkout aisle, where Alicia takes over driving the shopping cart again. She stops the cart in the aisle and begins to unload the groceries onto the belt, smiling at the cashier waiting to scan the items. "Penny, do you want to help Mommy?" Alicia begins to say, but she stops midsentence when she sees Penny staring intently at the candy shelves right next to her. "Mommy! Look! M&M's!"

Alicia laughs and shakes her head. Penny does this same act every time they're at the store, as though the little lady had never seen candy before. Penny looks back at her mommy with her usual wide, pleading eyes. Alicia nods, and Penny quickly looks back at the bags of candy, grabs one as fast as she can, and tosses it into the cart, a grand smile taking over her little face. Alicia reaches into the cart and grabs the bag of candy and puts it on the conveyor belt. Penny's eyes follow the bag intently as it travels down the belt to the cashier, as though it might disappear on its journey to the shopping bags. "Will that be all, ma'am?" the cashier asks as the bagger puts the last of the bags into the shopping cart. Alicia nods, still smiling. The cashier rings up the total and waits patiently while Alicia digs through her purse and pulls out her wallet. She hands over enough cash to cover the total, and the cashier hands back the change with her receipt. Alicia tosses the change and receipt into her wallet and puts the wallet back into her purse, checking to make sure Penny is still by her side. Penny's eyes are focused intently on one of the bags in the cart. Alicia is pretty sure it's the bag with Penny's candy in it.

Alicia exchanges pleasantries with the cashier and bagger and begins to push the cart toward the exit and her car parked outside. Penny stays right by the side of the cart, taking turns between looking around at the other shoppers coming and going and keeping an eye on the bag in the cart holding the candy. As Alicia reaches the trunk of her car and unlocks it, a familiar voice booms across the parking lot.

"Shouldn't you be making Colin do the shopping on a Saturday, young lady?"

Alicia laughs and turns to her left, where Mrs. Ellie is standing a few cars down from her. "And look at that precious little lady next to you! Come here and give your Meemaw a big hug!"

At the sound of Karen's voice, Penny's attention switches from the cart to Mrs. Ellie, and she takes off toward her. "Watch for cars, Penny!" Alicia quickly states, although she knows Karen would never let anything bad happen to the little girl. As Karen's outstretched arms wrap around Penny, Alicia turns back to the task at hand and begins to unload the grocery bags into the trunk of her car. Karen, now carrying Penny, walks over to her and, using her one free hand, helps unload the rest of the bags.

"Why are you working on your day off, sweetheart?" Karen asks.

Alicia chuckles and shrugs. "My work is never done, Mrs. Ellie, you know that."

Karen Ellie nods. "That's the truth, isn't it, dear? Why isn't Colin here helping out?"

Alicia puts the last bag in the trunk and pauses a moment,

smiling. "He's at home getting tools together for work on Monday. He has a big construction job starting up in Shelton and wants to make sure he's prepared. Honestly, though, he's probably just sitting at home watching some terrible B horror movie on TV."

Karen laughs and shakes her head. "Sounds like Colin."

Penny's voice interrupts their conversation, returning the focus to what matters most to her. "Meemaw, would you get my candy from that bag?" the little lady states as she points at one of the bags in the back of the trunk.

Karen laughs. "Of course, dear, I'd be happy to help," she says as she reaches into the bag and deftly pulls out the bag of candy. "What do you say, young lady?"

Penny, eager for her candy, begins to squirm in Mrs. Ellie's arms. "Please?"

Karen obliges the young girl and sets her down, handing Penny the small bag of chocolates right after both her feet are firmly on the ground. Penny takes the bag and mutters a quick thank-you before turning her attention to opening the bag and getting to the chocolate hidden inside. Karen turns to Alicia and laughs. "She's just like her mother was at that age, you know," she states.

Alicia shakes her head in disagreement. "No ma'am, I was never that polite."

Both women laugh at that comment while Penny, after getting the bag open and spilling only a few of the candies on the ground, happily munches away. Karen looks down at the happy little girl and then back toward Alicia, her eyes pausing on the way at a design scratched into the trunk lid of Alicia's car—a large C & A with a misshapen heart around the letters. Karen's smile grows as she speaks. "Honey, as a fan of your artwork, I would've expected better lines." Alicia laughs out loud, rolls her eyes, and closes the trunk lid. "I was eighteen, Mrs. Ellie, and I think my lines are perfect, considering I was using a screwdriver."

Karen winks at her as the trunk closes and looks toward the grocery store. "OK, dear, I need to get some supplies for the dinner rush tonight. See you Monday at five?"

Alicia nods, remembering she'll have to tell Colin later that she's working the late shift at Ellie's on Monday and he'll need to pick up Penny from day care when he gets back from Shelton. "Yes ma'am. I better get this little one home and get some actual dinner in her anyways," she states, pointing at Penny, who has gotten chocolate all over her fingers and smeared on one side of her mouth. She gives Karen a big hug and watches her head off toward the store.

Turning back to Penny, Alicia digs into her purse and finds a tissue. "How did you get chocolate all over yourself, young lady?" she asks her little progeny.

"I dunno," is her response.

Alicia carefully cleans up the chocolate from Penny's fingers and face, tossing the tissue back into her purse. "OK, messy one, let's get back to Daddy." Penny nods and heads to the passenger side rear door. Alicia follows, opening the door and lifting Penny into her booster seat. Alicia secures the straps and smiles at her little girl. "Are we happy we don't have to sit in the car seat anymore?" she asks.

Penny replies without missing a beat. "Every seat is a car seat when it's in a car, Mommy."

Alicia giggles and pinches her little girl's nose. "You are absolutely right, smarty-pants. Let's go see what Daddy is doing. I bet you he's watching TV right now."

Penny nods in agreement and turns her focus to one of the children's books on the seat next to her.

Alicia steps back and takes a long look at her little girl. *Definitely the best thing to ever happen in my life*, she thinks. Smiling, she closes the car door, walks around to the driver's side, opens the door, and gets inside. She starts the car and carefully backs out of the parking spot, steering toward the parking lot exit. After making sure the way is clear of any approaching vehicles, she pulls out onto the road and heads toward home.

The drive is quiet, with the radio softly playing some random top-forty song and Penny focused on one of her Dr. Seuss books. Alicia enjoys the partial silence while it lasts, and a few minutes later she's pulling the car into the gravel driveway next to Colin's truck. The crunch of gravel underneath the tires pulls Penny's attention from her book. "Mommy, we're home!" Penny announces, as though Alicia may not have noticed.

"Yes, sweetie, we are," Alicia says in agreement.

She turns off the car while Penny wrestles with getting the

clasp of her booster seat undone. "One second, Penny, and I'll let you out," Alicia says as she gets out of the car. She closes the door behind her and heads toward the passenger side, where Penny is struggling impatiently. Opening the door, she frees the little girl, who immediately pops out of the seat and out of the car as if on fire, racing off toward the porch steps and front door. "Be careful, Penny," Alicia says as her little girl reaches the steps and tries leaping over them all. "Tell Daddy to get out here and help unload the groceries!"

She hopes Penny hears her as the little girl disappears through the front door, yelling, "Daddy we're home!"

Alicia turns and walks to the trunk of the car, opens the lid, and starts to grab some bags. At the same moment, Colin appears in the front doorway and calls down to her. "Hey, beautiful, need some help?"

Alicia looks up at him and scoffs. "I am a strong, independent woman, and I do not need a man to get the job done." Colin laughs and nods, giving her a thumbs-up, and turns around to go back into the house. "However, if my loving husband doesn't get his butt down here to help me out, I am going to kick his butt into next week when I'm done," she adds as he disappears into the house.

A little voice from inside reaches her ears—"Daddy, Mommy said *butt*!"—immediately followed by squealing laughter from the little girl. Alicia sighs and chuckles.

Colin reappears in the doorway and heads down the stairs to the back of the car where Alicia is waiting. "Just kidding, gorgeous," he states, giving her a quick kiss. He hastily grabs the rest of the bags and heads back toward the front door. Alicia closes the trunk lid with her free hand and follows him, pausing at the passenger side of the car to open the door, reach in, and grab her purse from the front seat. She slings it onto her shoulder, closes the door, and hits the lock button on her key fob. The reassuring locking sound from the car's doors fills her ears, and she heads inside to help put away the groceries.

As she walks through the doorway, she sees Colin already in the process of putting everything away and Penny bounding around him, repeatedly asking when dinner will be done. "In a little bit, hummingbird," he says several times, carefully navigating around the little girl while putting the groceries in their respective cabinets.

Alicia closes the front door behind her and sets her purse down on the table next to the door. A voice on the television announces that tonight will be a "creature feature marathon," and Alicia internally groans. How the man she loves can enjoy watching these absolutely cheesy and predictable horror movies is beyond her. She makes her way into the kitchen and sets the two bags she's carrying down on the table, turning her attention to helping put the groceries away before getting started on tonight's dinner.

≈

At the same time Alicia is turning on the stove to cook dinner for Colin and Penny, Nick is wrapping up a purchase from a supply company on the outskirts of North Shelton. He waits patiently as the forklift driver loads the two pallets of hardwood planks into the bed of the truck he's rented. Nick is careful, as he has been for years. He picked up this truck from a rental company just north of Rockville and then drove the long miles from Rockville to Shelton to complete the purchase. By his calculations, he has only about one or two more purchases of this volume to go before he has everything he needs to begin work, minus a few small items he'll purchase here and there as he goes. He smiles to himself, knowing this is the way he needs to do it. Confident in the outcome. Confident in his plan.

This is the only way, he thinks.

The forklift driver finishes loading the last pallet and gives Nick the thumbs-up. "You are good to go, sir," he says. Nick nods and waits until the forklift driver has gone back into the supply store. He walks to the rear of the rental truck, pulls a black tarp from the back, and positions it over the hardwood pallets before securing it down on all four corners so it doesn't blow off or move during the drive. Satisfied the tarp is secure and the cargo is not visible to anyone who may see the truck, he closes the tailgate. He walks to the driver's seat, opens the door, and gets in behind the wheel. He starts the truck and closes the door, checking the rearview mirror to make sure no one's standing at the supply store's loading bay and watching him. He puts the truck in drive and pulls away from the store, making his way toward the main road, which will take him back to Orchard Lake.

Nick drives in silence, with the radio turned off, and listens to the tarp fluttering securely inside the truck bed. Miles begin to quickly pass. Once the lights of the city are behind him and the comforting darkness has taken over, with only the truck's headlights to light the way, he allows his thoughts to wander back to the day that changed his entire life. A day he has thought about every waking moment since.

≈

Nick fidgets at the door to her house, switching the corsage from hand to hand while he tries drying his sweaty palms on his dress pants without success. *Get a hold of yourself, Nick*, he thinks. *You have been to this house hundreds of times.* He takes a deep breath to steady himself, but once again his nerves take over. *But you have never been here as her date.*

He wipes both his hands off again on his pants and summons the courage to ring the doorbell. The chime echoes inside, and a muffled voice announces his arrival. The door promptly opens, and standing in front of him is his date, Alicia. She's dressed in the most amazing red dress he's ever seen, but what makes everything else seem like a blur is how happy she is to see him. Her radiant smile, which makes him weak in the knees every time he sees it, is glowing on her face, while her eyes are alight with the perfect spark of her existence. Almost completely lost in her beauty, Nick is able to stammer out how beautiful she looks and awkwardly extends toward her the plastic container he's been holding behind his back. He went to six different flower shops in Shelton before finding the perfect corsage—a blend of roses and sunflowers, adorned with red lace, to match the perfect woman currently standing before him.

The first part of the evening passes in a blur. Nick tries his best not to be nervous through the plethora of picture taking and Alicia's father's "you'd better behave" speech and then the drive to his mom's restaurant, Ellie's, for dinner, where his best friend Colin is waiting. His mom insisted they have dinner there instead of driving up to Shelton or Rockville, and most of the kids in his class already had plans for dinner at Ellie's anyways.

As they pull into the back parking lot of his mom's restaurant, he takes a deep breath. *Be patient*, he tells himself. The right time will present itself, and then he can finally tell Alicia what he's been wanting to tell her for as long as he has known her. He turns the truck off and stares off at the lake in front of him, gathering his strength and trying to calm his nerves. The light of the setting sun is reflecting off the calm, dark-blue surface of the lake, casting beams of red and orange all around.

Now, he tells himself, *tell her now.*

Nick looks over at Alicia, who is staring out at the lake, and extends his right hand across the seat of the truck, setting it down on top of her hands, which are clasped together on her lap. He feels her jump at the touch of his hand, and he momentarily panics as a thought he dreads every time once again crosses his mind: *What if she doesn't feel the same and this is a mistake?*

His logic tries to fight his panic. *No, Nick, you have kept this in long enough. She has to know.*

Just as he's opening his mouth to pour out everything, a loud voice from just outside the truck explodes into the cab and slams the door on his moment.

Nick quickly pulls his hand back, and for a second he allows the resentment that's been building for a long time to show on his face. But only for a second.

He swiftly regains his composure and turns to see his best friend's face right outside the driver's side window.

Colin. Alicia's boyfriend. The guy Nick wishes he were with all his heart. Not because Colin is popular or athletic or handsome. Not because Colin seems to have everything going for him.

No, Nick wishes he were Colin for one reason and one reason only.

Alicia.

Nick takes a deep breath. *There will be another chance tonight*, he reassures himself. He and Colin exchange banter as they always do, and after a few laughter-filled moments, his mom calls for them to come inside and the trio heads into the restaurant for dinner. Nick leads the way through the back door with Alicia and Colin in tow and continues on into the kitchen, where his mother is busy working and waiting for him.

"Yes, Mom?" he asks as he walks into the busy kitchen where she's standing.

She smiles at him and pulls him to a slightly quieter spot at the back of the kitchen. "Have you talked to her yet?" she asks.

The palms of Nick's hands are immediately sweaty again.

"No, Mom, I haven't had a chance to yet," he replies.

She stares at him, a stern look on her face. *No*, Nick thinks, *not* at *me. Through me. She always looks through me.* He fidgets a bit and lowers his head.

"What did I tell you, Nick? If you want something in this life, you have to take it. Take the opportunities when they present themselves."

He nods at her, looking down at the floor of the kitchen. "Yes, ma'am," he responds, "I am going to talk to her tonight and tell her, I promise."

His mother's eyes soften a bit, and she smiles at him. "Good boy. Now give me a big hug and go have fun with your friends, but first run these upstairs for me." She hands him a stack of completed order tickets from her apron pocket. Nick nods once again and looks at her. He can't wait until he's able to move out on his own and get away from his mother's rule. Away to where he can make his own decisions. His own choices. His own plans. He hugs his mother and heads out of the kitchen, quickly going up the stairs to their apartment on the second floor. His mother likes to review the orders in the evening to determine which menu items are selling and which aren't. He sets the tickets on the kitchen table and then heads back down the stairs and into the dining room to enjoy dinner with the love of his life and the guy he wishes he were.

Dinner quickly goes by, full of laughter and smiles, and before Nick knows it, they're all walking through the doors of the high school gym where their prom is being held. Knowing

33

Alicia is excited to see the band playing later, he leads the three of them to the tables at the front of the gym, where the makeshift stage area is. He picks one of the empty front tables and takes his tuxedo jacket off, draping it over the back of one of the chairs. Alicia sits down, and Nick watches Colin head off to get them all some drinks. After Colin is far enough away, Nick turns once again to Alicia with the intent to follow through with his plan of telling her how he feels about her. How he has always felt about her. How he will always feel about her.

However, the look on her face stops him from saying anything at all. A look of sheer panic has replaced her normal smile. *Something's wrong* is his first thought. This thought is reinforced even more by her response when he asks her if she's OK. *Of course I will always be there for you, no matter what*, he thinks, as similar words come out of his mouth.

Before he can find out what's wrong, Colin walks up, trying to carefully balance three drinks. Nick watches as Colin tries to set the drinks down but almost loses one. Colin's left hand darts out to catch the drink before it tips over, hitting the candle in the center of the table in the process. Although Colin saves the drink, he doesn't save the candle. The candle topples wildly in Nick's direction, expelling hot candle wax across the table and onto his tuxedo jacket.

A flash of anger races through him. His mother is going to kill him for getting the tuxedo jacket dirty, even if it wasn't his fault. He starts yelling at Colin for his stupidity.

Just as he's about to yell at Colin some more, Alicia blurts out a single sentence that hits him like a speeding freight train.

"I'm pregnant!"

Her words immediately erase any other emotions Nick is feeling and replace them with a void, as though all the oxygen has just been sucked out of his lungs. *Did she just say she was pregnant?* he asks himself, as if he can't believe what he just heard and his mind has to demand that his ears confirm it. He looks over at Colin, who seems to have frozen with his eyes as wide as they can go. He looks back at Alicia, and the direction of her stare answers any and all questions Nick may have had about who the father is. Because she's staring directly at Colin.

Forgetting about his tuxedo jacket, Nick pulls his chair out and sits down. Everything seems to be moving in slow motion. Colin still hasn't moved. Neither has Alicia. Nick looks around the gym at the disco balls and lights, at the decor and at all his oblivious classmates having the best night of their life.

He looks down at the table and the light-purple wax trail on the tablecloth. The wax has already hardened. He tries to take a breath, but he can't get enough air. He looks at the overturned candle, a slight trail of smoke rising from the snuffed-out flame. *Maybe that's why the candle is out now*, he thinks. *Because there's no more oxygen in the room.*

The song playing over the loudspeakers seems to mock him. Singing to him about an everlasting love.

If he had any air in his lungs, he'd scoff at the lyrics, because right now his everlasting love has someone else's baby inside her. The baby of the guy he's wished he were for as long as he has known Alicia. A sense of dark dread begins to fill Nick, starting in his heart and slowly expanding until it fills every inch of his body. *If she has Colin's baby, she will never want to be with me.* This thought sinks in deeper. Nick fights myriad thoughts all at the same time. Does he hit Colin for probably taking Alicia away from him forever? Does he yell at Alicia for not giving him the chance he deserves? Does he play the part of the best friend and congratulate them? Does he just leave now and disappear forever?

Alicia's voice breaks the silence among the trio while the hypocritical song continues to play in the background.

"Colin, please say something."

Like a lighthouse welcoming him home after a long journey at sea, her voice brings Nick back to a world where he's once again able to breathe.

Colin's voice follows hers. "What do you expect me to say? Am I the father?"

Nick looks from Alicia to Colin and back to Alicia, their words barely registering in his mind. Yes, Colin is the father. Yes, she is keeping the baby. No, her parents don't know yet and Alicia expects Colin there when she tells them. Nick patiently waits for Alicia to finally turn to him and tell him how much she needs him in her life. How much she will need his help with this baby and ask him whether, if Colin doesn't want to be the father, he will be there instead.

But those words never come. Nick sits there, stoically and quietly, while Alicia and Colin argue back and forth about the future. Neither of them mentions him. Neither of them even looks over at him to see how he feels.

In those moments, those painful minutes that keep going past one right after another with no end in sight, Nick feels something inside him snap, like a thick wooden board bent so far it finally breaks in two, raining splinters down all around it. And what has just snapped inside him leaves behind a sudden, vast emptiness.

In its place, something new begins to form. A darkness. A void. As black as a bottomless chasm impenetrable by any light. As the evening wears on and the band comes onstage and begins to play, as all the people around him dance and laugh and Colin and Alicia come to terms with their new future together, Nick finally comes to terms with his.

Because that void, that darkness growing inside him, is now talking to him. Comforting him. Reassuring him.

Telling him that if he wants something in his life, he has to take it.

Telling him that he has to seize the opportunity when it presents itself.

Nick finally finds his smile again as the evening grows to a close, after he's memorized every detail of everything around him. Because that darkness is giving him ideas of what he can do.

What he can do to fill the emptiness inside him.

What he can do to make everything perfect.

CHAPTER 3

THE PLANNING

Nick sets the dustpan down and begins to sweep the floor of the kitchen, per his mother's request. He thinks about the last several months.

He made himself scarce after prom. Not because he didn't want to see Alicia, but because the darkness, the voice from the void that comforted him at prom, told him not to. He already knew he had no intention of seeing Colin, at least for a while.

Both Alicia and Colin have come by the restaurant several times looking for him, trying to see how he's been doing, if he's OK. Each time his mother has done as he's requested and told them he's not here. Even on the nights Alicia is working or Colin is here with her eating dinner, Nick has made sure he isn't seen. Not available. Not home. Thankfully, his mother has been understanding and has covered for him, allowing him to keep his distance from the two of them.

Sometimes when he knows they're both in the restaurant,

he sits just out of sight near the top of the stairs and listens to all the sounds below in the restaurant. Listens to see if he can hear their voices, hear what they're talking about. What they're laughing about. On a few occasions, he has been able to make out Colin's laugh. What was Colin laughing about? About how he destroyed his best friend's only chance at love by getting Alicia pregnant? On those occasions, Nick can feel the fury building inside him, making him want to storm down the stairs and tell his so-called best friend that he's taken his future away from him. His future with Alicia. The voice inside him has kept him calm, though. Kept him focused on the plan.

Nick smiles when he thinks about the voice. It's as though something inside him is finally awake after being dormant his entire life, and now it is giving him strength he never knew he had. The voice from the darkness is giving him advice and telling him that all his wishes will come true as long as he listens.

He continues to smile while he sweeps the kitchen floor of the restaurant. The plan the voice is outlining to him has to work. It's almost fail-safe. But he will have to be careful. It will take time to set it up. It will take time for the right moment to present itself. The voice reassures Nick he has time. As long as he's patient, he will get what he wants. What he deserves.

A future with Alicia.

As Nick is finishing up the floor, his mother comes down the stairs and into the bar area. The restaurant is closed today due to a holiday, so his mother has him cleaning up the kitchen and prepping everything for tomorrow, when the restaurant opens back up. He hears the clinking of glass as she pours herself a drink.

After prom, he came home and told his mother about everything that had happened. About Alicia's pregnancy. About Colin thinking about proposing to her after he found out about the baby. And about him not being able to tell Alicia how much he cares about her. How much he loves her.

He also told his mother about the voice inside him and what it was telling him. What it was telling him to do.

He fully expected his mother to have him locked up for hearing voices in his head, but instead she surprised him by wrapping her arms around him and holding him close. "I will support you in everything and anything you ever choose to do," was all she said that night. Even after he told her what the voice's plan was.

He hears the clinking of the glass again. His mother's voice comes from the direction of the bar. "Have you figured out what you're going to do?"

He takes a deep breath. He's not sure how she'll react to what he's about to say. "Yes, ma'am. I am going to find a place to stay where I can work on everything. Where no one will find me." He takes another deep breath. "I need you to tell everyone I joined the military and was shipped overseas."

He's not sure how believable that last sentence is, but he couldn't think of any other story in which he could leave town and at the same time be so unreachable that no one would try to find him. Just saying he was going off to college would leave

Alicia and Colin believing they could get a hold of him. And he has no intention of going to college. Not now. Both Colin and Alicia are staying in Orchard Lake. He needs to stay in town as well.

But he's also not sure how his mother is going to react to him saying he needs to find a new place to stay. Living here at the restaurant is too risky, especially with Alicia working here. She might see him, ask him too many questions. The voice has told him repeatedly that that cannot happen. Not yet. She will see him again when it's time.

He stands still in the kitchen, holding the dustpan and broom, waiting for his mother's response.

The voice on the other side of the bar remains quiet. The voice in Nick's head tells him to be patient and that his mother will understand.

He hears the clinking of the glass once again, and finally his mother speaks. "Are you familiar with the old logging camp at the other end of the lake?"

Nick nods and then realizes his mother can't see him. "Yes, ma'am, I heard the stories about the accident there and how it's now haunted by the loggers who died."

He hears his mother laugh a bit at the last part. "Yes, honey, there was an accident and several people died. They shut that camp down shortly afterwards, and it's been locked up and abandoned ever since. What you don't know is that your momma owns that property."

The glass clinks again as his mother pours another drink.

"When you're done with your chores, go upstairs and get the large key ring on the far right of the holder. After you get the keys, head on out to the old logging camp road and follow it all the way until it seems to end. The road ain't there no more, but there is a still a pathway through the woods to the camp. The largest key on the ring will open the main door."

Her voice trails off after the last sentence as yet another clink of the glass can be heard.

Nick knew the camp was there, but it has been strictly off-limits to everyone due to what happened to the loggers years ago, before Nick was even born. As kids, he and his friends were also told that there were sharp, rusty blades all over the place just waiting to cut open a trespasser and that the ambulance would never get out there in time to be able to save someone from bleeding to death. For impressionable kids, even the braver teenagers, ghosts and death were both pretty strong deterrents.

He definitely didn't know his mother owns the property, though. She's never spoken of it before today. He knows better than to ask too many questions. "Yes, ma'am. Thank you."

She doesn't respond. Instead, he hears her glass being set down in the bar sink and her footsteps crossing the restaurant to the stairs that lead up to where they live. Each stair creaks its own song as she climbs the stairs, until once again the restaurant and kitchen are silent.

Nick empties the dustpan into the trash and puts both the dustpan and broom away in the far corner of the kitchen. He looks at the prep stations near the stoves and quickly takes note of what is low. Sliced carrots, diced tomatoes, diced onions, and sliced pickles.

He goes to the pantry and grabs the tomatoes and onions he'll need, walking back into the kitchen and setting them on the prep counter. He then crosses the kitchen and opens the walk-in fridge and gets a bag of carrots and an already opened jar of whole pickles. His mother always insists on cutting up fresh ingredients for her recipes, and over the years Nick has gotten pretty adept at using the wide variety of knives in the kitchen. He sets the remaining items on the prep counter and grabs one of the knives hanging nearby, testing to make certain the blade is sharp. He quickly dices the tomatoes and onions, filling both prep containers to the top. He slices up most of the carrots in the same fashion, and several of the pickles, until he's filled their respective prep containers as well.

Satisfied, he puts the unused items away and carries the knife and prep board across the kitchen to one of the two big dual sinks on the far wall, near the shelves with all the utensils and pans. He washes the knife and prep board thoroughly, dries them both, and then returns them to their original locations. He surveys the kitchen one more time to make sure he didn't miss anything.

Content that his mother will be satisfied with his work, he turns his focus back to what she told him about the old logging camp. He looks at the clock on the wall above the stoves. Just a few minutes past four. It won't be dark for at least two or three hours, which will be more than enough time for him to hike out to the camp and take a look around. He isn't sure why his mother told him about the camp, but maybe it was her way of suggesting someplace he can stay that's away from here. A place he can work on his plan.

Determined to find out what the old logging camp really holds within its walls, he turns and heads up the stairs. Reaching the top step, he stops and grabs the large set of keys on the far right of the key holder. He always thought these were just spare keys to the restaurant. He pauses before he turns back down the stairs. He can hear the television in the living room and nothing else besides the hum of the fridge and freezer in the restaurant below. He puts the keys deep into his right pocket and heads down the stairs for the back door. Once outside, he turns toward the main parking lot and begins walking up the road, leaving the restaurant behind him. He takes a right onto the main road in front of Ellie's and begins the two or so mile walk to the old logging camp road.

The walk is quiet. He doesn't run into anyone, car or pedestrian, on his trip there. Had he not been looking for the entrance, he might have missed it. The road is extremely overgrown with encroaching shrubs and overhanging branches. Nick stops at the entrance and looks down the road through all the overgrowth, wondering how far he can actually see. *Maybe sixty feet*, he thinks. He isn't sure how far back the road goes.

The voice in his head makes itself known again. *Go on*, it urges.

Nick takes a deep breath and steps onto the road, placing one foot after another, dodging branches and bushes alike. With each step, the initial hesitation he felt when first standing before the road slowly disappears. The voice becomes louder in his head.

Yes, this is already perfect, it tells him. He smiles in agreement. But then, he has been here before. He knew it would be perfect. It's obvious that no one has driven down this road in years. Maybe even decades. He continues down the overgrown road, listening to the birds in the trees above, who are clearly unhappy with his sudden presence in their world.

After what feels like an eternity, Nick reaches the end of the partially visible road. The rest of the way is so overgrown he can't even see the road anymore. He looks around for the path his mother mentioned earlier at home. The path he and Alicia saw years before, on an adventure, when they were here together. When they were still in high school. An adventure where he came to know he would love Alicia forever. But they didn't press onward down the path at that time.

He pushes the thought of their adventure from his mind and concentrates on the task at hand.

He sees a slight break in the underbrush and pushes the larger shrubs aside, which allows him to make out just the faintest hint of a path that leads deeper into the woods. The sound of the upset birds seems to amplify for just a moment when he initially pushes the shrubbery aside, and then suddenly they are quiet, leaving the woods around him completely silent.

The hair on the back of his neck rises as thoughts of ghosts and sharp rusty blades waiting to kill him race across his mind. *Get a grip, Nick*, he thinks. *Your mother would not have sent you out here if she thought you were going to die.*

He takes a deep breath and plunges into the thick overgrowth that has taken over the pathway. He winds his way down the path, trying to dodge branches and thorn bushes, until finally he crosses underneath a large branch stretching over the path. Just beyond this branch is the edge of a large clearing. The clearing in front of Nick is big and full of large, decaying tree stumps that dot the landscape in random places. In the center of the clearing is a large, warehouse-style building with a loading dock at one end. A dilapidated antique truck, almost completely hidden by the surrounding bushes and weeds, is parked next to the dock. In the center of the building is a large metal sliding door with some steps leading up to it. Nick digs into his right pants pocket and pulls out the large key ring, flipping through the keys until he finds the big key his mother mentioned. He looks at the ominous sliding door and back at the key. *This has to be the key that opens that door*, he surmises.

Confident he has the way in and excited because he's about to set foot in a place no one else may have been inside for a very long time, he puts the keys back into his pocket and steps from the tree line and into the clearing. He carefully makes his way through the tall grass, almost expecting either a hungry zombie logger or an angry rusty saw blade to leap out at him. Step by step he traverses the clearing until he reaches the concrete pad and mounts the steps in front of the large metal door.

He looks around. No flesh-eating lumberjack zombies. No attacking rust-covered metal blades.

Of course, he thinks, *they might all be waiting for me to open this door, and then they will all attack at once because I've set them free.*

Nick hesitates a moment before he reaches back into his pocket for the keys.

The voice makes itself known again and reassures him. *The only thing that should be feared here is you*, it tells him. Nick nods to himself. There is nothing here worth his fear. He reaches into his pocket and pulls out the large key ring, finds the necessary key, and inserts it into the keyhole on the large metal door. One turn to the right and Nick hears the heavy lock on the door disengage. The sound seems to echo both inside and outside the building, bouncing off walls and trees until the noise of the forest finally takes back over. He takes a deep breath and begins to slide the door open, the loud screech of metal on metal penetrating the evening quickly descending over the clearing.

After Nick finally gets the door all the way open, he looks into the darkness beyond. Dust filters through the few beams of sunlight coming in from the broken windows at the top of the building, revealing unused and long-forgotten equipment. A thick layer of dust covers the floor directly in front of him and for as far as he can see into the building.

No one has been in here in a very long time. The voice

inside Nick's head speaks up once again, saying just one word this time.

Home.

≈

A bump in the road jostles Nick back to reality. He glances in the rearview mirror to ensure that his cargo is still fully covered. Although he knows he might pass only one or two cars on his trip home at this time in the evening, he still has to remain careful.

One small slipup, one simple mistake, and all his work over the last eight years will be for nothing.

He's so close to finally bringing the plan to fruition. A couple more evening trips and the last of the materials needed will be in place. Then he can finally move on to the next steps. As the turnoff to the old logging camp road approaches, Nick smiles.

Soon, Alicia, he thinks. *So very soon.*

A few hundred feet before the road he will be turning onto, Nick turns off the truck's headlights and slows down. He has traveled this section of the road hundreds of times and knows every inch of it by heart. He's not worried about running off the road; he just has to be sure no vehicles are approaching from the other direction or coming behind him. He also has to be sure there are no pedestrians on the road, even though he's never seen one this far out of town at this time of night. Satisfied that no one is around, he makes the turn onto the old logging camp road and drives down the route slowly.

Leaving the truck's lights off, he grabs the flashlight lying on the seat next to him and turns it on, shining the dim beam out the front windshield. The beam gives him a small amount of light to finish navigating his way until he reaches the spot where the road ends and the path to the logging camp begins. He pulls the rental truck into a spot between two trees on the right and turns off the engine. He turns off the flashlight, plunging the cab into darkness. Nick takes a deep breath and smiles. The darkness has been his only friend for years. He waits for a little while, listening to the sounds of the forest around him and letting his eyes get used to the dark. A small amount of moonlight shines through the trees, giving Nick just enough vision that he doesn't need the flashlight for the rest of tonight's work.

He sets the flashlight back down on the seat, opens the driver's side door, and gets out. He heads to the back of the truck and unlatches all the straps for the tarp, removes it, and folds it back up before placing it back in the truck. Climbing into the bed, he reaches into his right pocket and pulls out a pocketknife. He cuts the securing straps to both the wood pallets and places the knife back into his pocket. Then he drags two of the boxes made of hardwood off the pallets, carefully sets them down on the tailgate, one by one, and hops down out of the bed. He takes another look around, ensuring he's still alone, and goes to the passenger side, pulling out a large camouflage tarp. He carefully covers the truck from front to back as well as its cargo and secures the tarp so it doesn't fall off.

Nick takes several steps back and looks at his handiwork.

The truck is almost impossible to see unless he's up close. Satisfied, he walks back to the truck and reaches under the tarp, grabbing both boxes of wood resting on the tailgate. He turns toward the pathway to the logging camp and carefully makes his way down the path, avoiding any snagging branches as best he can. Over the years, the path has been worn in quite a bit from Nick traversing from the camp to the road, yet he's always been slow and careful and has done his best not to make it too obvious that the path is there.

He reaches the edge of the clearing quietly and pauses before stepping out from the tree line, taking a look around to ensure no one is about. Content he's still alone, he steps from the end of the path and navigates his way to the logging camp. Once he reaches the door, he sets the two boxes of wood down on the steps and fishes a key ring from his left pocket, feeling through the keys for the larger of the set. Once he finds it, he quickly unlocks the door and puts the keys back into his pocket. Slowly he slides the door partially open, the metal-on-metal sound only slightly noticeable. He makes a mental note to grease the rollers for the door. It's too risky for the door to make noise every time it opens or closes right now, especially when he's so close to what he wants.

Nick picks up the two boxes of wood and proceeds into the darkness beyond the door. He doesn't need any light here. This is his home. He knows every inch of it.

Halfway into the building, he reaches another door. He repeats the process of setting down the boxes of wood and unlocking the door. He leaves this door slightly open as well and proceeds deeper into the logging camp. He navigates down a flight of stairs in the pitch-black, not missing a single step, and reaches another door. The process is repeated one more time, allowing Nick to enter a small room, approximately fifteen by twenty feet, with only a few pieces of furniture in it. Confident that no one will see any light now, he reaches to his left and flips a switch. Fluorescent lights overhead turn on, bathing the room in light. To his right is a table against the wall, currently covered in various blueprints and how-to manuals. In front of him is a large chest with a dust-covered sander on top of it. A sturdy wooden chair sits next to the chest. To his left, on the other side of the room, is another large metal door.

Nick smiles when he looks at this door. Beyond that door is his salvation. His plan. His way of showing Alicia that he is the loving husband she should have been with all this time.

Nick remembers the day he first found this room and the room beyond the metal door. It was as though something was finally answering his prayers and giving him something he wanted instead of always taking it away. Showing him that this plan was exactly what he needed to do to win her back.

It took him multiple years just to get the room beyond the metal door excavated enough for the dimensions he needed. Days of digging. Nights of hauling excess dirt out of the logging camp, spreading it around the surrounding forest and ensuring that it wasn't noticeable. Months of studying how to reinforce the ceiling so it wouldn't cave in on him while he was working.

Or while his plans were finally being put into action.

He would sleep in the room beyond the metal door most nights, feeling the cool dirt underneath him, hearing only his heartbeat in the complete silence. He has never wanted for food or water or money, as a simple trip to his mother's restaurant solves those problems. She even rents the trucks he's been using to secure the materials he needs to complete the task he's dedicated himself to. Nick still doesn't know why she helps him, other than her saying she would rather her son remain close than that she never see him again. She knows what his plan is. Knows what the outcomes might be, both good and bad.

Nick takes a deep breath, confident the outcome will be exactly what the voice told him it would be. Of course, over time, Nick has come to realize that the voice he heard was his own, coming from his own darkness and desire for vengeance. Once he came to this realization, the voice was quickly replaced by an even more intense determination to get back the love of his life at any cost. From that point forward, he just knew what he had to do. *Because I am the voice*, he thinks, smiling. *I always have been.*

He turns toward the metal door and crosses the room, once again going through the motions to unlock the door. He pulls the heavy door open, the metal framing along the bottom scraping across the concrete, creating a raspy scratching noise as the door follows the preordained path set by its hinges. Nick's smile gets bigger. A long hallway is before him, with lights hanging every few feet to light the way. These lights were already on. Nick has had no reason to ever turn them off, as none of their light escapes from the edges of the metal door when it's closed. He replaced a lot of the wiring the first couple years he was here, since many of the lights didn't work and he knew he'd need good, working electrical wires for what he was creating.

He reaches the end of the hallway, stopping at one final door. This door is new, solid, and similar to a standard windowless door you'd find in a gymnasium. Although there's a lock on this door as well, it's currently unlocked. He hasn't had a reason to use the lock yet. Nick installed the door shortly after he finished digging out and reinforcing the room. *Can't give away the surprise too quickly*, he thinks, laughing out loud a bit at the thought of calling his plan the surprise.

The plan. The way he is going to make Alicia his, forever.

The sound of his laughter seems foreign here, since he's barely said anything over the course of the last eight years while near or inside the room beyond this door.

Nick's smile remains on his face. *This room won't be silent for too much longer*, he thinks. He nods in agreement with his own thoughts and opens the door, stepping into the void beyond. He reaches out and flicks several switches upward, causing several large overhead lights to turn on with a burning intensity and chase away the dark from almost every corner of the room. The room is extremely large for an underground room. He was lucky the room was on the side of the logging camp that faces the mountain when he first discovered it, or he might not have been able to keep the scale of the room fully underground. *Just another sign that what I'm doing is right*, he thinks. To the far left of the room are several pallet-sized stacks of boxes, all of the same type of wood Nick is currently holding. There are also several smaller boxes full of nails and a variety of wood screws as well as the various tools he'll need to put everything together. Another door a little farther down on the left wall opens into a bathroom and shower room, which Nick has surmised was used as a locker room of sorts. Before he expanded the room, it appeared to have been used for equipment storage, with several large replacement parts for the now nonworking saw system at the dock of the building.

Assured that nothing has changed in here since his trip up to Shelton today, Nick walks over to the other boxes of wood and sets the two he's carrying down on top of the others. He will have several trips to make tonight so he can get all the boxes down here before dawn. He can't risk hauling the boxes in the daytime, and he can't risk leaving any in the back of the truck in the event a wandering passerby finds the truck and checks it out. Even now, after all these years, he must remain vigilant and cautious. He is too close now to make a mistake.

He takes a deep breath and begins making the trips back and forth from the truck to the large room, carrying two or three boxes at a time, making sure he is careful each trip not to make too much noise. Just as he has done many, many times before. Much to his satisfaction, he's able to get all the boxes moved into the room in only a few hours, well before dawn.

Nick takes a moment to survey his handiwork and then counts the stacks of hardwood boxes in front of him. One more trip to a supply store will be enough, which he can do tomorrow night. He just needs to find another store he can make the purchase from. Buying too much from a single store might raise suspicions, so Nick has made sure he's spread his purchases out over several stores. Eleven so far, to be exact. Hopefully this next one will be the last.

He turns away from the stacked boxes and heads toward the hallway. He needs to ensure that all the doors are closed and locked before he goes to sleep. As he makes his way down the hallway and into the smaller room, just as he's about to head up the rounded staircase that takes him to the main floor of the logging camp, he hears a sound coming from above him.

A sound he should not be hearing.

The familiar scraping of metal on metal coming from the main door as it is being opened the rest of the way.

CHAPTER 4

THE PUSH

Karen Ellie is a simple woman. She's happy with her small-town life, her cozy little restaurant, and her beat-up pickup truck. She never had any wish to drive a super-fancy car or live in a big mansion like the ones she sees on television.

She's happy with her down-to-earth comfort food menu and the modest home she's created above her restaurant. *You won't find any of that fancy overpriced city food here at my place,* she thinks.

She's even happy with her handsome little boy. Sure, he may not have headed off to college like she expected, but he has set his mind to something he wants to accomplish and he's working hard to make it happen. That's all a mother could want for her son.

Karen looks at the clock on the wall near the bar. Almost two in the morning. She closed the bar an hour early tonight, as there were only a couple of her regulars here and one was already falling asleep with his head on the bar.

She gets up from the stool behind the bar and pours herself another shot of bourbon, taking in everything around her. Her beautiful little restaurant, with plain tables and chairs out on the dining room floor and simple wooden bar stools at the bar. The only thing that isn't simple or plain in her little world is the artwork hanging on the walls all around the dining room. Hand-painted scenes of the town of Orchard Lake, the mountains surrounding the town, and even the lake itself, all painted by one of her most favorite employees ever.

Alicia.

Such a bright young woman, full of life and laughter and always with a smile on her face.

Karen smiles as she looks from painting to painting. *The young woman does have quite the eye for detail*, she thinks. *Although that same eye for detail completely failed to see how much she meant to my boy before she got all knocked up*. "That's OK, though," Karen says out loud to the empty restaurant. "My boy is going to show her just how much she means to him and what she's been missing all these years."

She finishes the shot in her hand and pours another one out of habit, still lost in her thoughts.

Karen wasn't sure how to react the night Nick came home after the prom and told her about what had happened, about the love of his life being pregnant with his best friend's baby. Karen pauses a moment in her thoughts and scoffs. "Best friend, my backside. My boy deserved better than that."

The empty tables and chairs around her remain indifferent, providing no response to her comment.

She especially wasn't sure how to react after her boy told her he was hearing voices and that they were telling him about some grand plan to win Alicia's heart from Colin. She didn't want to believe it was possible he suffered from the same affliction she had suffered from while his father was still alive, before her boy was born.

A voice inside her head. Speaking to her. Telling her what to do.

Ultimately, she did exactly what any loving mother would do. She pulled her little boy close, wrapped her arms around him, and promised she would always support him in everything he wanted to do.

It took her a bit of time to come to terms with what Nick was planning. In theory, it was a very sweet idea, and any woman would be honored to have a man do that for her. But her boy's idea of how to make it all happen required the type of commitment that only a dedicated mother could give, because there was no turning back from that kind of action.

So, once again, she did exactly what any loving mother would do. Went along with his plan and decided to do everything she could to help him out.

Karen's smile returns, and she finishes off the second shot. She's far too deep in to back out now. She knows it. She knew it the moment she told his friends he went off to the military. She knew it the moment she broadcast that he had been killed overseas. And she really knew it when they had his funeral right here in Orchard Lake.

Of course, the casket was empty. That's the nice thing about living in a small town most of your life—people don't tend to question what you tell them, especially when you're playing the part of a grieving mother. It was a beautiful ceremony, though, and the business at her restaurant tripled for a good six months afterward. Nick's death in the military was her idea, as she was running out of excuses as to why he was deployed in another country for so long and tired of answering questions about when he'd be coming home. And when people would ask her why she didn't have a military funeral for her boy, she would just tell them the government had already taken her boy's life and she didn't want to give them any more satisfaction. That statement pretty much ended any questions, and after a year or two, no one brought him up to her anymore.

She doesn't feel the need to talk about her boy with anyone anyway, as she knows right where he is. At the old logging camp. Right on the other side of the lake from her.

Right where she told him to go after he told her about his plans and she had some time to think about it. She knew the main room of that old logging camp was big enough for what Nick was going to do, although she was a bit surprised when she found out he was instead digging a room into the side of the mountain.

Karen pours another shot and raises it high. "Whatever makes my boy happy," she toasts, and then finishes the drink.

For a moment, she thinks about pouring another but shakes her head. "Can't have too many if I'm gettin' behind the wheel, right?" she asks the empty glass.

Her boy hasn't been by in a couple days to get any food or water, so she decided earlier today that she was going to take some out to him at the logging camp. Plus, she wants to see exactly how much he's gotten done on his plan since she started renting all the trucks and paying for all these building materials for him.

Karen sets the empty shot glass in the sink and turns away from the bar, walking around the back of the liquor display and into the kitchen. Several empty produce boxes are stacked up next to the walk-in fridge. She walks over, picks up one of the boxes, and sets it down on one of the prep tables, intent on filling it with supplies. She gets several bottles of water and a six-pack of cola from the walk-in and places them in the produce box. She then returns to the walk-in and grabs several ham-and-cheese sandwiches she made earlier in the day. Nick's favorite sandwich.

She knows he won't be happy she's coming out to the camp, since he did ask her to please leave him be there, but if it hadn't been for her, he never would've gotten this far with what he's doing.

And without her, he won't be able to accomplish what is to come.

Karen steps back from the prep counter and nods, pleased with the contents of the box. She carries it outside through the back of the restaurant, pushing the door closed behind her, and places the box of groceries in the bed of her truck. She walks around and gets behind the wheel, starts up the truck, and turns on the lights. She doubts she'll run into anyone on her way out there, since most of the town is asleep right now. She backs out of her spot, turns the truck around, and heads toward the road for the logging camp.

It takes only a couple minutes before she's turning onto the run-down overgrown ruts that are considered the road. The truck bounces and sways as she drives slowly over the various dips and bumps, the long overhanging branches along the route scraping the roof of the cab. A few minutes later she reaches the end of the road. She pulls the truck into a spot on the right between some trees and near what she believes is one of the latest of several different truck rentals she's rented for Nick. Although this one is covered with a large camouflage cover.

Karen smiles as she turns off her headlights. *Smart boy*, she thinks. *Guess I don't have to do all the thinkin' after all.* She grabs the flashlight out of her glove compartment, turns on the light to verify that the batteries still work, and hops out of the truck, closing the door behind her. At the bed of the truck, she picks up the box of supplies, holding the flashlight with one hand, making sure the beam is shining out in front of her. She walks across the road and heads down the pathway, which clearly has seen some use over the last several years, although it is still relatively overgrown and almost hard to identify in some spots.

Several scratches later from quite a few overly friendly

thorn bushes, Karen clears the path and steps into the clearing. There's enough moonlight out tonight that she's able to make out the building in the center, so she turns off the flashlight. She carefully navigates through the clearing to the door leading into the camp. The door is halfway open, and it's pitch-black inside the run-down building. Karen listens for any sound from within the building but hears nothing beyond the usual forest sounds all around her. The nightly symphony of crickets mingles with the occasional loud croak of a bullfrog from the lake, accented by the loud call of a loon. She wonders if Nick is even here right now. *Where else would he be if he isn't here?* she wonders.

"Nick, honey, it's your momma. Are you in there?"

Her unanswered question lingers in the air as though suspended by the heavy silence from inside the building.

She pauses a moment before deciding to go in. She hasn't been out here in a very long time, since shortly after Nick was born. That was a different time, though, and she did what she had to do to make sure Nick would be safe. A mother's love knows no bounds, the voice used to tell her, up until she finally acted on what it was telling her to do. And it was right.

Karen looks over toward the old truck parked next to the loading dock on the far end of the building, her eyes hardening as memories she hasn't thought of in years come flooding back.

Even with the moonlight it's difficult to make out the shape of the truck, but she can see it hasn't moved since she pushed it to where it currently sits. And only she knows what's buried underneath that truck.

As her memories remind her of an abusive past she's spent well over two decades forgetting, they also remind her of how satisfying it was to feel the butcher's knife when it was buried almost hilt deep into her husband's chest. The voice was right back then. It really was an almost orgasmic feeling, after suffering beating after beating from the worthless bastard she was married to. Granted, she was tough and resilient and was willing to put up with the abuse, because in a way, she did actually love him. He gave her Nick, her beautiful little boy.

But in the long days after his logging camp was shut down for good, he turned even more vicious toward her. And the night he decided, after a day of drinking, that he was going to lay his hands on her little baby boy, who was just crying because he was hungry, was the night the voice in her head said it was time. And before he could storm up the stairs to get to her boy, she grabbed the biggest knife in the kitchen and plunged it as far into his heart as she could.

Karen still wonders if he was able to see her smiling as she stood over him while he was bleeding out on the floor of the restaurant, watching as the light faded from his eyes and went out forever.

The voice helped her that night. Helped her get his body into the back of her truck. Helped her clean up all the blood. Gave her the idea of where to bury his corpse.

Of course, she went upstairs and fed her amazing baby boy before she did all of that, because he did, and always will, come first in her world.

Everyone in town knew he was abusive, so no one really thought much of it when she told them he'd left her. Of course she said she didn't know where he'd gone and she hoped to never see him again. She said she'd never bothered trying to file for divorce, since the restaurant and logging camp were in both their names, and she didn't want anyone digging into where he might have gone. Luckily, he was an only child and both his parents had passed long before she met him. It really did all work out, just like the voice in her head had said it would.

And that's why, when her boy told her about the voice in his head, she knew she had to help, no matter the cost.

Karen breaks her stare from the old truck and looks back at the door in front of her. Still no sounds from inside. She takes a look around the clearing and then turns on her flashlight, shining the beam through the half-open door and into the large room beyond. A well-worn path of footsteps leads farther into the building, and she follows this path using the flashlight.

The beam of light leads Karen farther into the dark building until she comes across a large piece of equipment, unused for years and covered in dust. She hesitates a moment in confusion, a slight furrow forming between her eyes. It isn't the large table with a saw in the middle that seems out of place, but the bright-pink backpack and flashlight lying on top of it.

Even more out of place, as she moves the beam from the table to the floor, is the set of legs sticking out from the darkness behind the table.

≈

When the familiar sound of the main door opening reaches Nick's ears, he freezes in the room downstairs. *They found me*, he thinks, *Alicia and Colin have found me.* Once again Colin is going to ruin everything he's spent all these years working on. A nervousness he hasn't experienced since high school begins to set in. He can feel the heat starting to radiate from his palms. He should have locked the door when he brought in the last load of wood.

He was careless, and now he's about to pay for that carelessness.

"Hello?" he hears.

An unfamiliar voice.

"Hello, is anyone here?"

The voice is soft. Feminine. Not Alicia's. Not his mother's. A voice he's never heard before.

Nick quickly reaches to his right and hits the switch on the wall, extinguishing the fluorescent lights above him, plunging the small room into semidarkness. The light from the hallway leading to the large room continues to light up a portion of the room near the open metal door. It's risky to close that door now without alerting whoever's upstairs of his presence. He quickly steps out into the dark hall to the stairway and quietly pulls the door to the small room closed, taking care not to make much sound with the latch. The small amount of visibility remaining in the stairwell from the hallway lights is gone, leaving Nick to stand in the pitch-black.

"Hell-o-o-o?" The person upstairs calls out again, their

voice echoing in the large room and bouncing off the narrow walls as it makes its way down the staircase and to Nick's ears.

A flash of anger rushes through him, quickly replacing any nervousness. *Who is this person thinking they can just come into your home?* he asks himself. *Are you going to allow them to get away with this? What if they want to ruin the surprise for Alicia?*

Nick's eyes harden at the thought that this person, this trespasser, might be here just to ruin what he is doing, what he is planning. He cannot allow that to happen.

As quietly as he can, Nick reaches into his left pocket and pulls out the key ring, trying to keep the keys from clinking against each other. All the keys are stamped with numbers that correspond to the door they open. He memorized the feel of each key years ago to ensure that he'd never need any light to find the right one. He feels the keys until he locates the one for the closed door behind him, then turns to face it. He finds the lock, inserts the key, and slowly rotates it until he hears the soft metallic click of the bolt sliding into place.

Turning from the door and back toward the stairs, Nick listens for any other sounds from upstairs and slowly puts the keys back into his pocket.

Silence.

Maybe the person left when no one answered them. Or maybe they're testing him and have slowly been moving toward him while he's merely stood here doing nothing. He shakes the thought from his head, and a smile begins to form on his face. He is the only one to fear here. This is his house. His home. His way to get the love of his life back, his one and only. And he will make sure no one stops him from his plan.

He reaches into his right pocket and pulls out his pocketknife, carefully opening it, muffling the click of the blade lock engaging. He steps forward, softly, one foot after another, until he reaches the base of the stairs. As he starts to climb the steps, noise from the room above makes him pause.

A soft, rhythmic thumping noise with a corresponding slight metallic clang persists for a few minutes, then stops, swiftly followed by the soft voice again. "C'mon, you fucking flashlight, don't die on me now. This place is creepy enough as it is."

Nick's smile grows bigger when he hears this. The darkness is on his side. It's helping him.

He carefully takes the steps one at a time until he's at the top of the stairwell. One slow step after another and soon he's standing at the partially open door that separates the stairwell and the main upstairs room. He looks through the gap of the partially open door into the large room. Moonlight, pouring in through the halfway open main door, partially illuminates and outlines the trespasser for Nick to see. The trespasser is standing next to the table saw closest to the main door, rummaging through a bag sitting on the table.

The figure speaks once again. "Where the fuck did my extra batteries go?"

He waits and watches the trespasser's silhouette through the gap in the door. He watches as it continues to rummage through the bag on the table, shifting things around while digging for the batteries it previously mentioned.

A calmness falls over Nick while he watches. A familiar focus. He knows what he needs to do.

He reaches forward with his left hand and pushes on the door lightly. The door moves silently on its hinges. The gap between the door and doorframe grows larger, little by little, until the door is open a bit farther than halfway. Just enough space for Nick to fit through.

The silhouette, still focused on the bag, doesn't sense the figure that just stepped through a nearby doorway. The silhouette doesn't sense the slow, soft footsteps coming up from behind it.

Instead, the silhouette finally finds the batteries they're looking for in the very bottom of their bag.

"Aha! Fucking finally!"

Those are the last words they ever say.

At the same time as Nick's trespasser locates what they're looking for; Nick is only a couple feet behind them. In a fast and calculated motion, he swings his right arm in a wide arc and buries the blade of his pocketknife deep into the right side of the trespasser's neck, driving the hilt far enough into the skin that it causes the tip of the blade to exit out the left side of their neck. The force of his swing causes this person, who is much smaller in stature than he, to topple over to their left and hit the dusty floor with a solid thud.

Still standing in the same place, Nick watches as his

trespasser kicks their legs and claws at the knife buried in their neck. He listens to the raspy gurgling sound they're making. It only takes a minute or so before they stop moving completely and one final rasp escapes their lips.

Nick takes a deep breath and audibly sighs. He didn't expect what he just did to feel as good as it does right now. He won this round. He was being tested. Being tested to make sure he would follow through with whatever he needed to do to complete the plan. And he won. He proved he could do whatever he needs to.

He looks down at the body near his feet and softly speaks to the only thing listening, the darkness. "Don't worry, Alicia, I won't let anything come between us. Never again."

Nick continues to stand there for a few minutes, allowing the feeling to continue to wash over him. The rush. The elation. One wave after another, as though the life leaving his visitor's body is creating aftershocks through the air. He closes his eyes and takes a deep breath, allowing the last of the rush to leave his body.

When Nick opens his eyes back up, a new thought surfaces in his mind. *What am I going to do with the body?*

It doesn't take him long to come up with a solution. He will just have to do a bit more digging in the room below and bury the body there. This person, this unwanted and unwelcome intrusion, can become one with his plan, forever able to witness how he shows his one and only love how much he cares for her. Nick smiles at how romantic the thought is. A permanent guest, always present to witness the love he and Alicia will share for all eternity.

Nick glances at the bag on the table, with what appears to be the trespasser's dead flashlight next to it. He will have to ensure those items are entombed with the body lying motionless at his feet. He'll also need to clean up the blood, but that will have to wait until morning.

Who is this uninvited intruder? he wonders. *Why were they here?* He looks at the backpack on the table. *Maybe the contents of their bag will tell me who they are.*

His smile falters a bit as one more thought crosses his mind. *What if someone comes looking for them?*

Nick hesitates a moment while he tries to figure out what to do in the event more people start showing up. People looking for whoever this is. A momentary sense of panic begins to fill him. He's too close to his goal, to what he wants. He takes a deep breath to calm himself.

He will not allow anyone to interfere with his plans. His mother will know what to do.

But first, he needs to move the body.

Just as he's about to bend down and pick up the body to take it downstairs, a quick flash of light from outside illuminates the inside of the building.

Nick immediately turns around and looks through the doorway and out into the clearing. A flashlight is swaying back and forth in the forest on its approach to the camp. The bright beam of light, illuminating the ground in front of the person holding it, reaches the end of the path and the edge of the clearing. The beam then crosses the clearing and nears the building, causing a flash of light to pierce the darkness enveloping Nick, momentarily blinding him, causing him to step back a few steps in fear that the light might expose him. The beam then shuts off and Nick is sure he's been seen. There isn't enough time for him to retrieve his pocketknife before this additional intruder is upon him, so Nick quickly steps to the wall to the right of the main door and picks up one of the old ax handles leaning there, just underneath several rusty bear traps with jagged teeth that are hanging from large hooks. As he positions himself to get a good swing at his next uninvited guest, he tells himself he might need to put those bear traps to use one day if uninvited people keep coming out here.

He waits until the second uninvited guest finally reaches the doorway to his home. They turn their flashlight back on.

Another voice reaches his ears. This time he recognizes it. His mother.

He waits before announcing himself and watches, safely hidden in the shadows by the wall, as the circular spot of light follows the pathway he's worn through the years of dust until it falls upon the table saw. He watches the beam illuminate the backpack, which Nick can now see is bright pink in color, and the shiny metal flashlight next to it. He continues to watch as the bright circle leaves the backpack and travels down the table to the floor, stopping on the legs and feet of his first uninvited guest.

"Lord Jesus, what the hell happened here?"

Nick lowers the ax handle and steps from the shadows of the wall, into his mother's line of sight. She jumps a bit when he appears in the light of her flashlight, then seems to quickly regain her composure. She shines the beam directly on him. "What did you do, and just who is that?" she demands.

He doesn't respond. Instead he lowers his head and, walking toward the door, beckons for her to come in. After his mother is fully inside, he grabs the handle of the main door and slides it shut, sealing off her flashlight beam from the outside world. He turns back around and faces her, waiting for the additional scolding he expects.

His mother sets the box she's holding on the table, near the backpack and flashlight, and shines her flashlight on the body on the floor, starting at the feet and finally stopping on the face.

"You made one hell of a mess, didn't you?" she asks, motioning at all the blood splattered on the floor and table with her free hand. She kneels down next to the body and moves some of the blood-covered hair from the trespasser's face. "Why, she's just a young thing," she exclaims, standing back up. She looks back at Nick. "I thought you were doing all this for Alicia. Who is this girl?"

Nick shrugs and finally speaks. "She was going to ruin everything, so I made sure she didn't."

His mother shakes her head in response. "Like I said, you made a damn mess, and that's about all you did." He watches as she moves the flashlight beam from the dead girl to the bag on the table. "Well, let's see if we can find out who this is." She walks over to the bright-pink bag and motions him over. "Get over here and hold this light for me."

Nick does as he's told and walks to his mother's side, taking the flashlight from her hand and aiming it at the bag. He watches as she opens the bag and searches around inside for anything that might tell them who this intruder is. After a minute or two of searching, she pulls out a small wallet. She opens it and pulls out one of the identification cards from its clear plastic window. It's a student ID from some high school Nick knows is hundreds of miles away. The photo on the ID is of a pretty, raven-haired girl with a large smile. According to the ID, she's currently a senior at the school. Karen pulls out the next ID card from the wallet, the girl's driver's license. The license lists her address as being in the same city as the high school.

His mother shakes her head back and forth and chuckles a bit, as if reminded of a joke. Nick doesn't have to wait long to find out why she's laughing.

"Well, I'll be. I know exactly who this girl is."

CHAPTER 5

THE DECISION

Alicia puts the last of the dishes from breakfast in the sink and turns on the water. She wiggles her fingers through the stream of water to find that perfect temperature—hot, but not so hot that it scorches her skin. She puts the stopper in the drain and pours some dish soap into the pool of water already beginning to form under the dirty dishes, watching the bubbles and foam rise along with the water, quickly filling the sink.

As she turns off the water, she hears a childish squeal of laughter from the living room behind her. She looks over her left shoulder and sees Colin tossing Penny into the air and catching her.

She laughs and yells at him over her shoulder, "I hope she pukes all over you because you're doing that so soon after breakfast." Colin laughs and tosses Penny in the air once again.

Penny is the only one to respond, between her laughing fits. "Hear that, Daddy? I'm going to puke on you!"

Colin gives his little girl a big hug and finally sets her down. "Well, little hummingbird, we definitely don't want that to happen, though it wouldn't be the first time."

They both continue to laugh as Alicia finishes up the couple of dishes remaining, setting them aside to dry.

She turns to her family, walks into the living room, and fakes a long sigh. "So what do you two goofballs want to do today?" she asks.

"Watch awesome scary movies on TV!" Colin says, winking at her.

"Ugh, Daddy, boring! Let's make cookies!" Penny says, giving her dad a thumbs-down. "Those movies are stupid."

Alicia laughs. "Mommy agrees, those movies are stupid."

Colin shakes his head and pretends to be hurt. "No fair ganging up on the only guy in the house."

Both Alicia and Penny giggle at him. "You know what?" Alicia asks. "It's supposed to be a beautiful Sunday today, and we've been cooped up in this house way too much lately. How about a picnic outside for lunch?"

Penny looks at her and asks, "Like, with the ants and bugs?"

"Yes, sweetie, with the ants and the bugs. In fact, they were going to be the main course, but you already figured it out," Alicia tells her little girl.

Penny gives her a funny look and shakes her head no. "No, thank you, Mommy, I would rather watch one of Daddy's stupid movies."

Alicia giggles and looks over at Colin, who's giving his

precious little daughter two thumbs up with a smug look on his face. "What if we don't invite the ants and the bugs and just have the picnic with the three of us?" she asks.

"OK, Mommy, I might be able to find the time to attend."

"Sounds fair enough to me," she tells her little girl. "What about you, Daddy? Can you make the time to attend?"

Colin stands up straight and strikes a pose with his right hand grabbing his chin and his left arm behind his back. "Why yes, my dear, I do believe I have that time available on my calendar, although I may have to cancel my afternoon tea with the royal princess," he states.

Penny immediately chimes in, "It's OK, Daddy. We can have our tea at the picnic."

Colin nods at Penny and bows with a flourish, eliciting another fit of giggles from the little girl. Alicia chuckles as well and confirms their afternoon plans. "So a picnic lunch it shall be."

The remainder of the morning is a typical one, with Penny playing in her room and Colin watching the morning news on the TV. Alicia busies herself with a few cleaning tasks she's put off most of the week, and before she knows it, lunchtime is upon them.

As she finishes mopping the kitchen floor, Penny comes running into the kitchen and loudly proclaims, "Mommy, I'm hungry." Colin, tearing himself away from the television, chimes in, "I'm hungry too, Mommy. When's lunch?"

Alicia laughs and looks at Penny and then Colin. "Mommy

clearly isn't allowed to have any time to relax today, is she?" she says. Both Penny and Colin shake their heads in agreement. "Fine, Mommy is hungry as well, anyways. Honey, would you go make sure the picnic table out back is clean?"

Colin stands up, salutes her, and responds, "Yes, ma'am. Captain Colin is on the mission. C'mon, little hummingbird, let's go make sure the picnic table is secured for the queen." Penny giggles and nods enthusiastically. Colin turns toward the front door, his little girl in tow, and heads outside.

Alicia watches them until the front door closes, smiling. *How did I end up so lucky to have those two in my life?* she asks herself.

She sets the mop in its bucket and places both in their normal spot in the far corner of the kitchen, then starts looking in the lower cabinets for the picnic basket. She finds the basket hiding in the back of the cabinet under the sink, behind the random assortment of cleaning supplies. As she's pulling the basket out and trying not to knock over any of the bottles of cleaning solutions, she hears her little girl laughing outside. She frees the basket from the cabinet and looks into the backyard from the window above the kitchen sink. Penny is chasing Colin around the swing set. Alicia smiles, shakes her head, and returns to what she was doing. She looks in the picnic basket and confirms that the tablecloth is still in it. *At least that's one thing I don't have to hunt around for*, she thinks. She sets the basket aside on the kitchen table and proceeds to make the sandwiches for the picnic. Bacon, lettuce, and tomato sandwiches for her and

Colin, peanut butter and jelly with the crusts cut off for little Penny. And a few extra pieces of bacon for Colin's sandwich, since he'd survive on nothing but bacon if she let him.

As she's finishing up the first sandwich and wrapping it in cellophane, she hears a knock on the window behind her. She turns around and sees her husband out of breath and red-faced, smiling at her and motioning for her to open the window. She reaches across the sink, unlocks the window, and slides it open. "If you're looking for oxygen, you won't find any extra in here," she tells him.

He laughs and shakes his head. "I just wanted to tell my beautiful wife that I love her and would love her even more if she'd grab me a cold beer from the fridge."

Alicia laughs and walks over to the fridge, grabbing both a cold beer and a juice box. She returns to the window and hands both to Colin. "The juice box is for your daughter, sir, not for you," she makes sure to point out.

He looks at her with wide eyes. "Why does she get the one with all the alcohol in it?" he asks.

Alicia pushes his forehead out of the window and shoos him away. "I'll be out in a little bit. Let me finish the sandwiches," she says, and closes the window on him as he blows her a kiss and disappears off toward the picnic table.

She finishes making the other two sandwiches, ensuring they're wrapped tightly in cellophane and placed neatly in the picnic basket. She grabs a couple apples and bananas from the fruit basket on the counter and places them next to the sandwiches. From the cabinets under the counter she pulls out a small cooler and sets it on the table next to the basket. She grabs several beers and a couple more juice boxes from the fridge, positioning them in the cooler to make sure they all fit when the lid is closed. After adding a handful of napkins, she steps back to admire her handiwork. *One family picnic, all set to go*, she thinks, smiling.

Alicia carries the cooler and picnic basket to the front door, which she carefully opens, and steps outside as the door closes behind her, her footsteps echoing from the open space under the wooden front porch. She proceeds down the steps and heads to the right, crossing the gravel driveway. As she clears the side of the house, the picnic table and Penny's jungle gym come into view out back. Colin is sitting at the picnic table, watching Penny and sipping the beer Alicia handed him earlier. Penny is swinging back and forth on the swing closest to her daddy, giggling and kicking her feet into the air.

"If she falls off that swing again," Alicia says, "it's your fault this time, Daddy."

Colin turns from Penny and gives her a thumbs-up. "I accept full responsibility for her having fun."

Alicia shakes her head and laughs as she reaches the table and sets the cooler and basket down on the bench seat. "Help me get the tablecloth on, would you, handsome?" she asks. She pulls out the tablecloth from the basket and unfolds it, giving one end to Colin. They lay it over the table, the bright white-and-red checkerboard pattern of the cloth a festive change from the dark wood. With the tablecloth in position, she places the picnic basket and cooler on the table and sits. Colin finishes his beer, setting the empty bottle to the side.

"Honey, would you please make sure the princess washes her hands before she eats?" she asks him.

Colin smiles and nods, turning to Penny. "Let's go, hummingbird. Time to wash up."

Alicia watches Penny as she brings the swing to a stop and hops off, chasing after Colin, who's already walking toward the house. As the two disappear around the corner, she pulls out the sandwiches and stacks them in the center of the table, then the fruit and napkins next to the sandwiches. She places the now empty picnic basket on the far end of the table, on the other side of the cooler. A giggle and the patter of little footsteps running up behind her announce that Penny and Colin have returned from the house. Before Alicia has a chance to turn her head in their direction, Penny sits down on the bench next to her.

"All clean, Mommy," the little girl announces, presenting her hands for inspection.

Alicia pretends to scrutinize them closely and suddenly exclaims, "Oh my, what is that?"

Penny lowers her head to look closer at her hands. "What's what, Mommy?"

"That. That right there," Alicia states with a concerned look on her face, without giving any indication of what she's looking at.

Penny continues to examine her hands, trying to figure out what Alicia is talking about.

Colin reaches the table, stands behind Alicia, and puts his hands on her shoulders, giving her a loving squeeze. He leans over Alicia's right shoulder and looks at Penny's hands as well. "Oh, wow, how did we miss that?" he asks.

Penny, thoroughly confused at this point, lowers her hands and sets them in her lap. She looks at Alicia and Colin, who are both trying hard not to smile, her brow furrowed. "Not funny, Mom," she states. Alicia and Colin erupt in laughter while Penny glares at them.

"Just kidding, sweetie," Alicia says, and leans forward to give her little girl a kiss on the forehead. Penny allows the kiss but then sticks her tongue out at Alicia as her mother pulls away. Not wanting to be left out of the kisses, Colin pecks Alicia on her right cheek, leans over and kisses Penny on the top of her head, and then walks around the picnic table and sits down on the other side. He reaches into the cooler and pulls out a beer, offering it to Alicia, who nods in return. Penny grabs her sandwich from the stack and starts to tear off the cellophane. Colin grabs his own beer and his sandwich. Alicia takes a deep breath and smiles. She opens her beer, setting the cap aside, and grabs a juice box from the cooler for Penny before getting her own sandwich. They eat in silence, listening to the birds and squirrels in the trees around them and enjoying each other's company.

Colin is the first to finish his sandwich, as usual. He gathers the cellophane discarded on the table from everyone's sandwiches and rolls all three pieces up into one large ball, tossing it into the empty picnic basket. He grabs one of the apples on the table and takes a bite. Midway through chewing, he looks over at Alicia and smiles. "Well done, Mommy. The sandwich was delicious."

Alicia smiles at him, finishes her sandwich, and looks over at Penny, who's found a way to get jelly on her hands. Alicia grabs one of the napkins from the table, turns toward her daughter, and cleans her hands with only a small amount of resistance from the little girl. "I can do it, Mommy; I'm not a baby anymore," the little lady exclaims. Alicia nods and gives the napkin to Penny, letting her finish up.

"Hey, isn't it time for some tea?" Colin asks as he finishes his apple. Penny looks at him and nods eagerly. "Why doesn't the princess go get her tea set and bring it out here so we can all enjoy some?"

Penny, needing no more encouragement, drops her napkin on the table and hops up, turns toward the house, and takes off running to get her tea set from inside. Alicia watches her go and then picks up her discarded napkin from the table, tossing it into the picnic basket with the cellophane.

While she cleans up after Penny, Colin turns toward the tree line at the edge of the yard behind him and throws the apple core into the woods. He turns back to her and smiles. "Hey there, beautiful, I love you," he says.

Alicia smiles in return as they wait for their little princess to come back with her tea set. "I love you more, handsome."

≈

Nick opens his eyes and looks up at the ceiling of the room. The large overhead lights are still on. He sits up and stretches, looking at the clock on the far wall of the room. Three hours of sleep. *I must have been tired*, he thinks, *I normally don't sleep for that long.*

He replays the last few hours of this morning in his head. With his mother's help, he moved the young woman's body down here and cleaned up as much of the blood as they could find. They worked together to dig a shallow grave and buried the girl in the back corner of the room along with her backpack and flashlight, sealing away any trace that she was ever here under several feet of dark soil.

His mother repeatedly told him he was extremely lucky and it might not be as easy next time. According to her, the young girl was a runaway who the TV news said has been missing for the last several months. His mother told him the police had stopped by the restaurant a while back asking if she'd seen the girl and that was it. They believed the girl was on her way to a friend's house several states away.

Nick finds comfort in what his mother told him about the young woman. The odds of someone else coming out here looking for her seem miniscule, which reassures him. He will still be able to finish his work. His plan.

He looks at the clock again on the wall. Nine in the morning. He wonders what Alicia is doing right now. He wonders if she's thinking of him like he thinks of her. *Is she wishing she were with me instead of him?* he asks himself.

Nick surveys the room, trying to estimate how much longer it will take to complete his task. Once the floor is done, he'll be able to finish up quickly. Just some finishing touches here and there. He hopes Alicia will appreciate it. He takes a deep breath. He hasn't seen her in several days; the last time was at the post office when she was checking her mail. Nick made sure he wasn't seen, being careful as he moved from tree to tree on the other side of the road. She always checks the mail on Thursdays before she goes in for her shift at the restaurant. Nick knows this from watching her over the years. Observing her. Memorizing her usual schedule. *What kind of loving partner would I be if I didn't know her schedule?* he thinks.

She heads to the post office on Tuesdays and Thursdays, shops at the grocery store on Saturdays, works at the restaurant Monday through Friday, and every few Sundays she has a picnic outside with the little girl and Colin.

"Colin." The name tastes like poison in his mouth. The bastard who took his future away from him without ever caring how it might hurt his so-called best friend. Nick spits into the dirt next to him as if to remove any taste the name left behind. He'll make sure Colin feels the same despair he has felt. The same loss. The same wishing, day after day, that his one and only were with him and by his side.

He wonders if Alicia is having one of her picnics today. *She has to be*, he thinks, *because she has them just so I can see her. So I can miss her. So she can show me what my future with her will be like.*

Nick breathes in deeply, allowing the earthy smells of wood and dirt to fill his nose. He wants to see her. No, he *needs* to see her. He exhales and smiles.

He stands up and heads out of the large room, turning the overhead lights off and closing the solid wood door behind him. He walks down the hallway and into the adjacent room, repeating the motion of turning off the hallway lights and closing the heavy metal door, the scraping sound of metal on concrete friendly and familiar. He repeats this process two more times until he's standing in the main logging camp room. The room is still dark, almost none of the morning light making its way into the room. Years ago he replaced all the broken windows in the main room and covered them with newspaper so limited light could get in.

Nick traverses the floor of the room and reaches the main door. He made sure all the doors were locked after his mother left early in the morning. After unlocking the main door, he slowly slides it open, stopping after a few inches to look into the clearing beyond. He makes sure there's no one outside and opens the door just far enough to fit through. He steps through the door and closes it behind him, making sure to lock it.

He crosses the clearing quickly, plunging into the forest via the pathway. A short trip later and he's standing at the end of the logging camp road, his rental truck still parked where he left it and still covered by the camouflage tarp. He walks over and removes the tarp, securing it in the cab. He gets in and starts the engine, backing up from the spot between the trees and onto the old road. He slowly drives down the deserted route and pauses for a moment before turning out onto the main highway to make sure no cars are coming from either direction. He makes a right turn instead of a left turn, as a left will take him past the restaurant and through the main road in town, where too many eyes might see him. Might recognize him.

Although, after this long, probably no one would recognize him. But he'd still be a stranger, and in a small town people notice strangers. They remember them.

He doesn't need anyone remembering him. Not yet.

Nick takes the long way around the town, not seeing anyone else on the road until he's a few miles away from the turnoff to Alicia's house. He pulls off the road to the left side of the highway and far onto the shoulder, bringing the truck to a stop. After he turns the truck off, he waits a moment, looking for any other traffic. One car approaches from the other way, and he lowers his head to hide his face. The car goes by without slowing, probably heading to a day of shopping in Shelton. From where he's parked, it's only a mile or two through the woods to the back of Alicia's house.

Excitement begins to build inside him. He will be able to see his one and only soon. His *one*, as he likes to think she is. As he knows she is. To see her face, her smile; to be able to hear her voice as the wind carries it to him. He tries not to think about how he will feel if she isn't outside today. If he isn't able to see her. Especially after he proved this morning that he's willing to do anything to make sure nothing comes between them. She owes him the time, the chance to see her. To show him how much she wants to be with him instead of the bastard she's currently with.

I'm coming, my love, he thinks. *Not much longer.*

Confident no other cars are coming, Nick exits the truck and heads into the woods. He slowly navigates his way toward Alicia's house, doing his best not to make any noise by stepping on any downed branches or leaves. He deftly moves from tree to tree, keeping a low profile, until he's only a few hundred yards from the edge of the tree line separating the forest from Alicia's backyard. He moves closer until he dares to go no farther in fear he'll be seen from the window in the back of the house. A window he knows is above the sink in her kitchen. He knows this because he's been in that house before, many times. Just like he knows that the left side of the bed is her side, because the smell of her hair and skin lingers on the pillow there long after everyone inside the house is gone for the day. Nick knows the inside of that house almost as well as he knows his own by now.

He settles in to wait, completely motionless now, to see if she's going to show him that she knows he's there. That she knows what he's done for her. That she knows what he will do for her.

To show him she's finally ready for him.

Nick doesn't have to wait long before the backyard has company. Colin, the little girl in tow, appears from the right side of the house, heading into the backyard. The little girl runs past Colin and toward the picnic table.

Nick's eyes harden at the sight of Colin. *You don't deserve her*, he thinks. *You never deserved her.* He watches and waits as the little girl chases Colin around the swing set and then begins to swing on one of the swings while Colin walks to the back of the house and knocks on the glass. The glass of the window slides open, and for a moment, just a moment, her face appears from the darkness beyond the window.

His Alicia. Her face beaming. For a moment Nick feels like her eyes are looking past Colin and into the woods. Looking for him. Longing for him. He fights the urge to move, to give her a hint of where he's watching from. *No, she knows you're here*, he tells himself. *She can feel her connection with you.* Nicks closes his eyes a moment and takes a deep breath. When he opens his eyes back up, Alicia is outside and walking toward the picnic table, where Colin is already sitting.

He watches as she sets down what she's carrying and they prepare for their usual picnic. The picnic Alicia puts on just so Nick can spend time with her. He continues to watch as Colin and the little girl go inside the house, leaving his Alicia behind.

Sitting alone.

She sent them away for you, he tells himself, his heart beginning to race. *This is the sign. She wants you to take her away from this hell right now. She's begging you to come save her.* Every muscle in Nick's body tenses up. Is it time? Is it finally time after all these years? The plan isn't completely ready yet, though. He still has work to do.

Do it now, the voice in his head screams at him.

Nick steels his resolve, pushing the indecision from his thoughts, and just as he's about to bound into action to rescue Alicia, Colin and the little girl reappear from the side of the house. Nick curses softly under his breath and glares at Colin. Once again, that self-centered bastard has ruined their plans.

Nick relaxes and waits. He can still be patient. He has been patient for a very, very long time. But now he knows. He knows Alicia is ready. She wants him to save her.

And save her he will.

He watches the picnic unfold as the trio's laughter and conversation reaches his ears. He watches as the little girl gets up to head into the house, and he watches as Colin suddenly turns toward him. He freezes, his head low, his eyes narrowing at the man only a short distance away from him. The man who took his love away from him. The man who will soon know what it feels like to lose that same love.

Colin throws something in his direction. Nick continues to stare at Colin, unblinking, as the object hits the ground only a few feet away from him on his right side.

Nick refuses to acknowledge the object. He watches as Colin turns back around to Alicia, and the little girl reappears from the house carrying a large teapot and several cups. As the little girl hosts a tea party, Nick takes in everything about Alicia. Her smile. Her laughter. The light in her eyes that he can see even from here.

Soon she will be looking into his face and smiling, laughing, and giving him her love.

He watches as the tea party wraps up and the three of them get up to head inside. The skies above are beginning to darken with the threat of rain. Alicia packs up the picnic and follows Colin and the little girl to the corner of the house, and they all disappear, out of Nick's sight.

It's time, he tells himself. Time to go get ready to finally save Alicia and bring her into his life where she wants to be. Where she deserves to be. Where she belongs. Forever.

He is turning to his left, getting ready to leave, when a young voice from behind him speaks.

"Hello?"

Nick pauses, the events of this morning flashing through his mind. Keeping his head low, he slowly turns it to the right and sees the little girl standing at the picnic table, holding a teacup in her right hand that must've been left behind.

"Is someone there?" she asks.

Nick wonders if he'll have to take care of this little girl like he took care of the young woman this morning. He knows he'd rather not hurt her, as she is part of Alicia, but he will not allow anyone to come between him and his one true love. Not even this child.

However, before he has to make that decision, Alicia's voice reaches them both from the window of the kitchen. "Penny, hurry up, sweetie. It's about to rain."

The little girl turns toward the house and responds, "OK, Mommy, coming." She runs for the house and disappears around the corner. Nick watches as Alicia slides the window closed and disappears from view.

Nick waits a moment longer to make sure no one else comes out to get something they forgot and then makes his way back toward the truck.

He needs to see his mother and let her know.

Let her know it's time.

CHAPTER 6

THE TAKING

The skies open up just as Nick makes it back to the truck, the rain coming down in torrential waves. By the time he's back in the driver's seat, he's soaked through. The rain doesn't bother him, though, as he has spent many nights in the rain, watching Alicia from a distance. The slight discomfort means nothing to him when it comes to her.

He starts the truck and turns on the windshield wipers, transforming the blurry green, gray, and brown watercolors in front of him back into visible shapes. He switches on the headlights and puts the truck in drive. The clock on the dashboard reads two fifteen p.m. Alicia's shift tomorrow doesn't start until five p.m., and he'll need to be ready to be her knight in shining armor.

He turns the truck around and gets back on the main road, once again taking the long way around town. The restaurant will be busy with the Sunday dinner crowd later, fresh from doing all their usual Sunday activities.

He will have to wait until much later this evening to speak with his mother.

Nick drives in silence, reaching the old logging camp road and turning onto it after making sure no one is around to see. The heavy rain, still fighting the windshield wipers, has already filled up the various ruts in the road, causing muddy water to splash on the truck as he drives through them. He'll need to wash the truck before returning it to the rental car company, just to avoid any unnecessary questions. He reaches the end of the road and pulls back into the same spot as before. He gets out, covers the truck with the tarp, and heads down the path to the logging camp.

He doesn't pay any attention to the rain. His focus is on the ground so he can make sure he doesn't step somewhere that will leave a footprint. He reaches the end of the pathway without any issues and pauses, surveying the clearing in front of him. Satisfied it's empty, he steps into the clearing and quickly crosses to the main door of his home. He unlocks it and steps inside, sliding the door closed behind him and relocking it. He repeats this process until he's standing once again in the large room at the end of the hall, the now permanent resting place of his first guest. He looks over at the corner where the young woman is buried and smiles.

"You will get to meet her soon, I promise," he says, as though answering a question.

Anxious to make sure he's ready for Alicia, he walks over

to all the boxes in the near left corner of the room. He digs through some of the closest boxes and removes a large roll of heavy-gauge wire and sets it aside. He continues to look through the boxes until he comes across several rolls of duct tape, which he sets down next to the wire.

He tries to think of whether he'll need anything else just yet. He looks at the wire and the duct tape and shakes his head. *No, these will be fine for now.* He picks up the items and heads out of the large room and back into the smaller room, setting the wire and tape down on the heavy wooden chair against the back wall, next to the metal storage chest. He already knows the storage chest is empty and locked, and the antique wood hand sander on top of it has no blades in it.

Nick walks over to the table lining the far back wall opposite the metal door and gathers up the various blueprints and how-to manuals he's spread around, doing his best not to get them wet. He takes them all back to the large room and into the locker room on the left, setting them down on a bench in the center of the room. He still needs these for his plan.

He returns to the room at the base of the stairs and transfers the wire and duct tape from the wooden chair to the table. He tests the chair to make sure it's sturdy, applying pressure to the wooden arms and legs to see if they'll provide any give. The chair is old and extremely solid. Nick is pretty sure it was made by the loggers who used to work here, as the surface is smooth but relatively unfinished.

Satisfied the chair will hold up, he takes a deep breath. He's ready. He has a lot more work to do to show Alicia how much he cares, but he knows she'll be patient with him like he has been patient with her. And when he's ready to show her his plan, she'll be ready to truly appreciate it.

He once again heads back through the large room to the adjoining locker room. The room is tiled from floor to ceiling, with several open showers on the right and several toilets on the left. A couple of sinks line the wall at the back, and his blueprints and how-to manuals are now stacked on the bench in the center. A single bulb hangs in the middle of the room, waiting to provide the room with its light. He flips on the switch, and the single bulb lights up, dispelling the shadows from either side of the room. Also on the bench are several sets of folded clothes.

Although Nick doesn't have much of a wardrobe anymore, he does ensure that he showers and changes his clothes on a fairly regular basis. His mother washes his clothes for him when he drops them off while picking up food and water.

Walking across the room, he looks at himself in one of the smudged mirrors above the sinks. His shirt is stained all over with blood. His face and hair are soiled with dirt that the rain wasn't able to wash away.

For a moment, and only a moment, he is thankful that he didn't save Alicia earlier today. She doesn't need to see him like this. But he knows she will love him no matter what he looks like.

Nick turns from the mirror and strips out of his dirty

clothes, setting them in a pile on the floor next to the bench. He walks over to the showers and turns one on, the ice-cold water pouring over his skin. He grabs a used bar of soap from the shelf in front of him and starts cleaning the blood and dirt from his body, lost in his thoughts of what he still needs to do.

He'll need to get the hot water heater connected for Alicia. She likes hot showers. At the moment, the hot water heater he purchased several years back is sitting unused in the far back corner of the room, next to one of the toilets. Nick has always preferred cold showers, so he never took the time to hook the heater up before. He makes note that he'll need to do that soon for her. He thinks about what else she may want but can't come up with anything.

She will have me, he realizes. *That's all she will want.*

This thought makes Nick smile as he finishes up his shower. He sets the soap back on the shelf and turns off the water, turning to his left. Along the wall are several metal hangers. On two of the hangers are towels. He grabs a towel and dries himself off, returning the towel to the hook.

He returns to the bench and grabs a set of clothes from the end, quickly putting them on, followed by socks and his work boots. He looks at his showered image in the mirror and runs his hands through his disheveled hair a few times, getting it to lie down evenly.

Finally looking presentable again, Nick gathers up his dirty clothes and leaves the locker room, turning the light off behind him. He closes the door and walks over to where the boxes and hardwood are stacked. He grabs one of the empty plastic bags from the floor and stuffs his dirty clothes in the bag, tying the top of the bag shut. He looks up at the clock on the wall. Just after five. The restaurant normally closes at ten, but the staff typically stays later, cleaning up and preparing for tomorrow.

Nick takes the plastic bag and exits the room, making sure to turn off the overhead lights and pull the door closed behind him.

He smiles. The next time he goes through this door, Alicia will be his.

He walks down the hallway, stepping through the metal door. He grabs the handle and pushes the large metal door closed. He walks over to the table and sets the plastic bag down on it. After he sets the bag down, he yawns, unexpectedly tired.

The events of the last day must have worn on him, knowing as he did that after all this time, he will finally have his love, his one, with him where she belongs.

Nick walks over to the wooden chair and sits down, yawning again. He closes his eyes, daydreaming about the happiness to come. About how his life will be perfect, how Alicia's life will be perfect. And about how Colin will finally feel the same pain that Nick has all these years.

Just as he thinks he is drifting off to sleep, he jolts back awake. He opens his eyes and lifts up his head, a soreness in his neck quickly making itself known. He rubs the soreness away with his left hand and stands up, not tired anymore. He wonders if he actually did sleep.

Nick stretches, trying to wake his stiff muscles up. As he begins to walk across the room to the stairwell door, he detours to his left and grabs the plastic bag with his dirty, bloodstained clothes in it. He then proceeds through the door to the stairwell and heads up the stairs and into the main room, making sure the doors are closed behind him. He doesn't lock any of the doors behind him this time. As he reaches the top of the stairs, he can hear the rain still singing its song against the metal roof above him, although that song is much softer now than it was when he first came home.

He smiles. Another sign he is on the right path. The rain keeps people inside and off the road.

He navigates around the equipment and to the front door, unlocking it and slowly sliding it open a bit. The clearing outside is pitch-black, which lets Nick know he actually must've gotten some sleep. With the darkness upon him, the restaurant will surely be closed by now.

He steps out into the light rain and pulls the door closed behind him. He leaves it unlocked, like the others. He wants to make sure nothing slows him down from getting his precious cargo home, and he knows she will not want to be held up by something as stupid as him fumbling for some keys to open a door.

There is no moonlight to light his way this time on account of the rain. It doesn't bother him or slow him down. He skillfully finds his way through the clearing, to the pathway, and down the trail until he finally reaches the hidden rental truck. He will need to return the truck soon and get a different one from another rental company in another city. Vehicle rentals that run more than a week might raise some questions, and Nick isn't planning on answering any questions. Thankfully, his mother takes care of all the paperwork in her name, and no one in the cities he picks the rentals up from have any idea who he is.

He plans on keeping it that way. He will still need supplies so he can complete the plan.

He sighs. Hopefully, when he is done with his work, he won't need another rental vehicle. *The rental truck merry-go-round, according to Mother*, he thinks as he sets the still-wet, folded-up camouflage cover on the floor of the passenger side of the truck along with the plastic bag containing his dirty clothing. He starts the truck, turns on the windshield wipers, and flips on the parking lights. The parking lights give him just enough light to see by so he can back out from between the trees and get the truck turned around and pointed down the old logging camp road. A damaged rental vehicle only leads to questions. He glances at the clock on the radio. Three in the morning. He really did get some sleep this time around, although it didn't feel like it and the soreness lingering in his neck says otherwise.

He puts the truck in reverse, and an unexpected lightning bolt of excitement rips through his body as it sinks in that today is the day. Finally, after all the years of being patient. After all the years of watching and wishing and planning.

Today, Alicia will be his. His one, finally with him where she belongs.

A smile takes over Nick's face as he backs the truck up and puts it in drive, carefully navigating through the ruts and dips of the old logging camp road. When he reaches the main highway, he ensures that no other traffic is coming and takes a left onto the road, finally turning on the headlights. The drive to the restaurant takes only a few minutes and then he's already turning into the parking lot. The parking lot is empty, as he expected, and he drives the rental to the back of the building, parking it next to his mother's truck and out of sight from anyone who may be passing by on the road out front. He kills the lights and the engine of the truck at the same time.

He sits there for a moment and watches the rain build up on the windshield, blurring any visible shapes in front of the truck. The smile is still on his face.

Nick exits the truck and quickly crosses the gravel to the back door of the restaurant, opening the door and stepping inside in one fluid motion. The kitchen light is still on, indicating his mother is still awake. Her voice, laced with irritation, reaches his ears before he moves any farther toward the kitchen from the back door hallway.

"You're late."

≈

Karen takes a deep breath and finishes the two cheeseburgers on the flattop grill, then transfers them to the plates already prepared. She sets the spatula down and grabs the loaded plates, taking them to the pass-through and setting them down on the counter. She checks the ticket to make sure the order is complete and hits the bell.

"Order up!" she announces, and her day-shift waiter makes his way through the restaurant to the pass-through. He smiles at her and picks up the plates, heading off to deliver them to the waiting diners.

Karen sighs. She'll have to remind him he needs to check the ticket before racing off with the food to ensure the order is correct. Although she rarely messes up a ticket, some of her less experienced line cooks have a habit of missing the smaller details, such as an order specifying no mayo or a special request for gravy on the side instead of on top of the mashed potatoes.

The customers are almost always locals, and luckily they're all very forgiving when something is missed; however, this is her restaurant and her name is on the outside of the building. She expects her employees to uphold her standards.

Today, though, it is only her in the kitchen. With the rain outside, business is slow, and right now there are only a handful of diners in the dining room. Her current waiter, a local high school boy still wet behind the ears, is spending more time chatting with the diners than doing anything else. She shakes her head and turns her attention back to the flattop, grabbing the scraper and cleaning the surface of any remaining burger or cheese remnants.

As she's scraping the flattop, she thinks about earlier this morning when her boy came by. She was already irritated because he was late by over an hour, as he normally shows up around two in the morning. Instead, he came strolling in past three. And then, when he told her it was time and what he needed her to do, a momentary panic raced through her.

This is your little boy, she told herself. *You will do anything to ensure he is happy.*

So she agreed and told him not to worry about it, that she would do what was necessary.

Karen looks at the clock on the wall in front of her. Almost four in the afternoon. Alicia will be here a little bit before five for her shift, which runs until about eleven on most nights. The kitchen closes at ten; however, Alicia always stays and helps prep for the following day.

Karen takes a deep breath and thinks about what she's going to tell Colin. She rehearses the conversation in her head. *Yes, dear, she was here for her shift as usual and then left to go home. Nothing seemed out of the ordinary. She never said anything about leaving or being unhappy.* She repeats it a few more times in her head, convincing herself of how believable it sounds. She knows Colin won't question it if it's coming from her.

Karen smiles. She is, in her own way, looking forward to seeing him suffer for what he did to her boy. For hurting her Nick and keeping Alicia away from him. As she is thinking about the satisfaction Colin's grief will bring her, Penny creeps into her mind. The poor little girl won't understand why her mother is gone. Not at first, anyway. But Karen is sure that one day down the road, when Alicia finally comes to her senses and realizes who she is really meant to be with, the little girl will be reunited with her mother.

Karen's smile gets a little bit bigger as she continues to imagine what the future will bring. Her boy will make an amazing father, and she is already the little lady's Meemaw, so it only makes sense that one day little miss Penny will be back with the family she should've been with all along. Maybe Karen will even be able to get her boy back under her roof and away from the logging camp, his loving family by his side. *No, not just his family*, she tells herself. *It will be your loving family too.*

She finishes cleaning the flattop and turns her attention back to the dining room. The last couple of guests are getting up to leave, and her young waiter is busy busing their table. The departing diners wave at her and she waves back, still smiling. The bell above the front door chimes, and then it's just her and her employee, who is currently putting the last of the dirty dishes in one of the crates on the dishwasher conveyer belt.

"Mrs. Ellie, did you want me to go ahead and wash these?" he asks. "I already cleaned up the tables in the dining room."

"Yes, that'll be fine, young man. When you're done, you can go ahead and clock out. I'll note you stayed to five so you get that hour of pay."

"Yes, ma'am. Thank you, ma'am!" he responds excitedly, and slides the crate of dishes into the dishwasher, closing the door and turning the machine on.

Karen nods and turns, walking out of the kitchen and into the bar. She cleans up the two glasses in the bar sink and sets them on the drying mat. As she's drying her hands on the towel hanging from her apron belt, her young waiter scribbles his hours on his time card next to the pass-through and waves good-bye to her as he heads toward the front door. "Have a great night, Mrs. Ellie!" he tells her. She nods and waves as she watches him leave, the chime above the door once again making its presence known.

Maybe not a great night, but definitely a night this town will be talking about for a very long time, she thinks. She turns around and grabs one of the lowball glasses sitting upside down along the liquor display, flipping it over and setting it back down on the bar. She grabs the nearest bottle of Jack Daniel's from the shelf and begins to pour it into the glass until it's just over halfway full. She puts the bottle back in its spot on the shelf and picks up the glass of whiskey. *The things we do for our children*, she thinks as she puts the glass to her lips and drinks until it's empty. She normally doesn't drink during work hours, but today is different. Today she needs the drink.

Karen sets the glass down on the bar and takes a look at the bottle, wondering if she should have another glass. She chooses not to pour any more just yet, deciding it will be better to wait until after the events of the evening are done.

As she's turning to set the empty glass in the bar sink, the chime of the front door rings and a family of seven makes its way into the dining room. Karen smiles at them as they file through the door, one by one. "Just have a seat anywhere. I'll be with you shortly," she says.

She walks to the end of the bar and grabs one of the order pads and a pen from the stack sitting on the shelf. She makes her way into the dining room and begins to take everyone's order. Halfway through the order, the door chimes again and Alicia steps through the front door. She waves quickly at Karen, nods, and heads toward the kitchen to get her apron after dropping her purse on the shelf at the end of the bar. Karen finishes taking the family's order and heads toward the kitchen, putting the order ticket on the wheel and rotating it so the ticket faces the kitchen. She puts the pad and pen back and heads into the kitchen to start making the order.

Alicia, who's just finished putting on her apron, gives her a quick hug. "I got them, Mrs. Ellie," she reassures Karen just as the front door chimes once again. Karen smiles and gets to work on the order as the dinner rush gears up to full swing.

Before Karen knows it, ten o'clock is almost upon her. The restaurant picked up for several hours as the locals in Orchard Lake braved the light rain to get some dinner on this wet Monday evening, which kept her busy filling orders instead of constantly checking the clock above the stoves. She puts the last order in the pass-through window and hits the bell. "Order up!" she yells, mostly out of habit. She knows Alicia started on her way to the window to grab the food the moment the bell went off. Karen turns her focus to cleaning up the kitchen and prepping for tomorrow.

She wonders what time Nick will be here, or if he's already here and just waiting outside for the rest of the patrons to leave.

She glances up and looks at the time. Twenty minutes after ten.

She takes a deep breath. She will know soon enough.

A sudden noise behind her makes her jump. She quickly spins around and sees Alicia at the dishwasher, unloading dishes from the busing tub and stacking them in the washing rack.

"You OK, Mrs. Ellie?" Alicia asks her. "You seem a bit jumpy tonight."

"Yes dear, I'm fine, just have a lot on my mind tonight, that's all." Karen looks into the dining room, relieved to see that the last of the customers have gotten up and are heading out the front door.

The door chimes one final time.

"Honey, I'm going to go ahead and lock up and close the restaurant for the night. Would you mind finishing up the dishes and some of the prep for tomorrow?" she asks.

Alicia smiles and nods at her. "Of course, Mrs. Ellie, I'd be happy to," she says as she slides the loaded washing rack into the dishwasher, closes the door, and turns it on.

Karen walks to the front of the restaurant and bolts the front door, making sure the lock is secure. She reaches over to the switch for the neon open sign and flips it down. She watches the bright-green light of the open letters turn off and the deep red closed letters turns on. She looks out the window in front of her to see if anyone is in the parking lot. From what she can see, the parking lot is completely empty. Alicia's car is probably parked next to her truck in the back of the restaurant.

She turns and walks back toward the kitchen, stopping at the end of the bar. Alicia's back is to her while she is busy unloading the now clean dishes from the washing rack and putting them away.

Movement from her right, in the hallway, catches her eye, and she glances in that direction.

Nick is standing in the hall, looking directly at Alicia, who's still focused on finishing up the dishes.

Karen tries to remember if she heard the back door open. She doesn't think she did. She wonders how long he's been there.

She looks over at her son and nods, feeling her heart rate rapidly increase. In his right hand is a white rag.

Karen watches as Nick carefully approaches Alicia, one step at a time. When he's about four feet away from her, Alicia turns to the prep station and sees Nick standing in the center of the kitchen. Karen sees the look of panic immediately cross Alicia's face as her eyes move from the man in front of her to the white rag he's holding in his right hand. Karen cringes at the scream that follows.

The next few moments seem to move in slow motion for Karen.

Nick, slightly caught off guard by Alicia's scream, hesitates before he reaches out and tries to cover the last few feet between the two of them. His hesitation gives Alicia a chance to turn and run. As Alicia begins to run toward the dining room to escape, Karen knows what she has to do.

She steps from the end of the bar and directly into Alicia's path, intercepting her before she can get out of the kitchen. She wraps her arms around the young woman and holds her tight. Alicia initially doesn't resist and instead screams for Karen to run, that there's an intruder in the restaurant. Karen continues to maintain her grip around the much smaller woman.

"Shhhhhh," she starts to say, over and over, while the panicked woman in her arms looks from Karen to Nick and back to Karen.

"What are you doing? Mrs. Ellie? Why won't you let me go? Please? What are you doing?"

Karen closes her eyes and continues to shush the woman in her tightly clenched arms, even when Alicia begins to fight against her grip, trying with all her might to break free.

"Shhhhhh." She keeps saying it, over and over, as Alicia's pleadings turn to anger and then finally to screams once again as Nick reaches them both.

Moments later, the young woman in her arms stops struggling and goes limp. "That's a good girl. It's going to be OK, I promise," Karen says to the now unconscious Alicia as she lowers her to the floor. Karen steps back and looks at her son, who's putting the rag away in his pocket. She smiles when she sees the look on his face as he kneels down next to Alicia and caresses her face with his left hand. "She's yours now. You better take good care of her," she tells her son. He looks up at her with the happiest look on his face she's seen in a long time and nods at her.

At that moment, the very second when she sees that look on her boy's face, Karen knows that what she just helped her son do is going to be worth every minute of what is to come, for as long as she lives.

"Once you get her to the camp, you need to come pick me up outside of Rockville," she tells him. "I rented a large unit in a storage facility just outside city limits. I'm going to drive her car out there and put it in the storage unit. You need to do this quickly. Colin is going to be calling here if Alicia isn't home by midnight, and I need to be here for that call. This means we have just over an hour and a half to get all this done. Get the address off the board in the hallway."

Her son nods at her and bends down, carefully picking up the unconscious woman. Nick turns and heads for the hallway leading to the back door.

She watches until the both of them disappear out of her sight, then turns toward the bar, where Alicia's purse sits.

She's going to need Alicia's keys.

CHAPTER 7

THE WAKE-UP

Nick pulls the rental truck into his usual parking spot among the trees and turns off the ignition.

A smile forms on his face as he thinks about finally being able to see his girl again. He doesn't like being away from the home they now share together, but he had to pick up some supplies in Shelton. He took a big risk going into town so close to the morning hours, but to him it was worth it. Still smiling, he grabs three bags with his right hand from the passenger seat and gets out of the truck. He closes the door and sets the bags down on the ground, then retrieves the cover from the bed of the truck and secures it over the vehicle. Satisfied, he picks up the bags and turns toward the pathway leading to his home. To his beautiful girl. He pauses a moment, allowing the feeling to wash over him. He is actually going home to his girl, to his love, instead of to an empty house.

Although he's anxious to be back home and with his love, he

takes his time walking along the pathway. Adorned on either side by the trees' leafy canopy, the path to the center of his life is actually quite beautiful today. The early-morning sun, hunting for breaks in the trees where it can shine down to the ground, leaves spots of glowing light at random intervals. It almost feels as though he's seeing it all for the first time.

He listens to the birds singing their songs in the trees and feels the breeze gently blowing across his face.

If there is a heaven, he is walking along the path leading to it. Of course, to him, his home and his girl are his heaven. His everything.

He begins to hum as he walks along, completely content. A few more steps and the path finally ends. He pauses a moment and takes in the sight as though he's finally reached a beacon that's been calling to him. His home is set in the center of a large open area, with a beautiful view of the lake that the town where he lives is named after. It wasn't easy getting his life to where it is now, but every sacrifice has been worth it. He steps from the path and into his yard, casually walking toward his front door, the bags in his right hand swinging back and forth with his stride.

Reaching the front door, he reaches up with his free hand and knocks. The sound echoes loudly inside his home. He knocks again, already knowing the response. Again, the sound goes unanswered. He should have known she wouldn't answer the door. *She must be busy taking care of our home*, he muses. He moves the bags from his right to his left hand and reaches into his right pocket, pulling out his key ring. He fiddles with the keys until he has the correct one and unlocks the front door. Putting the keys back in his pocket, he grabs the door and slides it open. A familiar, comforting screech comes from the tracks the door is set on. One of his favorite features of his home is his front door—a large metal door that can be slid fully open, revealing an opening big enough to bring almost anything through.

The bright sunshine from outside falls upon the interior of his home as the door opens. He smiles, seeing that everything is still in the same place it was when he left. He worries that every time he leaves home, something bad will happen to the picture-perfect life he's worked so hard to obtain. That something bad will happen to his home. And now he worries that something bad will happen to his amazing girl.

He takes a deep breath, breathing in the familiar smells, and listens for a moment. Beyond the sounds outside, the inside of his home is silent. His smile fades a bit. He was hoping he would hear his love calling out to him, welcoming him back home and telling him how much she missed him. "Honey, I'm home," he calls out. Silence continues to greet him.

He steps inside and slides the door closed behind him, cutting off the daylight from the room and plunging it into familiar darkness. He repeats the process with the keys, making sure the front door is locked. Although his home is well off the beaten path, with no nearby neighbors, one can never be too safe. He turns from the door and navigates around the various items in the room, finally reaching the door to the basement. Another cycle with the keys and the door to the basement is unlocked and open. He reaches into the dark and flips a switch, allowing the bare bulb overhead to light up the hallway and stairwell. He steps in, closes and locks the door behind him, and continues down the stairwell, finally reaching the door that separates him from his love. His heart begins to race.

On the other side of this door is his girl. His one and only.

The room on the other side of the door is silent. He wonders what she's doing. *Is she sleeping? Working? Reading? Maybe anxiously waiting for me to return?* He unlocks the door but then pauses and instead reaches over and turns the hall light off, plunging the hall into darkness. If she's asleep, he doesn't want to wake or worry her unnecessarily.

The anticipation of being able to look into her eyes again escalates from a want to a need. He needs to see her, to see the reason for all his happiness. The reason for the brightening of his once dull life. He slowly opens the door.

No sound greets him from the room now open in front of him. A sudden fear races through him. What if she's not here? What if she's hurt? The fear begins to resurface as panic. He quickly reaches for the wall and hits the light switch, causing the overhead lights to come on, bathing the room in bright white light.

His heart soars with elation. There she is, sitting in her favorite chair, eyes firmly closed from the sudden incursion of light into the room.

"Good morning, beautiful," he says. She sits in silence. He must've woken her up from her sleep. The urge to apologize strikes him, but he knows he shouldn't have to apologize for his passion and concern for her. His trip to Shelton was very early in the morning, primarily so he could avoid any traffic on the road. To avoid any prying eyes. It was early but not that early, maybe seven or eight in the morning, so she should be awake and ready to face the day. To take care of their home and to take care of him. Like the love of his life is supposed to do.

He hefts the bags still in his left hand and decides it's probably best if he just goes to work and lets her alone for a bit. He doesn't want to make her any angrier than she may already be.

"You have a good day today, my love, and I will be back before you know it."

He smiles at her, happy to be able to look upon her beautiful face again, wishing he could give her the world and make all her dreams come true. If she would only open her eyes and see his, she would see how he will be everything she has ever needed. *It's OK*, he tells himself, *there will be many days where I can gaze into her eyes and share my love for her.* He pulls the door behind him closed and locks it, then turns toward the large metal door set in the wall to his left.

Time to go to work and earn his right to have this amazing woman's love. He can't wait to show her what he's been working on for so long. Working on just for her.

He walks over to the metal door and unlocks it, pulling hard on the heavy door to open it. The loud metal-on-concrete scrape echoes through the room as the bottom of the door follows a familiar worn path on the floor. He steps through the doorway and pulls the metal door shut behind him, making sure to lock it once it's fully closed. One day he hopes he can leave this door unlocked, but for now he has to keep the surprise waiting for his love as just that, a surprise. The light from the room on the other side is now gone, left behind to keep his beautiful girl company.

Enveloped by the darkness, he turns from the door. The darkness is like family to him. Familiar. Comfortable. Reassuring. Although he could easily maneuver through the black void around him to get to his destination, he needs to ensure that all the lights are still working properly.

Reaching out to his right, he finds the switch on the wall and turns it on. A long hallway lights up as all the overhead lights turn on. Every ten feet hangs a bare lightbulb, straining to light its small section of hallway. This continues on for quite a distance, until the final hanging bulb is reached. This bulb, unlike the others before it, gets to cast its light on a door. And beyond that door is his work. His plan. His way of showing his love how much she means to him.

He treks down the hallway, finally reaching the door. Grabbing the doorknob, he twists and in one fluid motion opens the door. He knew this door would not be locked.

There was no reason to ever lock it.

The door swings open, and the last overhead bulb fights

valiantly to try to push light into the room beyond.

He steps through the doorway and turns to the left, hitting all three switches on the wall.

Large lights, hanging from the ceiling, quickly light up and illuminate the room he's standing in. Nick takes a moment and surveys the work he's already done. The walls and ceiling have been smoothed and painted a bright orange. Another door breaks up the smooth orange of the wall along the left side of the room. Stacks upon stacks of plastic-encased wooden planks randomly dot the floor of the room, waiting to be unwrapped and set free from their plastic prison. A large pile of metal poles rests on the floor to the far back of the room, next to a wide variety of boxes yet to be unpacked. A partially completed subfloor under his feet runs approximately sixty feet in front of him before it ends and reveals the dirt below. He smiles at how much work he's completed in the last twenty-four hours since his love came home to be with him. He expected his work on the floor to take a lot longer than it has, but she's here now. Right down the hall from him. He has found a new energy, a new vigor, which he didn't have before without her. That he didn't have when he was expanding the room. When he was doing all the digging, all the bracing, all the hauling of dirt and rock out of his home. Day and night. Until the room was just the right size, just the right dimensions.

Now his work is to finally put the room together and transform it. Everything has to be perfect. Perfect for his love so she can see just how much he cares about her and how much she means to him. He pauses a moment in his thoughts of the future and hopes she has a good day today. He wonders if she will clean the house, or if she will do some reading. He is letting his thoughts continue to wander when a loud pop from overhead brings him back to the present. He looks up toward the sound. One of the overhead lights is now dark.

He frowns. *Those bulbs were new, weren't they?* he asks himself. Turning toward the wall to the left, he sets the bags he's still holding down on the ground. He walks over to the wall where a large ladder is leaning and carefully maneuvers it around various stacks of planks and boxes of supplies until he's underneath the now burnt-out light bulb. He sets up the ladder and then walks back and fishes a new bulb out of a large supply box on the ground. He returns to the ladder, climbs up, and switches bulbs, careful not to drop either. Once screwed in far enough, the new bulb explodes in bright white light that announces its life to the room. He quickly finishes screwing the large bulb in before it gets too hot to touch and climbs down. A few moments later the ladder is back in its place against the wall and the burnt-out bulb in the wheelbarrow next to the door, which he uses as a scrap and garbage hauler. Satisfied, he walks over to the bags on the floor and picks them up, carrying them over to the various boxes spread around on the ground. He carefully empties the contents from the bags to their respective spots in each of the boxes and then tosses the empty bags into the wheelbarrow to join the burnt-out bulb. Satisfied that his supplies have been adequately refreshed, he can now continue.

He walks over to where the subfloor ends and bends down, picking up the hammer lying on the ground. Right where he left it before he headed to town for more supplies.

Time to get back to work.

As he works, his thoughts turn to what he's creating and who he's creating it for. His love. His life. He knows she will appreciate this when he's done. She will appreciate the years of work and planning he's put into this. The research to make sure everything is exact. A smile forms on his lips, and he begins to hum along with the sound of his hammer strikes. Nick loses himself in his thoughts as he works.

It won't be much longer before the subfloor is completed. A few more adjustments and a bit of cutting, and then the subfloor will be done. He glances over at the spot where his permanent guest is buried, now fully concealed. He smiles, happy his guest will get to see his love's reaction. To forever bear witness of their lives together. He stands up and stretches, admiring his work. Soon he'll be able to start laying down the wooden planks. A rush of exhilaration races through him as he starts to imagine how it will look when it's all done. Though he's anxious to continue working, a rumble in his stomach tells him it's time to get something to eat. He looks at the clock on the wall above the door, a large round white one with black block numbering, just like you'd see in school. Almost six in the evening. His exhilaration is briefly replaced by a flash of panic. His love must be starving, as he knows she'll wait patiently for him to return from work before eating. He sets the hammer down next to the last few pieces of subflooring and heads to the other door in the room. He opens it up and takes a look around. The solitary bench, with several sets of folded clothes, maintains its control of the center of the room between him and the sinks. He steps into the room and turns on the single light, then walks over to the first shower and turns on the spigots, adjusting the temperature until the water is mildly warm. It took him only a few moments to hook up the hot water heater to the connectors where the old one was, but it will take him some time to get used to a shower that isn't cold. His love won't have to worry about any cold showers. He strips out of his clothes, tossing them into a pile on the floor next to the door, and steps into the stream of water, grabbing a bar of soap sitting on the shelf on the wall.

He quickly washes the dirt and grime of the day away and turns off the water, watching the last few streams swirl around his feet and disappear down the drain.

Grabbing a towel hanging near the sinks, he dries off and then rehangs the towel. He walks over to the bench and selects one of the folded piles of clothes and gets dressed. He wants to make sure he isn't a mess when he goes home to his love. A quick look in the mirror and he's satisfied with how he looks. He heads out of the room, pausing a moment at the pile of dirty clothes to get his keys, then turns the light off and closes the door. He can deliver the clothes to be washed tomorrow. Another glance at the clock on the wall. Almost seven. He's going to have to apologize quite a bit for being late tonight.

But she'll be excited to learn about how much progress he has made today.

He quickly walks to the door that will lead him back to his love, opens it, and turns off the overhead lights, plunging the room back into complete darkness.

$$\approx$$

Darkness.

That's all she can see when she finally comes to and opens her eyes.

She blinks her eyes repeatedly to erase the visual fog of waking up. As she feels her clarity returning, she strains to see anything. Anything at all.

The darkness remains in control. No shapes, no outlines, not even the faintest sliver of light that would give her something to focus on. She tries to move her arms and legs, but there is no give, no movement. She's firmly bound to the chair she currently sits in. She fights back the panic that quickly begins to set in. Questions race through her mind. *Where am I? Who did this? Am I going to die?*

She takes a deep breath in an attempt to calm herself. The smell of dust and wood fills her nose. The stale air mingles with the light, lingering scent of the perfume she put on before leaving for work. The same perfume that her husband recently told her he would remember forever. She strains to get a sense of time, to determine how long she's been here. She remembers it was Monday evening and she had left her little girl and husband to go work at Ellie's, the restaurant she's worked at since she was in high school.

High school, she thinks. *That was only eight years ago.* So much has changed since then, and it feels like an eternity ago that she was telling the young man who is now her husband, on prom night of all nights, that she was pregnant with their little girl. And now, even leaving for work at Ellie's feels like an eternity ago. Alicia remembers arriving at the restaurant, parking her car in the back lot, and after grabbing a quick cigarette out front, going inside for her shift. She remembers an intruder in the restaurant at the end of her shift, and she tried to escape, but then Mrs. Ellie grabbed her and wouldn't let her go for some reason. The intruder put a cloth over her face, and then there was nothing. Nothing but waking up to the darkness currently enveloping her.

She strains to hear any sound at all. The overwhelming silence is broken only by the sound of her breathing and her heartbeat, which is slowly reaching a crescendo and becoming all encompassing.

Thump-thump. Thump-thump. Thump-thump.

The sound continues to expand until it feels as though it's reverberating off the walls. The floor. The ceiling. Expanding until there's no more air in the room, just the rhythmic thump of her heart.

Thump-thump. Thump-thump. Thump-thump.

The panic grows and begins to take over. *What if whoever did this can hear it as well?* she thinks. She wills herself to calm down. To breathe. To try to make sense of what's going on. And just when it seems like the thumping of her heart will overpower and crush her, the sound of a door unlocking fights its way to her ears.

The room is instantly silent again. Her heartbeat retreats back into her chest, leaving the space around her empty once more. The hairs on her arms and the back of her neck rise. The small click of a dead bolt sliding into its home seems to echo around her. She strains to hear the expected sound of a doorknob being turned. A door being opened.

It feels like hours pass until another noise finally permeates the silence. The slight creaking of hinges in front of her and a small click cause a whole new world of sensation as blinding white light explodes from above. Her eyes instantly squeeze shut.

A voice reaches her ears. "Good morning, beautiful."

She cringes and doesn't respond. Even with her eyes tightly closed, the light fights its way through her eyelids and demands her undivided attention.

The voice reaches her ears again, competing with the light for attention. "You have a good day today, my love, and I will be back before you know it."

Her captor's voice is foreign to her ears, but something about it has a familiarity. As though she's heard it before, a long time ago.

A new sound reaches her ears as heavy footsteps move from in front of her to the far right. A loud, raspy, scraping noise reaches out to her, begging for her to open her eyes and look.

She fights the urge and soon the sound stops, followed by a solid click. Silence once again takes over.

She finally opens her eyes, slowly, as the light reveals to her where she is.

The room isn't as big as she imagined it. Alicia looks around, taking in the sights. A wooden door breaks up the unadorned wall in front of her, shut tightly, closing her off from what possible escape may be on the other side. To her far left is a table, devoid of anything on top or below. To her immediate left sits a large, dusty metal storage chest with an equally dusty hand sander sitting on top of it. To her right is a large steel door set within a frame of the same material. Scrape marks mar the concrete floor where the door has been opened and closed many times.

She looks down at her arms and feet, securely tied with thick wire to the arms and legs of the chair she's sitting in. She tries to move each one individually. The left arm. Nothing. The right arm. Nothing. The left leg and right leg give her the same results. A frown creases her face. She still has no idea of how long she may have been here. A few hours? A day? A few days? Time here seems to melt into an unmeasurable object with never-ending shape or direction. She takes a deep breath and exhales. Dust and wood are the predominant smells in the air. She takes another deep breath and exhales once more.

As she contemplates her situation, the fear of never seeing her family again races across her mind. She wonders what her little girl is doing right now. If she is missing her mommy. Tears start to form in her eyes as she thinks about never seeing her baby's face again. Never being able to hold her tightly in her arms. Never getting to hear her squeals of laughter or wipe the tears away when she's upset.

Another deep breath and exhale. *Calm yourself*, she thinks, as the first tear races down her cheek. So many questions cross her mind in a nonstop flow of panic. *Is my husband looking for me? Where am I? Why did this happen? Who is my captor? Is Mrs. Ellie a part of this?*

As Alicia tries to organize the myriad questions running through her head, a new noise reaches her through the silence in the room. A muted, rhythmic thumping comes from somewhere beyond the steel door. She focuses her attention on the door and listens. The thumping occasionally stops, letting its echoes become overtaken by the silence, then starts back up again with the same cadenced pattern. She continues to listen, trying to determine how much time is passing by counting the thumps in her head. It isn't long before her focus on the constant, repetitive sound starts to cause her eyelids to get heavy. Soon her eyes close and she escapes her current captivity by way of her dreams.

The loud scraping of the large metal door being opened abruptly intrudes upon her dreams and quickly brings her back to her current reality. She opens her eyes, blinking against the light above, and looks to her right. Framed in the doorway is her captor, looking at her.

"Hello, dear. How was your day?" he asks, smiling.

She doesn't respond. He nods and steps into the room, grabbing the handle of the metal door and pushing it closed behind him, allowing a screeching noise to fill the room once again. Once the door is fully closed, he reaches into his pocket and pulls out a set of keys. Finding the right one, he inserts it into the keyhole, locks the door, and puts the key ring back into his pocket. She watches as he turns back toward her and walks up to her in her restraints. His right hand reaches out for the right side of her face, and she instinctively moves her head away as far as she can, forcing her gaze toward the table at the far left. The hand stops its approach and lowers just a bit. His voice reaches her ears.

"Is everything OK? I'm sorry I was late tonight."

She refuses to acknowledge him by continuing to stare at the table. By remaining silent. By declining to make eye contact.

"Are you hungry?" he asks. She continues to ignore him, as though her current act of rebellion will convince her captor to release her and let her go. Let her return to her family and her life that he's ripped her away from.

He continues to speak as though she's responding. "I agree, I'm hungry too. Let me go get us some dinner. What would you like tonight?" he asks. Her stomach, clearly not agreeing with her silent protest, rumbles a bit. Out of the corner of her eye, she can see a smile form on his face as he hears the sound. A tinge of anger races through her.

"That sounds perfect. I was just thinking that we haven't had that for dinner in ages," he says, still smiling at her. His hand is still motionless in the air, only inches from her face. It finally moves forward once more, and although she has her head as far back from him as it can go, the hand still finds her. It caresses her right cheek softly, smelling of wood and soap. "I told you before and I will tell you again. I will always be here for you."

The tone in his voice, coupled with the feeling of his hand still caressing her right cheek, causes her to cringe in disgust. The hand pauses its petting motion for just a moment and then resumes its path from her right cheekbone to her chin line. Each touch makes her wish even more that he would stop. That he would realize this is not what she wants. Just when she begins to think she can't take it anymore and feels like screaming, the hand stops and pulls away slightly. He takes a step closer to her, his feet now almost touching hers. He extends his right index finger and slowly moves her hair behind her ear and shoulder, repeating the motion several times. Apparently satisfied that her right ear and neck are now fully exposed, her captor takes that same finger and traces it from the top of her ear to the bottom lobe, lightly touching her diamond stud earrings. A Christmas present from Colin, whom she is terrified she will never see again. Leaving the earring, the index finger jumps from her ear to her neck, slowly tracing a path along where her jugular is located. It crosses where the top of her T-shirt meets her collarbone, continuing downward on her shirt, moving over the top swell of her right breast. It stops when it reaches the upper edge of her bra, not moving any farther downward. Her captor takes a deep breath and pulls his hand away from her. She hears him sigh, and his voice reaches her ears.

"I'll be right back, my dear. Don't miss me too much, OK?" The last words out of his mouth make him laugh a bit, the sound disgusting her instantly. A tinge of anger grows, and she finally pulls her gaze from the table to her captor, turning her head forward and looking directly into his face. Into his eyes. His smile instantly heightens the disgust.

His laughter lingers in the air. She watches as he turns away from her and heads to the wooden door about fifteen feet away from where she's sitting. He once again fishes the key ring out of his pocket and, after finding the right key, inserts it into the lock. The following click echoes through the room. He puts the keys away, grabs the doorknob, and with a swift turn pulls the door open. The hallway beyond is pitch-black, and she's unable to see more than just a few feet into it as the overhead light tries making its way beyond the room.

The anger in her is slightly tempered by a bit of sadness as she realizes that even the light above her is unable to escape this room.

Her abductor steps through the wooden doorframe and into the darkness beyond. A click sounds, out of reach of the light, and a bare, solitary light bulb turns on and illuminates the hallway. The stark light from the bulb gives her a view of a possible escape route. An unadorned hallway leads to a set of steps that curve to the left and quickly disappear out of view. Standing in the center of that hallway, in front of a switch on the wall, is her captor. He looks over at her and walks back to the door, grabbing the handle.

"Be back soon, gorgeous," he says as he smiles at her, pulling the wooden door closed. A solid click from the dead bolt tells her that the hallway and stairs on the other side are locked away from escape. She releases her breath, not realizing she's been holding it in. She looks around again, desperately hoping to see something that may offer her a way of escape. Nothing promises the solace she's searching for.

She struggles once more against her bonds, looking for any possibility of movement from the thick wire restraining her. As expected, there is no movement. Mingling with disgust, anger, and sadness, her frustration makes itself known.

Alicia finally speaks for the first time since she woke up here. Not so much speaks as yells. At the top of her lungs, releasing all the emotions building up inside her.

"Fuck you!"

CHAPTER 8

THE HAPPY COUPLE

"Be back soon, gorgeous," Nick says, smiling as he pulls the door closed behind him and locks it. Alicia is upset; he could tell. He wanted to tell her about all the work he was able to get done today, but she didn't want to talk. She is hungry, and so is he, and he feels terrible that she had to wait so long for him to wrap up his day and now has to wait even longer while he goes and gets food. He should have brought something back with him last night or even earlier this morning instead of waiting until now.

He shakes his head, disappointed in himself for letting her down, and vows to do better from now on. He quickly climbs the staircase and unlocks the door to the main part of his lovely home. He steps through the door and closes it, ensuring it's locked as well. He follows the familiar path around his decor and furniture until he reaches the grand entryway. He unlocks the door and slides it open, the familiar screech of the metal a welcome sound to his ears. The sun has almost fully set, and the large trees surrounding his yard cast elongated shadows over the grass from the dying light.

He pauses a moment before closing the large metal door behind him. For an instant it almost sounds like a voice is calling out to him from inside his home. From his love.

He hesitates, straining to hear anything else. *Is she calling out to me, telling me she loves me and forgives me?* The only sounds he hears are the sounds of the evening forest. He must've been imagining it. Shaking his head, he chalks it up to merely wishful thinking. He slides the large metal door closed and locks it, continuing his journey to get dinner for his one. His love.

Nick quickly walks across his yard and to where the pathway starts. He plunges into the forest, heading toward where the truck is parked. The setting sun dips completely below the horizon, and with the thick canopy of branches above, it's almost completely dark along the path. He smiles, happy that he knows every inch of this pathway by heart and doesn't need any light to quickly make it to the vehicle.

A few more steps and he reaches the end of the pathway where it meets the road. He pauses a moment, cautiously, and looks around. The truck is tucked away in its normal parking spot, as expected. No lights penetrate the enveloping darkness. No unexpected sounds reach his ears.

Satisfied that he is alone, he steps from the pathway and onto the road, quickly traversing the distance to the vehicle.

After removing the camouflage cover and tossing it onto the passenger side floor of the cab, he walks to the driver's side. He grabs the door handle and hesitates a moment. *I will need to get another rental vehicle soon*, he thinks, and reminds himself to mention this to his mother as he gets in the truck, putting the key in the ignition and turning it on.

The engine comes to life. He takes a deep breath. The scent of Alicia's perfume lingers in the cab. He hopes that smell never disappears. Content now, he reaches into Alicia's purse sitting on the passenger seat and pulls out her cell phone. He has no reason to bring the phone into the house because he doesn't want any interruptions when he's with his love, so he left it in the vehicle. The phone is currently turned off. He turned it off in the restaurant's parking lot before he brought Alicia home so it couldn't be tracked. If Colin has the phone's GPS traced, the last location it will show will be the parking lot of the restaurant. He smiles, looking at the phone in his hand. He wonders how many times Colin, now Alicia's ex-husband because she is finally with Nick, has tried to call the number, only to get her voice mail each and every time. He wonders if Colin is finally finding out what it's like to lose her, like Nick found out years ago. *That's OK, though, because I won't ever lose her again*, he tells himself as he puts the cell phone back into Alicia's purse.

His smile's still on his face when he turns on the parking lights and carefully backs out of the spot, aiming the truck down the road toward his destination. Nick allows himself to be transported back to the perfect world he now lives in. His driveway is fairly long, which keeps his home secluded from the rest of the world. He prefers it that way, though. Visitors would only interrupt his time with his one and only and cause problems—although his last visitor did become a permanent resident of the home he now shares with his love.

The drive to his destination is quick, and he's careful not to draw any attention to the truck when he pulls in. Luckily, although the parking lot is full, there's no one outside at the moment. He drives around to the back side of the building and pulls in next to his mother's truck. He stops the vehicle and turns off the lights, leaving the engine running. He looks around, making sure there's no one outside who may see him, and quickly opens the door and steps out. Loose gravel crunches underneath his feet. A couple steps and he reaches the bed of his mother's truck. She told him late last night, while he was picking her up from the storage unit, that she would put some food in the bed of her truck for him and Alicia and he could grab it when he was able.

Just as his mother promised, sitting in the bed is a brown paper bag with a couple of large plastic containers inside. He grabs the bag and retreats back to his truck.

He sets the paper bag down on the passenger seat and turns the lights back on, quickly backing out to exit the parking lot. He breathes a sigh of relief that there's still no one in the parking lot as he leaves the restaurant, and he doesn't pass any other cars on the road while headed to his driveway. He makes the necessary turn, kills the headlights, and heads down the bumpy road. One of these days he's going to come out here and fix the bumps and ruts. Maybe even pave it.

She would like that, he thinks. A beautifully paved driveway, lined by lush trees, leading to a scenic pathway that takes you to a picturesque home with a happy couple living in it.

Maybe one day, he muses, *when she is ready*.

He reaches the end of the driveway and pulls into the spot where he normally parks. He turns off the parking lights and the engine, plunging the world around him into complete darkness and silence. His thoughts return to when they first saw this spot, their future home, together. It was well over a decade ago. They were just kids then, still in high school, running wild and free. Of course, his love wasn't his love back then. She was dating another man, her now ex-husband, who was never worthy of her affection. He pushes the thoughts of her previous lover from his mind, although the thought of Colin's suffering greatly pleases Nick, and thinks about that day he spent here with Alicia. Their haunted adventure, she called it. They actually walked the entire length of the rutted, run-down driveway, chatting and admiring the denseness of the forest around them. The path to the logging camp was a bit more overgrown back then, as no one was taking care of the beautiful home before his mother gifted it to him. By the time they reached this point, where the road ended and the pathway began, Alicia was too scared and didn't want to go any farther toward the logging camp, claiming this was about as much of the haunted adventure as she could handle. Of course, it was the adventure in which he came to know he would love her forever.

A smile crosses his face as he reminisces.

He remembers how the branches from the overgrown shrubs on either side of the road would snag her long beautiful hair while they walked, and how she would squeal a bit when she pulled her hair back. He remembers how, as they got closer and closer to the end of the road, she began moving closer to his side and began avoiding the spots on the ground where the sun wasn't shining. And most of all, he remembers how beautiful she looked as the rays of the morning sun cascaded down her smiling face.

He also remembers how, as they were standing here at the end of the road and not daring to go any farther, she leaned over and kissed him on the check, telling him how much she appreciated having him in her life.

It was in that moment, with that soft kiss, that he knew he would do anything to be able to give her the world. To make her happy. To make her his.

Of course, life always has other plans, and she ended up marrying another man. A man who did not deserve her, did not appreciate her. A man who did not love her like Nick loved her. If Alicia only knew for how long Nick had suffered without having her in his life while she was with that other man!

The smile on his face falters a bit. He tries not to think about Colin, the man who ruined everything for him in high school by taking Alicia away from him. The man whom he swore would pay for his actions. One day, he thinks. One day that man will pay for what he did. For how he hurt her. For how he hurt Nick.

The smile on his face is fully gone now, replaced by a scowl. His heart rate increases slightly with the coming anger. *No,* he thinks, *now is not the time to think about this.* He pushes the thoughts away and concentrates on the present. Alicia is with him, and he is with her, and now they have everything they ever wanted. And Nick can find solace in the fact that Colin is finally learning what it's like to lose Alicia.

He feels the calm begin to return, slowly washing the hatred away. His pulse returns to its usual rate.

The smell of the food reaches his nose, and his stomach rumbles, bringing him back to the present. He thinks about his love and how upset she probably is by now at having to wait so long for dinner. A frown causes his brow to furrow. *I feel like I can never do anything right when it comes to her recently,* he thinks, *but one day I will get it right. I will make it right. And then she will see how she means the world to me. She just has to be patient for a bit. I'm new to being a husband.*

His last thought helps clear the furrow from his brow. He is confident that it's only a matter of time before his love realizes that everything he does, everything he is doing, is for her. He grabs the paper bag from the passenger seat next to him and opens the door, but he pauses before he gets out of the vehicle. He sets the paper bag back down on the seat and opens it up, putting Alicia's purse on top of the plastic containers. He gets out of the truck, once again repeating the action of covering the rental fully with the cover. Pleased with his efforts, he carries the bag down the path, the excitement of seeing his girl once again beginning to overpower any hesitation or doubt he may have. He enjoys the sounds of the forest around him. The noises of the night, his mother would always call them when he was just a child. Now that he's an adult, they are a comfort to him, a reminder of less complicated times.

His home, framed by the faint light of the moon, comes into view as he reaches the end of the path and steps out of the forest. The place is completely dark, with no light visible from any door or window. To a passerby, it would appear as though it were abandoned or no one were home. He prefers it that way. Guests are only an intrusion into their happy life, as he has learned previously, and he knows his mother specifically selected this location for him as his home because of how remote and far away from the rest of the town it is. He crosses his yard and reaches the door, deftly maneuvering the bag of food while getting the keys out of his pocket. The usual process of unlocking, opening, closing, and locking is repeated twice and overly hastily, with him pulling the second door closed too hard, slamming it shut instead of simply closing it. He hopes the sound doesn't scare his love waiting just down the stairway ahead of him. He carefully walks down the steps until he reaches the door separating him from the love of his life. His one.

Light from the other side of the door fights the darkness

of the hallway where he's standing, illuminating the doorframe as though leading to a bright heaven beyond the pitch-black. His bright heaven. The bright heaven where his love is happily awaiting his return.

He listens for a moment before unlocking the door and stepping into that heaven. His love is silent on the other side. Not a single sound reaches his ears. His thoughts start to race as he panics for just a moment.

Is she OK? Did she somehow hurt herself? Is she lying on the floor, in pain and unable to move or speak? Did she finally have enough of my mistakes and leave me? Or worse, did someone kidnap her and take her away from me?

The panicked thoughts in his head continue growing until the sound of a chair scraping on the concrete floor reaches his ears from the other side of the door. Reassured but still worried that something may have happened, he quickly inserts the key and unlocks the dead bolt.

He grabs the doorknob and swings the door open, anxious to see his love and her beautiful face again.

≈

Alicia waits and listens.

For any response to her outburst. To her finally breaking her silence. To her finally openly acknowledging her situation and expressing her anger.

No sound reaches her ears in response. Her captor is either already out of hearing range or merely ignoring her.

She frowns, still feeling his lingering touch on her skin. She finally returns to her thoughts for a moment. *Why is he doing this to me? What did I do to deserve this? Why me?*

Although she doesn't recognize her captor, there is something familiar about him. A nagging feeling in the back of her mind tells her she has seen that face before.

She takes another look around, looking for anything she might be able to use to improve her current situation. Anything that might help her get out of the chair she's currently imprisoned in. Anything that might help her escape this nightmare.

Her eyes skip over the various objects in the room and finally return to the metal chest to her left. Maybe there is something in there than can help her. *But how do I get it open?* she wonders. She struggles against her bonds to no avail. They don't seem like they're going to loosen up from just her squirming back and forth as hard as she can.

"Damn it!"

Her voice surprises her; she didn't expect her words to sound as loud as they do in the relatively small room. Frustration grows inside her. She continues to fight against her bonds, working her body left and right, right and left, hoping for any give in the heavy wire bindings holding her arms and legs securely against the chair.

She continues to struggle over and over until she finally has to stop, soaked in sweat and out of breath. Her bonds, still secure, give her no chance at freedom. On top of it all, thanks to her struggling, she now has to pee. Pushing the sudden pressure in her bladder from her mind, Alicia tries to slow her breathing and regain her composure. She takes another look around the room. Everything is still the same as it was before, with the exception that she's now a couple feet farther toward the center of the room. Toward the door that may lead to her freedom.

Her struggling must've caused her to somehow edge the chair forward a few feet.

A glimmer of hope springs alive in her chest. If she can move the chair, maybe she can get to the door and escape. In the back of her mind, she knows she heard the door lock, but the hope that is now growing out of control inside her is screaming that the door is unlocked and if she can just reach it, she can find a way to get it open and escape to freedom.

Escape to her little girl. Escape to her husband and her life. Escape this terrible nightmare she's woken up in.

Alicia resumes her struggling. Left. Right. Right. Left. Every other forceful squirm rewards her with a slight scraping noise from the feet of the chair on the dusty concrete floor.

One scrape. Two scrapes. Three scrapes. She continues her efforts until a new noise invades the room. The sound of a door, far away, slamming closed.

She stops all her movement as a large rupture of fear rips through her mountain of hope. She listens intently and strains to hear any other noise, any other sounds. Nothing but silence.

She wonders if what she heard was just her imagination. Just her fear trying to hold her back from her freedom. She will not let her fear stop her from escaping, and she resumes her fight against her bonds.

Before another satisfactory scrape reaches her ears, the dead bolt in the wooden door in front of her clicks loudly, signaling that the bolt has retreated. The doorknob begins to turn, and all her hope, all her fantasy of freedom, is quickly snuffed out and replaced by fear.

Her captor is going to know she's been trying to escape. She's well over six feet away from where she was when he left her.

The door opens wide, and for an instant her eyes lock with the eyes of her captor. The urge to scream races up her throat, causing all the small hairs on her arms and the back of her neck to stand up. For a brief second, something tells her she has seen those eyes before.

His eyes are cold, though. Hollow.

But he's smiling at her. The stark contradiction makes her uneasy and even more frightened than she already was. She forces herself to look down at the ground, pulling her eyes away from his gaze. She concentrates on the dirty concrete at her feet.

"Hey there, beautiful. I'm so sorry I'm late with dinner." The tone of his voice matches his smile. The words, though, are unwelcome as they reach her ears, but her fear has sapped all her strength to speak. "I see you were busy while I was out getting us something to eat."

She doesn't respond. Even though she is forcing herself to stare at the ground, she can see him turn and walk toward the table at the left side of the room, leaving the door in front of her open. She looks up and leftward, in his direction, hoping not to see his eyes looking into hers again. Relief floods through her when she sees he's not looking at her. Instead, his back is to her, and he has set a paper bag down on the table and is unpacking the contents. She sees him pull out a large plastic container and set it next to a water bottle already extracted from the bag. He reaches back into the bag for the rest.

A quick surge of hope hits her as she looks back at the open door in front of her. A dark hallway extends beyond the door. And at the very edge of where the light reaches, she can make out the beginning of the steps going upward. The urge to start struggling again takes over, coupled with another to start willing the chair as fast as possible toward the allure of freedom in front of her.

For just a moment, she can feel freedom wrapping its arms around her, pulling her close and welcoming her back, happily pointing her home and toward her family.

She tenses up, getting ready to put all her effort into being free, when movement from her left catches her eye.

"Something on your mind, my love?"

She looks to her left and sees him standing at the table, now facing her. Watching her. Staring at her. She doesn't respond.

"I know, I know. Meat loaf again. How about we have your favorite food for dinner tomorrow night?" The smile returns to his face. "We both know how much you like a good burger. I promise tomorrow that I'll go grab a couple from your favorite restaurant for dinner, with fries and lots of ketchup, just the way you like them, OK?"

A surge of fear races through Alicia as his most recent words cause chaos in her thoughts. *How does he know what I like?* She strains to remember the last time she had a burger, despite her lost sense of time from being here. *Was it one week? Two weeks? Has he been watching me?*

Another, sharper spike of panic pierces through the jumble of questions and fears all fighting for control of her thoughts. *Has he been watching my family? My husband? My little girl?*

Alicia is pulled from her thoughts by the sudden movement of her chair being pulled back to where it was originally. She looks at the hallway in front of her and feels the despair begin to grow inside her with every inch she moves farther away from the doorway. The backward movement finally stops. A moment passes and she suddenly feels two hands on her shoulders.

She stiffens, terrified of what may happen next.

"I know, my love, it's been a long day. You are incredibly tense." He begins to massage her shoulders, softly, working his hands from her shoulders to her neck, moving his fingers and his thumbs in a circular pattern.

Alicia closes her eyes and wills him away with all her strength. To have him remove his hands from her body. The caressing of her shoulders and neck, which would normally feel good, only causes revulsion. She fights the urge to squirm away from his touch, fearing she might anger him.

His voice breaks the silence, and his fingers stop their circular dance on her neck. "I've kept you distracted long enough. Let's eat."

He steps from behind her and walks over to the table, grabbing one of the plastic containers and one of the water bottles. She watches him as he turns back toward her, holding each item carefully in his hands. He walks back over to her and squats down just to the left of her, setting both the container and the water bottle down on the chest next to her. "I bet your ex-husband never took the time to spoil you and feed you like this, did he?" he asks. Alicia doesn't respond, the worry growing in her when she hears her captor call Colin her ex-husband. "I'm sorry. I shouldn't have brought him up. I just want you to know how happy you make me and how I hopefully do the same for you," he tells her.

Still scared of what may happen if she says anything, she remains quiet. He reaches over and grabs the container, setting it on her lap. The warmth from the bottom of the plastic radiates through her jeans and onto the skin of her legs. He opens the container, revealing a slice of meat loaf, some mashed potatoes, some green beans, and a plastic-wrapped set of utensils with a napkin inside.

A homestyle meal. She momentarily wonders if he got this from Ellie's. Even worse, did Mrs. Ellie meet him somewhere and give it to him? Alicia isn't sure she wants to know the answer to that question. She doesn't want to consider the possibility that the woman who is like a second mother to her and Colin, like a grandmother to her daughter, would have a part in allowing this man to abduct her.

The smell of the food reaches her nose, and her stomach

involuntarily growls in anticipation. Her sense of time is distorted, as though she's been in this room for a lifetime already. *When was the last time I ate?* she wonders. *Yesterday? A week ago?*

She watches as he removes the plastic from the utensils and sets everything back down on the storage chest with the exception of the fork. Using the fork, he cuts off a small bite-sized portion of the meat loaf and stabs it with the plastic tines. He guides the fork toward her mouth, pausing a moment until she opens her mouth to allow herself to be fed. She chews the first piece slowly, the taste on her tongue truly waking up her hunger and letting her know just how famished she is. The taste of the meat loaf is familiar, and she's pretty sure she knows exactly where the food came from.

Definitely Ellie's. Her place of employment. And the last place she remembers being before waking up here.

As he guides a second piece of meat loaf into her mouth, she tries to gauge the time between when he left and when he got back. *How long did it take to get the food?* she wonders. *It couldn't have been more than an hour, was it? Two, maybe? That means Ellie's has to be somewhat close to where I'm being held, right?*

Her thoughts are interrupted by another bite of food directed into her mouth. She chews it and swallows, already opening her mouth for the next bite, still mostly focused on her thoughts. If she's close to Ellie's, then there is a chance she may be found, as she knows Colin will do everything in his power to find her. Her parents will as well.

The feeding ritual continues, one piece after another, until all that's left in the container is a couple of green beans. Finally, with a full stomach, she's unable to eat anymore and refuses the last bite, shaking her head and looking down at the ground in front of her. He sets the fork in the container and the plastic container down on the chest, on top of the spoon and knife. He grabs the water, twists off the cap, and offers it to her. She looks up from the floor and at the water bottle, nodding slightly. He carefully aligns the bottle with her lips and tilts it upward, allowing some of the room-temperature water into her mouth. She drinks slowly at first, then greedily, her thirst as ravenous as her hunger was.

His voice fills the room once again. "Easy there, beautiful. Don't want you to choke on it."

He pulls the water bottle from her lips, the last few drops spilling down her chin and onto her shirt. "I'm sorry, my love, I didn't mean to do that." He sets the water bottle down on the chest, next to the almost empty plastic container, and digs the napkin out from under the container. He carefully dries her chin and wipes the corners of her mouth. Alicia doesn't avoid his hand, allowing him to clean her up. He pauses a moment after he's done wiping her mouth, and she watches his gaze move from her face to her chest, where a few dark spots have formed from the water dripping. She watches as he stares at her for an uncomfortably long time, not breaking his gaze or blinking, the napkin still suspended in midair only a couple inches from her mouth. His eyes are intently focused on the wet spots just above her breasts. He doesn't react, he doesn't move. He just stares.

The reality of what might happen next suddenly sets in, and she feels the immediate need to act. To prevent the next possible step in this unwanted situation. To ensure that this nightmare she has woken up in does not become worse.

Panic races through her body as she stares at his eyes, which are still staring at the water spots. On her chest. She does the only thing she can think of to get his attention, to distract his mind from whatever sick manifestations it may be dreaming up.

She finally speaks to him, hoping that the words that come out of her mouth make sense and are enough to get her captor's attention.

"Thank you for dinner. It was delicious."

CHAPTER 9

THE REALIZATION

Colin opens his eyes and blinks a few times, trying to clear the post-sleep haze. Once the world is back in focus, he looks over at the clock by the phone. Seven o'clock in the evening. He looks over to his right and sees Penny still fast asleep on the couch, snuggled up with her bear under her favorite blanket. Both of them were up most of last night when Alicia didn't come home after her shift at work.

He quietly gets up out of the living room chair he fell asleep in and walks over to the phone on the table by the door, checking to see if there are any missed calls from Alicia.

The number three is flashing on the display. Any vestige of exhaustion quickly vanishes, and he hits the play button as fast as he can. The first message is from his foreman up in Shelton asking if he's planning on coming to work tomorrow since he wasn't there today. The second is from the Orchard Lake Police Station letting him know they have issued an all-points bulletin for Alicia and her car and they'll contact him if they hear or see anything. The third message is from Alicia's mother, letting Colin know she hasn't heard anything from Alicia and for him to contact her immediately as soon as he hears from her. The fleeting surge of elation he feels is quickly squashed at the end of the last message.

"Daddy? Did Mommy call?" a sleepy little voice behind him asks.

Colin turns around and looks at Penny, now sitting up on the couch and rubbing her eyes. "No hummingbird, Mommy didn't call yet," he tells her. He picks up the phone and dials Alicia's cell phone number again. Just like the last thirty times he's called her number since last night, the call is sent right to her voice mail. He tries it once more, with the same result. Right to voice mail.

"Is Mommy mad at me?" the little voice from the couch asks him. Colin looks at his little girl and shakes his head no. "No, sweetie, Mommy is not mad at you at all," he reassures her.

"Then why didn't Mommy come home?" she asks.

"I don't know, little hummingbird. I don't know," is the only response he can think of.

When Alicia didn't come from her shift, Colin's first call was to her cell phone, which sent him right to voice mail. He presumed that maybe her phone was off because she was still at work, so he called Mrs. Ellie. Mrs. Ellie confirmed that Alicia had been there for her shift, had helped prep for the next day, and then had left around eleven. She seemed shocked when he told her that Alicia hadn't come home from her shift and he wasn't able to get a hold of her on her cell. She promised she'd call Colin immediately if she heard from Alicia and told him that if he needed anything at all, he should just call. Colin then proceeded to call Alicia's parents and their friends and make no less than ten additional calls to Alicia's cell phone. When five o'clock in the morning rolled around without Colin hearing from her, he called the police station and filed a missing-person report. He then loaded Penny in his truck and, instead of taking her to school, spent most of the day driving all over Orchard Lake, stopping in every parking lot so he could go into every business in town and ask if they'd seen her and driving down every residential street in and around town looking for her car.

As his efforts to locate Alicia turned out to be futile, and with Penny upset in the booster seat next to him, he drove them home, where they both had some lunch and ended up falling asleep.

He steps away from the answering machine and heads into the kitchen, skirting around the table and going right to the fridge. He opens the door and pulls out one of the beers on the second shelf, letting the door close on its own. He turns back toward the living room, sets the beer on the kitchen table, and looks at Penny kneeling on the couch. She peers at him from over the back of it, her eyes wide.

The look on Penny's face is a lot like Alicia's when she's scared about something. Slightly arched eyebrows over wide eyes full of worry and concern.

Seeing that look is when Colin's strength finally gives out. Unable to hold it in anymore, he sits down on the floor of the kitchen with his back against the refrigerator, puts his head in his hands, and begins to sob uncontrollably. He doesn't know why Alicia wouldn't come home to him and their beautiful little girl. He doesn't know where she is or why she isn't responding to him or to her parents. His thoughts race from one scenario to another. *Did she leave me? Leave her family? Was she unhappy? Or did something happen to her? Was she kidnapped? Is she hurt?*

He continues to sob as his thoughts cycle through a chaotic series of what could have happened. He doesn't notice a very concerned little girl getting down from the couch. He doesn't notice the sound of soft steps as little feet approach.

What he does notice is little arms wrapping as far as they can around him. "It will be OK, Daddy," Penny tells him as her own tears cascade down her face.

Colin takes a deep breath and wraps his arms around his little girl, holding her close.

Several minutes pass while Colin regains his composure. He lets his little girl go and wipes the tears from her cheeks. "You are absolutely right, little hummingbird. It will be OK," he tells her. He gets up from the floor and looks at the beer on the table, not sure if he's interested in it anymore. He looks around the quiet kitchen and nods. Penny is going to need dinner. They both are going to need dinner. There isn't anything else he can do right now, at least nothing he can think of. "OK, little lady, what would you like for dinner tonight?" he asks.

Penny looks up at him and appears to think for a minute. "French fries!"

Colin raises one eyebrow. "French fries, huh?"

"Yes! French fries and spaghetti," she says.

Colin finds a laugh hiding inside him and lets it free while shaking his head. "Sweetie, that sounds like a terrible combination."

Penny shakes her head too. "No it isn't, Daddy. It's delicious," she says, getting up off the floor and crawling into one of the chairs at the table. Colin grabs the beer on the table, deciding he's going to have it after all. He twists the top off and takes a long swig. As he is lowering the beer, Penny hops up from the chair and proceeds to get a juice box from the fridge. Juice box secure, she returns to her chair.

"So let's see what we can do for dinner, since it will definitely not be french fries and spaghetti," he tells her. Penny sticks her tongue out at him and frowns. Colin smiles and digs through the cabinets until he finds a box of macaroni and cheese. "How about mac and cheese, hummingbird?" he asks, looking back at her. She nods her head with enthusiasm.

"Young lady, would you kindly get me a pan from under the counter while I make a quick phone call?" he asks.

"Yes, Daddy," she says. "Are you calling Mommy again?" she adds.

"No, sweetie. I have to call my boss and let them know what's going on so they don't fire me."

Penny nods and hops off the chair, making a beeline toward

the cabinet holding the large cookware.

While Penny is busy digging through the pans, Colin walks over to the phone on the table near the front door. For a moment he hopes to see the number one flashing on the answering machine, announcing a message from Alicia, saying he shouldn't worry and she'll be home soon and just had some car troubles. His hope is short-lived, as the answering machine displays a solid zero. He picks up the phone and, despite what he told his daughter, tries Alicia's cell phone again.

Voice mail once again. He stopped leaving messages after the first five.

He sets the headset down and picks it up again, dialing the number to his foreman. His boss's voice mail comes on, and Colin explains the current situation and why he wasn't at work today. He apologizes and requests a call back, as he is going to need a few more days off work for now. Content with his message, he hangs up the phone, fighting the urge to call Alicia's cell once again.

"Daddy, I found the pan!" the little girl announces as a loud clatter erupts from the kitchen.

Colin heads back into the kitchen and sees Penny kneeling on the floor with several pots and pans spread out around her. She's holding the one they normally use for the mac and cheese.

At least she found the right pan, he thinks, a weak smile forming on his face.

"Good job, young lady," he says as he takes the pan from her outstretched arm. "Make sure you put the rest of those away."

She nods and begins placing the various cookware back in the cabinet. One she finishes, she stands up and heads to her seat at the kitchen table.

Colin fills the pan up part of the way with water and puts it on the stove, turning the burner on. While he waits for the water to start boiling, he takes another drink from his beer, finishing it off. He tosses the empty bottle in the trash and gets a fresh one from the fridge.

He finishes making dinner in silence, with Penny's attention focused on reading what's written on the back of her juice box. As he is setting a bowl in front of her along with a spoon, she breaks the silence. "Daddy, do you think Mommy is having dinner right now too?"

Colin bends down and kisses the top of his little girl's head, taking a moment before he responds. "I'm sure no matter where Mommy is right now, she is having a great dinner and thinking of us, just like we are thinking of her."

He hopes what he just told Penny is true.

He puts his own bowl on the table and sits down, slowly taking a few bites. He watches as Penny digs in, working on finishing off her bowl. He follows suit, and once he is done, he asks her if she wants more. Penny shakes her head, and Colin gets up and grabs her bowl, adding it to his, and puts both bowls in the sink. He puts the remaining mac and cheese in a plastic storage container and places it in the fridge. The pan finds a new home in the sink with the bowls. He will wash the dishes later.

"Want to watch some TV, hummingbird?" he asks. Penny nods, jumps down out of the chair, and races off into the living room to turn the TV on. By the time he reaches the couch, she's found some animated show Colin hasn't seen before. He moves her blanket over and sits down on the end of the couch and reaches over, stealing the remote from her.

As he's searching the channels for a good movie to watch, Penny crawls across the couch with her bear and blanket in hand and snuggles up against him, making sure the blanket covering her arms is fully wrapped around her teddy bear. He puts his arm around his little girl and finally finds one of the cheesy B horror movies he enjoys so much. When the cartoon switches to the movie, he hears Penny groan next to him.

"Daddy, these movies are terrible," she tells him.

"Would you rather watch the cartoon?" he asks her. She nods, her head resting against his chest. "OK, hummingbird, we'll watch the cartoon," he says. He switches the channel back and sets the remote down on the arm of the couch to his left. He watches as a variety of animated animals chase each other around and play pranks on each other, all while slowly losing himself back in his thoughts about Alicia. Thoughts about where she is right now and if she's OK. Thoughts about why he hasn't been able to get a hold of her and why she hasn't called him.

The last question that crosses his mind, before he falls asleep, is how he is going to be able to do this without her.

≈

Karen finishes pouring her morning coffee and returns the coffeepot to the maker. She drops a couple of sugar cubes into the hot black liquid and grabs a spoon out of the utensil rack, stirring the coffee until the cubes are fully dissolved. Setting the spoon down on the counter, she picks up her coffee and walks out of the kitchen and into the dining room. She doesn't open the restaurant until nine, so she has a couple more hours to relax before the usual Wednesday breakfast customers show up.

She takes a sip of the coffee and looks out the front windows of her restaurant.

The parking lot is empty in these early-morning hours. No cars pass by on the main road where the parking lot connects to the highway.

She takes another sip of her coffee, turns toward the bar and kitchen, and thinks about what has happened over the last few days. In a way, she felt terrible lying to Colin about Alicia. He really is sort of a second son to her.

But then, in a different way, she felt a deep satisfaction in hearing the same pain and panic in his voice that she hasn't felt since the day her husband spent his last few breaths begging for his life.

Her son is happy. Truly happy for the first time in years. That means more to her than anything else on this planet.

Karen smiles, thinking back to the other night that made her son so happy. She didn't run into any other traffic when she was driving Alicia's car out to the storage unit. She's had the unit for well over a decade, as she initially rented it to store all of her husband's stuff after he was gone. Once people finally stopped asking her questions about him leaving her quite a few years after he disappeared, she sold off everything inside the storage unit, but she never did get rid of it. Little did she know how useful it would be once again.

Now it stores Alicia's car, hidden under a car cover and secured by a steel cable and a heavy-duty lock.

She hopes that Alicia comes to her senses sooner rather than later and she can pull the car out of storage, but she will ensure that it stays in there as long as it takes for that young woman to finally realize that Nick is the man she is going to be with. The man she *should* be with. They can't have Colin or one of Alicia's friends seeing the car and asking questions.

Of course, Karen played the part of concerned friend and employer. She answered the questions exactly as she should have. Expressed just the right amount of concern and worry. Offered just the right amount of support.

Since she had already gone through almost the same scenario with her husband, this time was much easier. She was much more prepared.

She wonders how her little boy is doing. She knows he came by sometime yesterday evening and picked up the food she left for him in the back of her truck, as her truck bed was empty when she went to go check it after she finished closing the restaurant last night.

I wonder if I should make some more plates for them tonight, she muses to herself.

She takes another sip of her coffee and nods. Her boy is going to have his hands full for a bit, so it would be best if she made sure he didn't have to worry about food for now. She will make sure to put another bag in the back of her truck later on this evening.

Karen finishes the last couple sips of her coffee and heads toward the kitchen, stopping at the sink and placing her empty cup in it. She wonders when the police will show up, as she knows they will sooner or later to ask her questions about Alicia's disappearance. She already knows what she's going to tell them. Same thing she told Colin when he called her asking her if she knew where Alicia was.

She glances at the clock on the wall. Getting close to opening time. Karen turns from the kitchen and heads up the stairs at the far end of the dining room, listening to the familiar creak of each step as she makes her way into her home above. As she gets to the top of the stairs and steps into her smaller personal kitchen, she notices a plastic bag on the seat of one of her kitchen table chairs. She pauses, momentarily confused, until she remembers this is the bag of clothes Nick brought over a few nights ago.

The clothes stained with the runaway's blood on them.

Karen has been so busy the last few nights that she hasn't had an opportunity to dispose of them. That amount of blood doesn't just wash out.

A tinge of panic suddenly surges through her as a thought crosses her mind. *What if the police want to search the restaurant, since this was the last place Alicia was seen?* she wonders. *Even worse, what if they find that bag?*

She can't allow that to happen. *Stupid*, she tells herself, *So stupid for just setting that there and forgetting about it.* She frowns, forcing the panic away, and grabs the plastic bag. She turns around and heads back down the stairs and into the bar, grabbing a pack of matches from the stack on the end of the bar and putting them in her pants pocket. She continues forward, into the hallway toward the back door of the restaurant, pausing momentarily to grab a bottle of lighter fluid from the storage shelves in the hall. She then proceeds out the door and into the back parking lot, plastic bag in her left hand and lighter fluid in her right.

There is a large steel fifty-five-gallon drum in the far back of the parking lot that Karen occasionally uses to burn excess garbage. She walks over to the burn bin and tosses the plastic bag inside. Popping the top on the lighter fluid, she sprays a good portion of the container all over the plastic bag. Once she's satisfied that she's soaked the bag and contents enough, she sets the lighter fluid container on the ground and digs the matches out of her pocket.

She strikes one of the matches and watches it roar to life, the flame slowly working its way down the length of the small wooden stick toward her fingers. She tosses the match into the drum and quickly steps back a few steps. A brief moment passes, and then a large ball of flame erupts out the top of the burn bin, the heat washing over her entire upper body.

"A bit early in the morning to be burning trash, isn't it, Mrs. Ellie?"

The voice behind Karen makes her jump. She whips around to see who's there. One of the deputies from the Orchard Lake Police Department is standing next to the back door of the restaurant. "I apologize if I spooked you. I tried the front door, but there was no answer," he says when he sees her face.

Karen swiftly regains her composure. "No worries, Deputy. I just wasn't expecting any company before I opened up the restaurant," she responds, forcing a smile.

The deputy nods. "Completely understandable, ma'am. I only came by this early because I wanted to speak with you about the disappearance of one of your employees and figured that early morning would be better than during business hours or afterwards. Do you have some time to answer a few questions for me?"

She nods and motions toward the back door. "Let's go inside, if that's OK? Would you like a cup of coffee?"

The deputy smiles and nods. "Yes, ma'am, I would love one."

Karen walks to the back door, steps inside, and holds the door open for the deputy. She leads the way into the kitchen and grabs a fresh coffee mug from the rack. "Cream? Sugar?" she asks the deputy, who is now standing in the center of the kitchen behind her.

"No, thank you. Black is fine," he responds. She pours him a cup and turns around, carefully handing it to him. He takes the cup with a smile and continues to look around the kitchen.

"Thank you. I know you're a busy woman, so I won't take too much of your time. Mind telling me about your employee Alicia and the last time you saw her?"

Karen nods and smiles, explaining how Alicia showed up for work as usual. She tells him it was busy that night and that at the end of her shift, Alicia helped prep for the next day and then left to go home. Or at least Karen believed that was where she was headed.

The deputy nods occasionally as Karen talks, taking a sip of his coffee from time to time. When she finishes her account, the deputy waits a moment before speaking again. "Did she make any indication she was unhappy with her home life? Unhappy with anything here at work? Any marital issues or issues with other people that she may have mentioned?"

Karen shakes her head no. "No, Deputy, she never said anything of the sort to me, and I have known that young woman since she was just a wee one." She waits for the officer's response.

The deputy finishes his coffee and offers the cup back to her, which she accepts. "That's some mighty fine coffee you brew, Mrs. Ellie." He looks around the kitchen one more time and sighs. "I'm sorry to have disturbed you, ma'am. I appreciate you taking the time to talk to me. I'll be on my way now."

Karen nods at him. "Anytime. I hope she's OK. She is one of my best employees, and she's like family to me." She points toward the front door. "I have to open up the restaurant, so

I'll walk you out." She sets the deputy's cup down and heads toward the front door.

She reaches the door and unlocks the dead bolt. Pulling the door open for the deputy, she turns to him, now only a couple steps behind her, and asks him, "Do you have any idea what might have happened to her?"

The deputy looks at her and then out the front door to the early morning beyond. "We haven't found any indication of any foul play. Maybe she was unhappy with her home life and just left. I know how close you were to her. If I hear anything, I will let you know."

Karen nods and smiles. "Thank you."

He steps out the front door and walks off toward the squad car in the parking lot. Karen closes the door behind him and watches through the door window until he starts the car up and begins to leave.

She waves at him as he pulls away and out of the parking lot.

Well, that went about as expected, she thinks, pleased that they might believe Alicia just left town. She relocks the front door, then rushes through the dining room and down the hallway to the back door. Once outside again, she hurries over to the large metal drum and looks inside. Most of the flames have died down, and only charred remains of the clothing can be seen.

Karen bends down and picks up a metal bar sitting next to the burn bin and pokes it around inside, moving the ash and char to reveal some unburned portions of Nick's clothes. She sets the bar down and picks up the lighter fluid again, spraying another healthy amount over the remaining unburned pieces in the drum. Once again she sets the lighter fluid down a safe distance away and pulls the matches from her pocket. She strikes the match, allowing the head to flare up and then settle into a steady flame. She tosses the match into the drum and another fireball rises high, flooding her surroundings with its heat. She watches as the flames burn, slowly decreasing until she can't see any of the fire in the drum anymore from where she's standing. She steps closer and picks up the lighter fluid, then crosses the last foot or so until she's standing at the edge of the burn bin. She looks inside to find almost no remnants of the contents of the plastic bag, and what does remain is mostly ash.

Karen doesn't want to think about what kinds of questions would've been raised if the deputy had seen any of those bloodstained clothes, although she's pretty sure she would've been able to talk her way out of it by making up some excuse about cutting herself while cooking. *Still, better safe than sorry,* she thinks.

She heads back inside the restaurant, returning the lighter fluid to its spot on the wall shelves. Walking into the kitchen, she grabs the deputy's coffee cup and sets it next to hers in the sink. She turns on the water and washes both cups, putting them both on the drying rack. She looks at the clock on the wall. Almost nine. She hurries upstairs and makes sure she looks presentable for the day, a task she was trying to do earlier before she saw the plastic bag on the chair. Happy with how she looks, she heads back downstairs to the front door. She unbolts it once more and flips the switch to turn on the green open light. She walks through the dining room to the bar and grabs an order pad and a pen, sticking both in her back pocket. She pulls out the matches, not needing them anymore, and puts them back on the stack of matchbooks on the counter. Before she has a chance to go check the hallway calendar to see who's working later this morning for the lunch crowd, the front door chime loudly announces her first customers of the day.

Karen turns toward the sound and puts on her best smile.

"Welcome to Ellie's!"

CHAPTER 10

THE PUNISHMENT

A licia shifts the best she can in the wooden chair, trying to ease the pain in her lower back that set in several hours ago and the numbness that constantly returns to her legs, hands, and buttocks. *Or did it set in several minutes ago? Several days ago?* she wonders. She has no actual concept of time anymore. The room she's being held captive in reveals none. Only the coming and going of her captor gives her any sense of what time it might be.

She guesses it's evening when her warden leaves through the door in front of her and returns with food, but other than that, he spends most of his time beyond the metal door. Pounding away at something, seemingly forever. Alicia is afraid to find out what's beyond that metal door and if whatever it might be will ultimately involve her.

She sighs and takes a deep breath, the smell of her own urine filling her nose. She can't remember how many times she's had to use the bathroom, but she does remember the feeling of when she finally couldn't hold it anymore. In the cold pitch-black of the room, she remembers the initial warmth that filled her seat and ran down the leg of her pants just as her own tears were running down her face. The fact that she pissed herself doesn't seem to matter to her captor. She shakes her head and tries to keep the tears away. *I wonder if he'll finally notice when I shit myself.*

The pounding from beyond the metal door stops, drawing her attention away from her own filth. A few moments later and the large metal door begins to swing open on its designated track. Her captor comes into view. "Good afternoon, beautiful," he tells her. "I hope you're having a good day so far today."

Alicia lowers her eyes and stares at her lap, the strong smell of urine once again reaching her nose. She frowns and speaks up again, trying to be as polite as she can through the constant rage and fear she's felt since the night her captor abducted her.

"Can I please get cleaned up soon?"

Her warden, who's walking toward the table against the wall, pauses a moment.

"Of course, sweetheart, I am so sorry. I've just been so busy with work lately. I promise to make it up to you. Let me go clean up the room for you a bit, and then we can get you cleaned up and in some fresh clothes."

Alicia cringes a bit when he says *we can get you cleaned up.* She scolds herself when she realizes what she just invited him to do. *So instead of sitting in your own filth and trying to think of a way out of this, you just invited this monster to take your clothes off and probably rape you.*

She watches as he heads back through the metal door and down the hallway, leaving the door open this time. She follows him with her eyes, taking in the hallway as he walks down it. A plain corridor, with no decor on the walls and stark uncovered bulbs every few feet to light the way. Her captor stops at a wooden door at the very end of the hallway and opens it, stepping into the dark beyond and closing the door behind him.

Well, now you're going to find out what's beyond that door, she tells herself, *unless you think of a plan to get out of here first.* She looks at the wooden door and tries to remember if he locked it the last time he passed through it. She moves her arms and legs the best she can, trying to get the feeling to return. Her best chance to escape is going to be when he unties her to clean her up. If he unties her. A new thought enters her mind. *What if he just grabs a hose and hoses you down while you sit here in the chair?* She forces the thought from her mind. No, he wouldn't do that, not with the way he's been looking at her. Not with the way he has touched her. He wants to see her naked. He probably is planning on raping her sooner or later. It's not like he kidnapped her to hold her for ransom. She and Colin have little to no money, and they have only a couple thousand set aside for Penny's college fund so far. Plus, he knows what her favorite food is, which means he has to have been watching her. He may already know they don't have much money.

Which means he wants her.

She twists around in her chair some more, wiggling her toes and fingers to make sure they all respond properly. She glances around the room, looking for anything she might be able to use as a weapon. The only thing her eyes can find is the old hand sander sitting on the metal chests to her left. *That will have to do*, she tells herself. She hopes she has enough strength and coordination to move quickly enough to grab the sander and hit him hard enough to give her a chance to get away.

Happy with her plan, she waits until the wooden door at the end of the hallway finally opens up and her jailer comes back into view. He walks down the hall toward her, and as he passes under each of the hallway lights, his face alternates from fully visible to hidden in shadow.

His face, when hidden in shadow, causes a spike of fear in the pit of her stomach.

He steps through the metal door and walks toward her until he's standing in front of her, his boots almost touching her shoes. "You ready, beautiful?" he asks her.

Alicia nods. *You can do this*, she tells herself.

Her captor kneels down and reaches both hands out to her left leg, pausing as his fingers settle on the first knot of the thick wire. He looks up at her and into her face. Into her eyes. His voice reaches her ears, different this time. Harder than the overly caring voice she's been hearing. "I am going to untie you. If you try anything at all to get away, there will be repercussions. Repercussions you will not like."

The spike of fear in the pit of Alicia's stomach rises into her chest. Is he trying to say he will do something to her? Or worse, is he going to do something to Colin or Penny? The underlying rage inside her since she opened her eyes in this hell fights the fear for control of her emotions. *This monster will not have the chance to do anything to me or my family*, she tells herself, forcing as much bravado into her resolve as she can.

He's still staring at her, hasn't moved since he spoke. He's waiting for her response. She nods and he smiles, the hardness of his voice immediately gone and replaced with the familiar, softer tone. "Thank you, gorgeous. I knew you would understand."

She waits and watches as he unties her left leg and then her right, setting both of the now coiled-up metal bindings to the right of her chair. She continues to wait and watch while his hands move to the bindings on her left arm, slowly undoing them and coiling up the wire. He repeats the process with her right arm and once again sets both of the coiled-up wires to the right of her chair, stacking them on top of the bindings already there.

Once she's fully free, Alicia tries not to give her captor any indication of what she is about to do. If he thinks she's going to try something, he might subdue her again and stop her, and she doesn't want to find out what he meant by repercussions. With him this close, Alicia quickly weighs the possibility of being able to grab the hand sander to her left fast enough to swing it at him. Afraid he'd be upon her by the time she was able to grab the sander, she skips that step in her plan and decides to just throw herself at him, grabbing his head with her hands. She can use her momentum to topple him backward while he's still squatting down, push his head backward as hard as she can, and bash it against the concrete floor, repeating the process until he's not moving. Or even better, not living.

Now, she screams at herself in her head. *Before he has a chance to stand up!*

With all her might and as fast as she can, Alicia clumsily grabs the sides of her captor's head and pushes herself forward out of the chair in an effort to send him hurtling backward to the hard concrete floor.

After sitting in the same position so long, her stiff and unused muscles don't respond with the force she expects. Her initial momentum does force her captor backward, but only onto his backside before he realizes what she's attempting. He quickly grabs her upper arms and twists to his left, slamming her onto the concrete. Pain shoots through her right shoulder, which has borne the full brunt of her fall. Alicia tries to free her left arm from his grip and kick at him with both legs. Her efforts are unsuccessful, and soon, completely exhausted, she stops struggling.

She stares at the concrete floor directly in front of her, terrified to look at her captor. The smell of dirt and dust, now only a couple inches away from her face, fills her nose.

It's a moment before her captor moves, still maintaining his iron grip on her to ensure that her struggle is over. Continuing to hold both of her upper arms, he shifts back onto his feet. In one fluid motion he stands up and takes her with him, lifting her from the floor and violently slamming her back into the chair. When he finally speaks again, any hint of the prior softness is completely gone.

"I really wish you wouldn't have done that, Alicia."

She continues to stare at the floor, at his feet, avoiding his eyes. His fingers, which feel like steel talons, let go of her left arm, allowing the circulation to return to that part of her body, and he bends down, grabbing all four coils of wire and dropping them into her lap. He lets go of her right arm and grabs one of the bindings. For a second Alicia thinks about trying again to escape. He's standing up this time, though; the pain in her right shoulder is angrily throbbing at her, and she doesn't feel any of her prior energy. Another attempt might result in an even worse outcome.

Without any resistance, she watches as he quickly and tightly rebinds her arms and her legs. He checks his work and confirms that she's once again firmly secured to the chair.

He doesn't move from his position directly in front of her once he's done reconfining her to her wooden prison. He speaks to her again, his voice as iron as his grip was on her arms.

"I hope you understand that this is for your own good. So you know, without a doubt, that there are consequences for your actions."

Alicia continues to stare at the floor but is able to see him reach into his right pocket and pull something out. She forces herself to stare at the floor, to not see what he might now have in his hand.

A loud click echoes through the room.

The sound causes the fear inside her to grow exponentially, and Alicia closes her eyes as tight as she can. She doesn't want to see what is about to happen.

"This is going to hurt me more than it is going to hurt you, Alicia, I promise."

She keeps her eyes tightly closed. She hears her jailer move from in front of her to her right side. A brief moment passes before she feels his warm hand settle on top of her right hand, which is resting on the end of the wooden chair arm. She freezes, afraid to move.

The warm and unwanted touch of her captor's hand caresses her, slowly tracing each one of her fingers from knuckle to fingertip, starting with her thumb and ending with her pinkie finger. As he reaches the tip of her pinkie finger, he pauses.

Alicia keeps her eyes squeezed shut. His touch disappears from her hand and she hears him sigh. In that same moment, his touch is once again upon her hand, although it's not a soft caress this time.

No, this time he forcefully grabs her pinkie finger and pulls it toward him and away from her other fingers. She feels one of the knuckles pop a little. In that same motion an exploding pain surges through her hand and races its way up her arm, overtaking the throbbing pain in her shoulder so much that it disappears. Bright white and red spots fill her vision through her clenched eyes, and a pain like molten lava takes over her right hand.

Unable to keep her eyes closed anymore, Alicia looks at her right arm, where the spreading avalanche of pain is racing away from her hand and up her arm. Her right hand is covered in bright red blood, which has splattered all over and is pooling on the floor next to her foot. Blood pours out of where her pinkie finger used to be.

Alicia tries to focus on her hand and her now missing finger, but the avalanche of pain has made its way to her head. Her vision begins to get fuzzy at the edges, then starts to turn to black.

Soon the black takes over completely, and she drifts off to a place where the angry fire of her right hand can't find her.

≈

Nick slowly washes his hands off, watching the blood as it mingles with the water from the faucet and the two liquids conduct a circular dance around the drain, finally disappearing together into the darkness of the pipe below. The fantasy that everything is perfect now in his life has been shattered by Alicia's actions.

Once he finishes cleaning his hands, he turns the faucet off, watching the flow of the water reduce until only a couple drips remain. He reaches to his right and grabs the towel hanging from the hook nearest the sink. As he dries his hands, he looks at himself in the mirror.

A haggard face looks back at him, with disheveled hair and

angry eyes. Several droplets of blood are splattered across the left side of his face and on the shirt he is wearing. He raises the towel and wipes his face clean. Once he's cleaned the blood from his face, he returns the towel to the same hook.

Why did she have to do that? he asks himself. He specifically told her not to do anything, and she agreed not to. Then she tried to escape. Tried to hurt him.

Nick frowns, the anger burning in his eyes finally visible on his face as well.

Why did she lie to me?

He continues to look into the mirror at the face reflected back at him. He looks into his own eyes and at the fire within. Anger and disappointment over Alicia's actions fuel this fire currently raging inside him. A fire that feels like it will continue to grow the longer he stares into the eyes staring back at him in the mirror.

He pulls his stare away from the one in the mirror and takes a deep breath, looking down at the sink. *No*, he tells himself. *She now knows what happens. She now knows you're not afraid to punish her, no matter how much it might hurt you inside to do it.*

He takes another deep breath, trying to suffocate the fire within him. *It's going to take time. Colin has poisoned her for years against you. You have to be patient and show her you are the one she belongs with.* Nick nods at himself in the mirror, finally looking up from the sink and into the eyes staring back at him. The fire is gone. He turns from the sink and looks around the bathroom. He removed anything that could be picked up and used as a weapon when Alicia asked to clean herself up earlier. A change of clothes for her is sitting on the bench in the middle of the room. When he went to Shelton the first day she was here, he picked up a couple sets of unisex shirts and pants for her to wear. As time goes on, he will learn her sizes and be able to go buy her what she wants to wear, but for now, these will have to do.

He looks at the lower half of the shower wall on the left side of the room and at his latest addition to the decor. A heavy-duty metal ring sticks out from the wall, a thick chain attached to it. At the end of this chain is a wide metal clamp with a lock. A similar ring and chain are attached to the wall in the adjoining large room through the doorway in front of him, and this additional ring-and-chain set is located not very far from the main door to this room. He installed these new features late yesterday and tested both of the chains and rings to make sure they don't move at all from the walls they're mounted on. He hopes that one day Alicia will once again realize she loves him and he won't need to use these anymore, but until then he needs to make sure Colin's grip on her doesn't pull her away from him. Not until he can break that grip completely and forever.

He walks out of the shower room, leaving the light on behind him, and into the large adjoining room beyond. He looks around at the work he's accomplished this week. The subfloor is done, with all the dirt below now hidden from sight and the hardwood flooring already started in the far corner of the room.

Right above where their permanent guest resides. As well as Alicia's purse and cell phone, which were a couple of late additions to the last portion of earth still exposed before he finished the subfloor.

He estimates it will take him two days or so to complete the floor, and then he can begin on the last few big projects for the room. After he wraps those up, he can do the finishing touches and finally show Alicia what he's been working on and how much she means to him. His grand plan to win her love back. He smiles, excited to get to work again now that he's so close to finalizing what he's been working on for her. But first he has to deal with the situation at hand.

After Alicia passed out, Nick rushed back here to grab a small propane torch, a metal bar, and a work glove for holding the metal bar. He returned to Alicia and, after using the propane torch to heat the metal bar until it was glowing, was careful to cauterize the jagged, fleshy stub where her pinkie finger used to be to stop the bleeding. He made sure to take extra care not to burn any of her other fingers or his own in the process. He then returned the torch and bar to their spots and proceeded to clean himself up.

Now it's time to go clean Alicia up.

He breaks free from his thoughts and turns toward the large stack of boxes in the corner of the room. He walks over and, after finding the right box, pulls out a first-aid kit. He tucks it under his arm and crosses the rest of the distance to the wooden door. He steps into the hallway, then quickly makes his way into the room where his beautiful woman is waiting.

As he enters the room holding his love, he looks over at her, feeling a tinge of guilt for what he had to do. *This isn't your fault*, he tells himself, *this is her fault. She openly lied to you, and she needed to be taught what happens when she lies.* He nods to himself, in agreement with his thoughts.

Nick takes in the sight before him. Alicia's head is limply hanging down, her chin on her chest. Her hair cascades down either side of her face, concealing her features from his view. A large pool of blood is spread out on the floor under the right side of her chair, staining the concrete. Blood is splattered all over Alicia's right pant leg and shoe as well as all over the right arm and leg of the chair. Nick will need to clean up as much of that as he can, although the blood that's soaked into the concrete floor should act as a good reminder to her of what happens when she lies.

He kneels down next to her in the chair, the blood on the concrete soaking into his pants where his knee meets the floor. He sets the first-aid kit in her lap and opens it, taking out the bottle of antiseptic, a small bottle of water, and a clean cloth. Nick carefully douses Alicia's hand with water, uses the cloth to wipe the blood and dirt away, and then applies the antiseptic, ensuring that the stub of burnt flesh where her pinkie used to be is thoroughly cleaned. He returns the two bottles of liquid and cloth to the kit, then pulls out a small container of petroleum jelly and a bandage. He applies a light layer of petroleum jelly to the wound and then bandages it. Satisfied with his work, he returns the items to the kit and closes the lid. He stands and walks the kit over to the table, setting it down next to the blood-splattered remains of her pinkie finger. He returns to Alicia and quickly unfastens her restraints, stacking each coil of wire on top of the metal storage container to his right. Nick is confident that if she does wake up, she won't be able to put up much of a fight trying to get away. Unless, of course, she needs another lesson taught to her.

Once she's free from her bonds, he leans in and puts his arms as far around her midsection as he can, the top of her head pressing into his upper chest. He pulls her to him and hefts her onto his right shoulder, being careful not to lose his balance.

With Alicia's limp body secure, Nick turns toward the hallway and the large room beyond. He carefully carries his love down the hall, through the large room, and into the shower room. He slowly lowers her body onto the shower floor, reprimanding himself for not laying a towel down first so the cold floor wouldn't bother her.

I will know better next time, he tells himself, unhappy that he's made another mistake with her.

Once Alicia is laid down on the shower floor, he grabs the metal clamp on the end of the heavy chain and pulls it over to her legs. He rolls up her pant leg and attaches the clamp to her right leg at the ankle, making sure the locking mechanism is fully engaged. He reaches into his pocket and pulls out the key ring, quickly locating the key to the clamp. He inserts the key and turns it to verify that the locking mechanism for the clamp disengages. Content that the mechanism works as expected, he relocks the leg clamp and puts the keys back in his pocket. He stands up and walks past Alicia to the hooks on the back wall where the towels are hanging. He grabs the one he previously used to dry his hands.

He lays the towel down on the ground next to her, stretching it out to its fullest length. Once the towel is covering as much area as it possibly can, Nick slowly and carefully moves Alicia from the tile floor onto the towel. "See, my love? I learn from my mistakes," he tells her.

He stands up, proud of his work. He hopes that when she comes to, she'll appreciate all his hard work and how he's taken care of her so far. As he turns to go clean up the blood and the chair, he pauses. A thought he previously did not consider comes to mind.

How is she going to get her pants and panties off to clean herself up when her leg is chained up?

Nick considers his options.

He could take her clothes off for her now and then rechain her, but then she wouldn't be able to get her clean clothes on later. He could leave her unchained completely, but then what if she tries to run again when he opens the door? He doesn't want to have to keep cutting off her fingers, at least if he doesn't have to. A slight furrow creases his brow. No, she stays chained up for now. She will be able to slide her pants and underwear off and down along the chain if she needs to so she can clean up. She will have to just deal with not being able to put on clean pants for now. When she can prove to him that she isn't going to try to run back to Colin, then he can consider letting her shower without the chain.

Nick steps out of the shower room and closes the door behind him. He pulls the keys from his pocket once again and locks the door, just in case Alicia somehow finds a way to escape the leg clamp. He tests the knob to make sure it's locked and then heads back toward the hallway, pausing once again at the boxes of supplies. He grabs a large rag and a spray bottle of cleaning solution and heads down the hallway and into the smaller room. He moves the wooden chair closer to the table against the wall. He sprays down the chair, using the rag to carefully clean the splattered blood and the urine from the arms, legs, and seat. Once the chair is clean, he turns his attention to the large bloodstain on the floor. He sprays the stain and scrubs the concrete with the rag, doing his best to clean up as much of the blood as possible.

As Nick expected, the unsealed concrete floor has soaked up a good amount of the blood and a large red stain remains, only now a darker red than previously. He hopes Alicia has learned from this and won't try anything like that again. Hopefully the stain on the floor will be a reminder to her anytime she's in this room. He grabs the chair and returns it to where it was previously positioned. He wipes down the bindings with the rag, cleaning up any of the blood that found its way onto them.

As he finishes the bindings and sets them back down on the metal chest, he steps back and surveys his work. Besides the large red stain on the floor, everything is back as it was.

Time to go see if Alicia is awake yet.

Still holding the rag and spray bottle, Nick walks over to the table and picks up Alicia's pinkie finger, feeling the soft skin between his fingers. He puts her finger in his pocket, next to the pocketknife that claimed that same finger. He sprays the table with the cleaning solution and wipes it down with the rag as well, removing any of the blood that remained from her finger. Holding the rag and spray bottle with one hand, he grabs the first-aid kit still on the table with the other. He turns toward the large room at the end of the hallway and makes his way back toward where his one and only is waiting for him.

As he approaches the large room, he hears a pounding sound coming from the shower room door on the other side. *Someone's awake*, he thinks. He steps through the doorway and places the rag and spray bottle on the floor next to the various boxes of supplies. He walks over to the shower room door and stands in front of it, listening to his love on the other side.

He listens to her pounding on the door. He listens to her begging for someone to help her and set her free. He listens to her ask why this is happening to her.

Smiling, Nick responds to her last request.

"Because I love you, Alicia. And soon, you will realize you love me."

The room on the other side of the door in front of him goes completely silent.

CHAPTER 11

THE CHANCE

When Alicia opens her eyes again, she is on her back. Above her is a tiled ceiling and showerheads on the wall to her left. Her right hand and shoulder are both throbbing in unison. She looks down at her body, afraid she might have been stripped naked while she was unconscious.

Seeing that she is still dressed in her clothes, she breathes a sigh of relief. She breathes even easier when she realizes she's not bound to the chair anymore. She slowly sits up and looks around. There is a large bench several feet to her right, with a row of toilets and a hot water heater on the far wall. In the middle of the wall in front of her is a door, and when she turns to look behind her, she sees several towels hanging on the back wall and a couple of sinks with dirty mirrors above them. The room reminds her of a very basic locker room.

She also notices the large chain mounted to the wall, which is attached to a clamp on her right leg. She lifts her leg and tests the weight of the chain. The chain is as heavy as it looks, and Alicia is sure it's securely bolted into the wall.

She looks down at her right hand, which is currently bandaged up. Even with the bandage, it's obvious she doesn't have her pinkie finger anymore. She's afraid to see what her hand looks like now. The pain is constant, a nonstop throbbing with occasional spikes up her arm. She reaches over with her left hand and rubs her right shoulder. The skin is tender and painful to the touch but nothing is broken, which brings her a small bit of comfort. She figures she'll have a large bruise there for several weeks.

With her left hand, she carefully pushes herself up off the floor and slowly walks over to the bench, allowing her legs to remember what muscles to use for walking. The chain drags on the ground behind her as she reaches the bench and sits down. She looks around the room again for anything she might be able to use to escape. The only items not bolted to the walls or the floor are the hanging towels, the towel on the floor, a couple bars of soap on a shelf under the showerheads, a stack of clothes on the bench next to her, and two rolls of toilet paper on the toilet tanks. Even the mirrors, which are polished metal and not glass, are bolted to the wall.

Unless she can knock her captor out with a bar of soap, her options for escape are virtually nil. She looks at the clamp on her leg. It is locked and fairly tight. The only way she's getting out of the clamp is either with the key or by smashing all the bones in her ankle and foot to slide it off her leg. If she needs to run to get away, the latter is not an option.

She wonders what part of the building she's being held in, or if she's still in the same building as before. Maybe he moved her to a different location while she was unconscious. *Only one way I can find out*, she thinks.

Alicia stands up from the bench, once again stretching her legs and waking up stiff muscles she hasn't used since she was bound to the chair. She walks over to the door, her metal leash again scraping against the tile of the floor as it travels with her.

She tries the knob. Locked, of course.

As frustration begins to set in once again, Alicia decides it's time for her to get some answers. Enough of being quiet.

She begins to pound on the door, yelling for her captor. Yelling for anyone. Yelling to be set free. Yelling to know why she's locked in here and chained to the fucking wall.

As she's catching her breath, getting ready to continue yelling, she hears her captor's voice from the other side of the door. The soft version of his voice.

What he tells her chills her to the bone, and she wonders to herself, *Does he really think he loves me? Has he convinced himself I want to be here like this?* In one sentence, one single statement, he answered most of her questions.

She lowers her left hand and doesn't respond. Silence takes over the room again. Her thoughts are scrambled and she tries to think of something to say. Something to do.

She glances over at the showers and then down at the chain

attached to her right leg. The first solid thought that comes to her mind quickly leaves her lips.

"How am I supposed to get my clothes off to shower when I'm attached to the wall by a chain?"

She waits quietly for a response. After a few moments, he responds.

"You can slide your clothes down the chain. Wash them if you want to, then put them back on if you prefer. Or keep them off and when I come in there, I can put clean clothes on you. Either way, the chain stays on until you prove to me I can trust you without it. Clean yourself up and then let me know when you're ready to come out."

Alicia looks down at the chain again and knows she definitely does not want her captor seeing her naked or putting anything on her at all, although she knows she will need to be prepared for the day that might actually happen, with or without her consent.

She turns from the door and walks over to the showers, stopping in front of the closest one with a bar of soap on the shelf. She carefully takes her shirt off and tosses it onto the floor, taking care not to bump her bandaged hand or strain her already bruised shoulder. After a bit of struggling with her left hand, she's able to get her bra off and throws it on top of her shirt. Her shoes and socks quickly join the growing pile of clothing. Her pants are a bigger challenge. To get them off, Alicia undoes the buttons and then, using her left hand, pushes each side down until they're at her ankles. She frees her left leg from her jeans; but she's unable to get the cuff of her right pants leg down and over her foot due to the clamp of the chain. After a couple of unsuccessful attempts at getting the cuff to stretch far enough over her heel, she stops trying and figures she can clean up just as easily with them at her ankle as she could with them on the chain. She repeats the process with her panties, looking over at the door repeatedly, hoping she doesn't hear the lock disengage or the door begin to open.

Finally near a toilet, Alicia walks over to the nearest one with her metal leash, her pants, and her underwear all dragging along behind her right leg. She finally alleviates the recurring pain and pressure from her abdomen letting her know that more than just urine needs to come out. After finishing her business and flushing the toilet, she stands up and walks back to the showers. She picks the towel up from the floor and tosses it onto the wooden bench. She turns on the water and adjusts it to the temperature she likes, then steps into the stream of water, taking care not to get her bandaged right hand wet.

Alicia closes her eyes and just stands under the water for a few minutes, taking in the comfortable feeling of the water striking her body. For the first time since she was abducted, she feels a sense of relaxation as the hot water cascades down her body, the heat helping ease the tension in the stiff muscles of her back, her arms, and her legs.

She opens her eyes, uses her left hand to grab the bar of soap on the shelf, and begins to lather herself up. She washes away the blood and the dust. She washes away the dirt and the urine.

For just a brief moment, she also washes away the thoughts of her current situation.

Her fleeting mental escape is cut short as she sees her pants and underwear on the floor, now soaked through. As she finishes washing her legs as best she can, she squats down and uses the bar of soap to scrub her clothes. The process takes time, as she can only do so much using just her left hand while trying to keep her right one from getting wet. She also digs into the pile of clothing a few feet away and pulls out her socks to wash them as well.

Just as the shower water starts to lose its heat, she returns the bar of soap to the shelf and then with her right leg slides her clothes over and directly into the stream of water, rinsing off as much of the soap and grime as she can.

This will have to do for now, she thinks as she turns the water off. She walks over to the wall and grabs one of the towels hanging there. She awkwardly dries herself off with just her left hand, leaving almost as many spots still wet as she was able to dry. Satisfied enough, she drops the partially damp towel onto her soaked clothes on the floor and with her left foot steps the towel down onto her clothes, trying to absorb as much of the water as possible. Once the towel is completely soaked through, she tosses it over with her shirt and grabs the towel from the bench, repeating the process of trying to absorb as much of the water out of her wet clothes as possible.

Once the second towel is just as wet at the first, she bends down and adds it to the growing pile of laundry. She slowly pulls her panties back up, followed carefully by her pants. Buttoning her pants back up takes both of her hands and using her right hand causes the ever-present throbbing pain to grow into a searing reminder that her pinkie finger is no longer there. She puts on her damp socks and then retrieves her dirty shoes from the laundry pile, slowly putting them back on one at a time. Retying her shoes also requires use of both her hands, again reigniting the searing pain in her right hand, causing her to tear up as the pain spikes up her arm.

As she regains her composure and the pain subsides back to a steady throb, Alicia looks through the clothes stacked on the bench. A couple of basic T-shirts and two pairs of sweatpants. The clothes are only a couple sizes bigger than what she usually wears. She considers trying to put her bra back on, but the slightly baggy T-shirt will hopefully conceal her breasts enough to not give her captor any ideas. She opts for just the shirt and puts it on, carefully guiding her right hand and arm through the corresponding sleeve.

She turns and looks at herself in the mirror. She looks like she hasn't slept in days, and the shower washed away the remnants of the makeup she was wearing when she went in to work on Monday.

She wonders what day it might be now.

Alicia runs her left hand through her damp hair a few times, unknotting a couple spots and pulling it back and out of her face. She walks to the door, dragging her leash along with her, the scraping of the metal against the tile in sync with each movement of her right leg.

She takes a deep breath and pounds against the door, waiting for her captor's response.

After her third time hammering on the door, a voice on the other side acknowledges her.

"Are you all cleaned up now? Happy and smiling?" the voice asks.

Alicia raises her left hand and gives the voice on the other side the middle finger, although her words don't match what she really wants to say. "Yes, I'm all cleaned up, thank you."

She hears a key being inserted into the lock. The door opens and the doorway frames her captor. "Are you going to behave now?" he asks.

She nods, looking everywhere but at his face to avoid his eyes. He steps into the room with her, forcing her to step back a few steps, the chain following her. He closes the door behind him and looks around the room. She sees him point at the clothes and towels on the floor.

"I will make sure those are cleaned for you. Are you OK with still wearing those jeans, or would you like a pair of the pants I bought for you?" He points from the clothes on the floor to the clothes on the bench.

Alicia hesitates a moment before responding. Although she's afraid of what he might do to her without any clothes on, she also senses a possible opportunity to escape. Her leg strength has returned, as has her balance. She quickly decides that any chance to escape, regardless of the consequences, is better than what might be in store for her if she remains his prisoner.

In her best begging voice, which has always worked with Colin, she responds to him. "I would really like to be able to wear the pants you bought me." She forces herself to look into his eyes and smile after she speaks.

The moment she sees him smile back, she adds as sweetly as she can, "Please?"

Her captor's smile gets even bigger and he nods, digging into his pocket for the keys and then quickly squatting down by her right leg. She waits for the moment she hears the clamp lock open and then springs into action.

Summoning all the strength she has, Alicia swiftly plants both her hands on her captor's right shoulder and pushes as hard as she can to his left. She fights to ignore the sudden explosion of pain in her right hand. Her captor, who's focused on taking the clamp off her leg, is thrown off balance and topples over. As he falls, the side of his head hits the end of the wooden bench.

Breathless seconds pass while Alicia waits to see if her captor, now immobile on the floor, moves. She frantically looks around for something to hit him with if he starts getting back up, then sees the key ring on the floor near her now free right leg.

Run! the voice in her head screams.

Alicia bends down and grabs the keys. She turns toward the door, and a few steps later she's standing in the large room beyond.

She locates another wooden door to her right, open to

the hallway beyond. Alicia takes off as fast as she can for this hallway, racing away from her captor and toward her freedom.

≈

Anger.

The first emotion Nick feels when he opens his eyes is anger. Anger that he was stupid enough to believe she wanted him. That she wanted him to help her out of her clothes.

Something Nick has wanted to do since the very first day he saw her.

Ignoring the pain coming from the side of his head, he pushes himself up off the tiled floor to a sitting position and looks around the room. Alicia is gone, as are his keys.

The second emotion he feels is panic when it sets in that Alicia is gone.

He shakes his head, trying to clear the dizziness. He can deal with his injury later. Right now he needs to locate Alicia and get her back here. This time he'll ensure she stays chained up forever.

Nick grabs the bench with his left hand and steadies himself as he gets to his feet. A wave of dizziness washes over him. He takes a deep breath and tries to focus his vision, fighting the sudden nausea.

After the dizziness passes, he heads out of the shower room. He looks up at the clock on the wall. Just after six in the evening. He tries to cut through the fog in his head. *What time did I put her in the room? What time did she finish her shower?* His thoughts find no answers. Before heading down the hallway and into the room where he initially kept her, he stops at one of the nearest boxes and grabs a familiar white rag and a small plastic container of liquid, stuffing them both in his pocket. He hurries into the smaller room. The door to the stairwell is open. He quickly goes up the stairs, finding the door at the top open as well as the large main door out of the building. Nick quickly checks the main room to make sure she's not hiding behind some equipment and then heads toward the open front door. He notices the keys still hanging from the lock. He grabs them and puts them in his pocket, then steps outside and slides the door closed behind him. As he's turning from the door, he pauses. If she's still inside the building and he leaves the door unlocked, she could still leave anytime and he wouldn't know until he returned.

He pulls the keys out of his pocket and locks the main door. *Just in case*, he tells himself.

Nick turns away from the door and surveys the area. The clearing is empty, and he doesn't see any movement anywhere near the tree line. He wonders if she might've headed toward the lake in hopes there was a boat on the water or even followed the edge of the lake to the restaurant, although that is several miles away. He looks at the pathway, which she could have easily seen from the building. If she was in a panic, she might have just chosen the route with the least resistance. Hoping he is right, he quickly crosses the clearing to the path and plunges into the forest. He swiftly navigates the path, and as he clears the last portion, he can see that the camouflage cover has been pulled off the truck and lies on the ground behind it. The driver's side door is open and the interior dome light is on. She definitely came this way, and it must've been recently or the dome light would have already automatically turned off.

He hurriedly checks inside and under the truck, finding nothing. He collects the camouflage cover and tosses it into the bed of the truck. He's thankful she left the keys behind, since the truck key happens to be on the key ring. If she'd been able to leave in the truck, there would have been no chance for him to find her before she either got back to Colin or reached the police.

She has to be fairly close, he surmises. The dome light doesn't stay on for that long. *Five minutes? Three?* he wonders. There's no time for wondering.

He gets behind the wheel of the truck and starts it up. The restaurant is probably busy right now with Wednesday's dinner crowd, and there will be a full parking lot. If she went this way, she'll be heading toward the restaurant. He hurriedly backs the truck up, turns on the headlights, and heads down the old logging camp road, taking the bumps and ruts at a speed that tests the limits of the suspension, jostling him from side to side. The back-and-forth movement causes the dizziness from earlier to come creeping back. Just when he thinks the dizziness is going to take over, the highway comes into view. He slows the truck just enough to make the left turn for the restaurant without losing control, and then he accelerates down the road.

He soon sees what he's searching for.

Alicia, on the left side of the road, running slowly toward the restaurant.

As he approaches her, she slows her pace and turns to him, waving her arms in an attempt to get him to stop. Although there's still some daylight left, the headlights of the truck must be stopping her from seeing him in the cab or realizing the truck is the same one she left behind moments ago.

Oh, I plan on stopping, trust me, he thinks. He slows the truck and brings it to a stop on the opposite side, off on the shoulder. He watches as Alicia takes a couple steps toward the truck, clearly winded and only about sixty feet away. As he opens the door she stops in her tracks, her eyes finding their way past the bright headlights and to his face. Her look of relief is immediately replaced by panic and she turns to run, slipping and nearly falling in the process.

Nick wastes no time.

He exits the truck and throws the door closed behind him as he takes off down the road after his love, who has now regained her footing and abruptly veered off the road into the forest. All his careful planning, all his steps to avoid running into anyone, all the work he has done all these years will be for nothing if he doesn't get her back. The fantasy of the last couple days, where he was finally experiencing such happiness with his one true love, will be gone forever.

Nick quickly reaches the spot where Alicia left the road and follows her into the woods. He sees her cutting around the trees ahead of him about forty feet away. He pushes himself to go faster, doing his best to make sure he doesn't trip on something that will let her get farther away.

Thirty feet away from her. Twenty feet away from her. He can now hear her panting, gasping for air, begging for the strength to get away.

The parking lot of the restaurant is slowly becoming visible through the trees ahead. Two people and a small child can be vaguely seen standing outside, next to a truck Nick has seen many times before.

Ten feet away. Nick can smell her perspiration. He can feel the heat coming off her body. The parking lot is getting closer, the people standing outside coming into focus. If he doesn't catch her soon, she'll be out of the trees and into full view at the far edge of the parking lot.

Five feet away. Three feet away. As the parking lot grows closer and the chances of losing her grow ever greater, Nick dives forward with all his might to grab her, to stop her from making it out of the woods. As his arms wrap around her and his weight and momentum cause her to fall forward with him, he hears her yell one word.

"Colin!"

In the same moment, they both hit the ground, Nick nearly on top of Alicia. He hears all the air exit her lungs, the wind knocked out of her. She's motionless under him, exhausted, trying to catch her breath while unable to speak. Nick pulls out the rag and bottle from his pocket. He fumbles with the lid, splashes some of the liquid on the rag and the rest all over the ground. He tosses the bottle aside and quickly places the rag over Alicia's nose and mouth, watching her eyes get wide and then slowly start to close.

Once her breathing slows, Nick removes the rag and places it back into his pocket. He looks up and through the brush to see if the people in the parking lot heard her. They're close enough to the edge of the woods that he's able to identify the three people standing in the parking lot.

His mother, Colin, and the little girl.

Colin is looking in their general direction. His mother has her hand on Colin's shoulder and is saying something Nick is unable to hear. The light is beginning to fail, and most of the forest around Nick is now dark with shadows. As long as he doesn't move too much, Colin won't be able to see him or Alicia on the ground. He wonders how he's going to get her out of here with Colin there. Thankfully, Colin doesn't look his way for very long before he turns his attention back to Nick's mother. Nick waits while they finish up their conversation and Colin helps the little girl into the truck, buckling her in. His mother, as she turns toward the restaurant, briefly looks his way and surveys the area while walking back toward the front door. Colin gets into the truck, the headlights come on, and the vehicle starts up. As the truck is turning to leave, the headlights momentarily illuminate the spot where he's lying. He holds his breath as the truck pulls out and away from the parking lot. Once the truck is gone, Nick takes advantage of the temporarily quiet parking lot. He pushes himself off the unconscious Alicia and picks her up. He carries her on his shoulder and turns back for his waiting truck. He skillfully navigates the trees and heavy underbrush, taking care not to bump her against anything.

By the time Nick reaches the truck, night has set in. The truck's headlights are still on, casting a luminous glare for a couple hundred feet. He crosses the highway and walks to the back of the truck, where the red taillights leave a sinister glow in stark contrast to the bright white of the headlights. He lowers the tailgate and softly places Alicia into the bed. He grabs the cords used to secure the cover and tightly binds both her hands as well as her feet. He closes the tailgate and grabs the camouflage cover, opening it up. As he's covering up his one and only, a new light pierces the darkness from behind him. A set of headlights is rapidly approaching.

He quickly checks to ensure Alicia is fully covered by the tarp as the distance between the back of the rental and the encroaching headlights dwindles. *Just keep on driving*, Nick thinks, *and mind your own business.*

Unfortunately, the approaching vehicle slows down and pulls off the road behind Nick. He turns toward the vehicle, shielding his eyes from the car's headlights, and waves them on.

The car remains motionless. In response to Nick's motion, a light bar on top of the car turns on, casting an alternating pattern of red and blue light all around the surrounding tree line. He immediately feels heat radiating from his palms as a surge of panic races from his fingertips to his toes.

Nick contemplates his options as he continues shielding his

eyes from the lights, waiting for the officer to make their next move.

It could be that it doesn't appear as if he's doing anything wrong and the officer is just stopping to see if he needs help. If he plays it cool and the officer doesn't run the tag or ask for identification, Nick should be able to talk his way out of this. If he can't, he has his pocketknife in his right pocket, provided he can catch the officer off guard. A missing police officer would really cause some issues, though, not to mention the problem of what to do with the police car itself. *Handle this*, he tells himself, *because that is exactly what Mother would tell me to do.*

He looks at the misshapen lump under the tarp in the truck bed, still partially hidden in the darkness but also now partially illuminated by the flashing red and blue lights. He hears the car door open and then close, and the officer walks into view, just a few feet away. He remains quiet as the officer breaks the silence.

"How are we doing tonight, Nick?"

CHAPTER 12

THE PRESENTATION

Karen sits down on her stool behind the bar and takes a sip out of the lowball glass in front of her. The whiskey goes down smooth, with just a slight lingering burn. She smiles at the feeling and takes another sip.

One of her line cooks, having just finished prep for tomorrow, walks by the end of the bar, heading toward the front door. "Have a great night, Mrs. Ellie!" he tells her.

She nods at him and continues to smile as he walks through the dining room and out the door. The door chime sings its last song for the night, letting her know she's now alone in the restaurant.

She gets up from the stool and walks over to the front door, locks the dead bolt, and turns the neon sign from open to closed. She looks out the window at the parking lot and watches as the taillights of the line cook's car exit the parking lot and disappear onto the highway. Satisfied, she turns from the window and heads back toward the bar, turning off the dining room lights as she goes. She glances at the clock in the bar and continues on into the kitchen. Once there, she crosses to the shelves lining the hallway and takes a loaf of bread from the several stacks stored there. She sets the loaf of bread on the prep table and grabs the other ingredients she'll need to make some ham-and-cheese sandwiches. It takes only a few minutes before she has four sandwiches finished on the prep table. She wraps the sandwiches tightly with plastic wrap and sets them inside a paper bag, then pulls a few colas and water bottles out of the walk-in and places them in the bag with the sandwiches.

She admires her handiwork and glances at the clock. She has about an hour before he'll show up. She heads back to the bar, resumes her spot on her stool, and takes another sip of the whiskey, savoring the flavor. She looks over her simple little restaurant and thinks about all that has happened in the last three months.

First, her boy killed that stupid runaway. Luck was definitely on his side that night. That girl could have been anyone. A local just out exploring. A hiker with a family nearby. She even could've been a ghost story hunter on a writing assignment. No, as luck would have it, this girl was a runaway who'd been missing for quite some time, and the police had long ago given up on thinking she was still in the state. Not that the girl didn't deserve her fate. *You don't go sticking your nose into other people's property*, Karen thinks. Of course, if it weren't for his momma, her Nick would've been lost as to how to handle the situation afterward.

She takes the last sip of whiskey in her glass and nods, talking to the empty restaurant around her. "That boy would be completely lost without me."

Karen sets the glass down on the bar and grabs the nearest half-empty bottle of whiskey from the shelf behind her. She pours herself another glass, placing the bottle down on the bar instead of returning it to the shelf, and continues her journey through her thoughts.

When her boy finally told her it was time to reclaim Alicia, she was both nervous and excited. She knew how much this meant to him, how much it was going to mean to him, and she knew she was going to do whatever it took to make sure her little boy got exactly what he wanted. What he should have had all along.

It might take some time for Alicia to come around, since she has been held captive by Colin for so long, but she will be much happier with her life when she remembers how great Nick is.

Karen sighs and looks at the glass of whiskey sitting on the counter, hesitating to take another sip. It might take some time for Alicia to forgive her for what she's done. For not letting Alicia run when she wanted to run. Karen may never forget the look on Alicia's face when the young woman looked up at her with pure panic and confusion in her wide eyes while stuck in Karen's embrace. *It was for your own good, Alicia*, she thinks. *One day you will realize what I did was in your best interest and you'll thank me for it.* She wonders if maybe Alicia has already forgiven her. It has been several weeks now without any incidents. Her boy has been smiling each time she has seen him lately.

Of course, the week after her boy claimed Alicia as his own was a bit of a roller coaster where she watched her boy go from happy to rejected, from rejected to angry, and then back to happy again. And if it wasn't for her, he would have failed miserably in his plan.

Karen first had to play the part of the concerned friend and mother figure with Colin, which was easy enough to do, since it was Colin's fault her boy had been heartbroken for years and years. His pain didn't bother her at all. In a way, she enjoyed it. *Still do*, she thinks. If it weren't for Colin, her boy would've had Alicia by his side years ago versus having to wait so long for the right time. Colin took Alicia away from her boy in high school, so it's only fitting that her boy has taken Alicia back away from him. But she will continue to play the part of the concerned mother, the concerned friend. She will continue to express her sympathy for Colin's loss and continue to nurture little Penny as she grows up. Once Alicia comes around, then little miss Penny can be reunited with her mother and start calling the right man Daddy. The thought of that day makes Karen smile, and she takes another sip of her whiskey.

Of course, she was a bit surprised by the officer who came out to speak with her. It wasn't who she was expecting. Karen fully figured the chief would come by to speak with her, especially since they had a shared past. The timing of the officer showing up threw her off guard as well, but she would've been prepared for him had she not forgotten to take care of her boy's clothes earlier instead of deciding to do it that morning. A stupid mistake she will not make again. She made sure to call the chief later that day and find out why he sent out a deputy instead of coming to see her in person. His response was simple—he didn't feel it was necessary, but if there was something he needed to know about, she needed to tell him.

That same evening the chief came to visit her, and over a few glasses of top-shelf Scotch, she got him caught up on everything that had happened. His initial reaction was as she expected, and she kindly reminded him about their past. Their shared past in which he was having an affair with a woman out of town. A woman who was threatening to tell the chief's wife about that very affair. A scandal like that in a small town where gossip spreads like wildfire would easily ruin his career, since most of the town's inhabitants of voting age frown upon adultery. One night the chief invited the woman to have a late-night dinner and conversation at the restaurant, and Karen was nice enough to help the chief find that woman a new place to lay her head.

Right next to where her husband currently lays his head. *Well, what was remaining of his head at the time, after the bugs and worms had their way with it*, she thinks.

The chief knew about Karen's husband and what had really happened, and he knew she was just the person to help him out of the situation. And help him she did. She never did ask for anything in return, just enjoyed the unspoken agreement between the two of them.

Karen takes another sip of her whiskey. The chief knows about her boy and where he's currently living. He played along with the military story and attended the funeral in his full dress uniform. He knows that she'll do anything to make sure her boy is happy. And now he knows about Alicia and what happened. She knew it would be best that the chief be informed of what had happened so he could make sure the investigation into Alicia's disappearance was guided in the right direction.

A direction that doesn't lead to her and her boy.

She didn't tell him about the runaway, though. The chief is a nice enough guy and one of the few people privy to most of her secrets, but he doesn't need to know everything. Just enough to make sure he can step in to protect her and her son when she needs him to.

Like the night Alicia got away. The chief was nice enough to call her and tell her he ran into her boy a mile or so down the road from the restaurant, covered in sweat and hiding something under a tarp in the back of the truck he was driving. The chief made sure her boy left quickly and that no other cars came across them.

She shakes her head; she should've known it was going to happen one day and isn't sure why she was so surprised when it did. *Maybe because I didn't expect it to happen the first week*, she thinks. She smiles and finishes the small amount of golden liquid remaining in her glass. She grabs the bottle of whiskey sitting on the bar and pours another while glancing up at the bar clock. Thirty more minutes until her boy is supposed to show up.

The evening Colin brought little miss Penny to see her came as a bit of a surprise. Karen didn't expect Colin to come by for the first week or two. He explained that he needed to get Penny out of the house a bit as well as drop off some missing-person flyers he had created to hang up around town. Playing her part was easy enough to do—agreeing to hang as many of the flyers as he wanted in the restaurant and even offering to hand them out to every customer if he desired her to. She may have played her part too well, though, as he broke down crying while they were standing in the parking lot. Right after she put her hand on his shoulder to console him and tell him everything would work out, a distant voice escaped from the tree line at the far edge of the parking lot.

A voice Karen immediately recognized.

A single word that, upon its release from the trees, drifted across the parking lot and to her ears. To Colin's ears.

"Colin."

She fought the urge to immediately look in that direction, as she could see Colin had heard it too. She watched as he turned toward the sound and asked her if she'd heard something as well. No, she hadn't heard anything at all, she said, asking him what he'd heard. When he told her he'd just heard Alicia yelling his name, she told him again that she hadn't heard anything and that there had been many times over the years where she had mistaken the call from one of the loons down at the lake for the sound of her boy yelling her name. This seemed to pull Colin's attention from the tree line back to her, and he shook his head in agreement and told her she was probably right and that he hadn't been sleeping much lately. She told him to go get some rest and that she would call him immediately if she found anything out. He agreed, and she gave both him and little Miss Penny big hugs and sent them on their way. As she was walking back to the restaurant, she risked a glance at the tree line where the sound had come from, and for a brief moment she saw, mostly concealed by the underbrush, her boy's face looking back at her.

Once Karen was back in the restaurant, she immediately called the chief from her cell phone and asked him if he'd be nice enough to check out the highway outside the restaurant for her and make sure everything was safe. His response reassured her that he knew what she was referring to. He said he was currently on his way back from Rockville and should be in the area in about twenty minutes or so. She thanked him and told him to call her if he saw anything, to which he agreed.

She wasn't sure what the chief might come across. He might come across her boy taking care of his business. He might come across Alicia. He might come across nothing at all. Either way, if Alicia really was free, her boy might need the extra help.

Thankfully, when the chief called her a bit later, it turned out her boy had taken care of things on his own.

She takes a sip of her latest pour. Her smile turns into a

quick laugh. She would've liked to see the look on her boy's face when the chief pulled up behind him. To see if he was calm and collected or if he was in a state of panic.

It was a lesson he needed to learn, she surmises. *It isn't just him he has to watch out for now*. It was a good reminder that he needed to be extremely careful and not make whatever mistake he'd made that had led to Alicia's getting free in the first place. Her boy did thank her later the following night, at least, when he showed up to get food for the two of them.

"That's what a good mother does, my son. She takes care of you, even in ways you don't expect," she tells the empty restaurant.

Another glace at the bar clock lets her know he should be here any minute. Karen finishes the remainder of her whiskey, and after rinsing out the glass in the bar sink, she puts both the glass and the bottle of whiskey back on the shelf where they belong. As if on cue, she hears the back door to the restaurant open and close. She gets up off the bar stool and walks to the edge of the bar and then into the kitchen. Standing in the hallway, next to the shelves with the various loaves of bread, is her boy. Her pride and joy.

"It's about time you got here," she tells him, even though he's actually on time for once. The smile on his face doesn't falter.

As she walks over to the prep table where the bag is sitting, her boy speaks with clear excitement in his voice.

"I finished it today. I'm ready to show her what she means to me."

≈

Alicia yawns and stretches, rubbing the sleep from her eyes. She sits up and looks around her small prison. A prison she has been living in for what feels like years. She lost count of the days quite some time back, but she does know she's been in here for at least several months now.

Her captor refuses to let her out of this room. He refuses to remove the chain on her right leg. "Can't have you pulling another stunt like you did before," he told her after she woke back up in here. After she was so close to freedom. So close to her family.

She remembers the fire in her chest, the pain in her legs, from her efforts to get away. She remembers spotting the parking lot of Ellie's and then miraculously seeing, standing in that same parking lot, the two people that mean more to her than her own life. She remembers yelling Colin's name so he could see her, so he could save her, and then she was on the ground and unable to breathe at all. She doesn't remember anything past that beyond waking up in here, once again chained to the wall.

Every day has been the same after that, chained in this room with the door closed and locked. With no real sense of day or night, she has slowly begun to lose count of how long she has been here. The only things that change are the food and the noises from the room beyond her cell.

Alicia sighs and stands up, stretching out her legs, and thinks about her current existence.

For hours on end, her warden hammers away and moves

things in the large room beyond her tiled prison. In the evenings, or at least she thinks it's the evenings, he unlocks the door and carefully enters with her dinner, always wary of her and her movements. His conversation is cheery and laced with compliments. He tells her she looks beautiful. Tells her how much he cares for her. Tells her how he can't wait to show her what he's working on for her. His plan, as he calls it.

The tone of his voice never matches his face. Never matches his eyes. The only time his voice matches his eyes is when he's punishing her.

Alicia looks down at her hands. The two stubs on her right hand are almost fully healed over now, and the stub on her left hand is still healing. Luckily, the pain isn't keeping her up at night anymore. After she escaped, her warden showed her how much he appreciated it by cutting off her right ring finger. She tried one more time after that to get away, to make it to her freedom and back to her family that's in her mind every moment of every day. She only made it to the small room before the stairway by the time he was upon her and subduing her once again. She lost the pinkie on her left hand for that attempt. After that, she stopped trying to get away and resigned herself to her current plight.

Just as all hope for escape was finally leaving her thoughts, her captor told her his work was done. That it was time for him to show her what he had done for her and how much she means to him. He told her before she went to sleep, and she was left worried about what he meant, but his words also reignited the almost dead flame of hope inside her that she may be able to escape this hell.

As she stared at the tiled ceiling of her prison last night, with the hard cold floor as her usual bed, that almost dead flame inside her grew. The more she thought of Penny, it grew. The more she thought of Colin, it grew. It grew until it filled every inch of her body, screaming to be given another chance to break free. She knew, at that moment, that she would seize every opportunity she had to get away from this nightmare. For as long as she was alive. When she finally did drift off to sleep, the raging fire of hope burning through her body, she chastised herself for ever thinking of giving up.

Alicia yawns one more time and walks over to the nearest sink to brush her teeth. Her captor won't allow her to have a toothbrush, but he does at least make sure she has toothpaste. Using her right index finger, she rubs the paste across all her teeth, doing her best to clean them. Once that's done, she turns the water on and cleans off her finger, then bends down and rinses out her mouth. As she stands up straight again and looks into the mirror, the lock on the door behind her clicks and the door slowly opens. She doesn't move from her position at the sink, instead looking in the mirror at the sudden reflection of her captor in the doorway behind her as her prison door opens farther. As usual, the lights are off in the large room beyond, and Alicia is unable to see any farther into the space than just a couple feet beyond her warden's body.

She refocuses her attention to her captor's reflection in the mirror. In his left hand is a large, rectangular white box, which, after a couple steps into the room, he sets down on the wooden bench.

"When you are done cleaning up, please look in the box and put on what I got you. I have a feeling you are going to recognize it and love it," he tells her. "In a couple more hours I will come and get you, and then you will finally see what I have done for you and how much you mean to me."

She nods at him in the mirror, knowing he won't leave until she acknowledges him. After her nod, he smiles at her and then backs out of the room, pulling the door closed behind him and locking it. Alone again with her thoughts, Alicia turns from the mirror and walks over to the white box. It's a standard cardboard garment box. She takes the lid off and looks at the red dress neatly folded in front of her. Confused, she reaches down and pulls the dress from the box, holding it up in front of her. The dress looks exactly like her prom dress from high school. She looks back down into the box. A receipt is still inside. Setting the dress down on the wooden bench, she grabs the receipt and reads it. It's from the same consignment shop in Shelton that she sold her prom dress to years ago. In fact, the date on the receipt is about the same time she may have actually sold the dress. She sets the receipt back in the box and looks at the dress again. *That can't be the same dress, can it?* she asks herself. *And if it is, how would he have known it was mine?*

Her thoughts about the dress trail off as new realizations set in. Her warden either knew her in high school and was at the prom as well, or he's been watching her for so much longer than she initially presumed. Her mind churns with new questions and confusions. She scrambles to put the pieces together until a new thought rises above all the others. One that, the more she thinks about, makes perfect sense. One that explains why her captor knows what her favorite food is, and about this dress, and why Mrs. Ellie helped him.

She knows her captor. And her captor knows her.

"But that's impossible," she says to the empty room, as though trying to justify her thoughts. "He died in the military. I was at his funeral."

It can't be Nick, she thinks. *Why would Mrs. Ellie lie to me about his death? And if it really is Nick, why would my childhood best friend kidnap me and keep me prisoner?*

The more Alicia thinks about it, the more it makes sense. Nick wasn't the same after he found out she was pregnant. He refused her calls and refused to see her. He refused Colin's calls and wouldn't see him either. Then he left and he was gone. Mrs. Ellie didn't speak about him much after he left, and Alicia stopped asking questions about him after a while.

The new stream of questions running through her mind doesn't stop, and she imagines a thousand different scenarios. None of them seem like they can be real, even if they make sense given the present circumstances.

She tries to focus on the now, the present. Although her captor has never answered her before when she asked him who he was or why her, he might give her those answers tonight.

And if it is Nick?

She doesn't have an answer for that question yet. She also doesn't have an answer as to why she doesn't recognize him. *Could I have really forgotten what he looks like?* she wonders. Her captor is gaunt, with haggard features. The Nick she remembers was heavyset, with a cherubic face.

A knock on the door to her left jolts her out of her thoughts and back to reality. "Let me know if you need anything, gorgeous," the voice on the other side of the door tells her.

She looks down at the dress and back at the door, the fire of hope in her still burning. Answers. Escape. Both of these things wait for her beyond that door.

Alicia takes a deep breath and strips out of her clothes to shower. She's been wearing T-shirts and sweatpants since her last escape attempt. Thankfully, the sweatpants are easy to slide off, all the way down to the base of the chain where it meets the wall and out of the water from the shower as long as she uses the shower closest to the towel hooks. She hasn't worn socks, shoes, or underwear since her last attempt, as putting them on only to take them off again was a painful chore with her missing fingers.

She quickly showers and dries herself off, returning the damp towel to its hook. She picks up the red dress from its spot on the wooden bench and slides it down past her head and arms, straightening and smoothing it out once it's fully on. The dress still fits, if it really is her actual prom dress from high school. She looks at her reflection in the mirror, and for a brief instant she sees her younger self looking back at her. A younger self whose biggest worry was whether Colin was going to leave her or not.

Now her biggest worry is whether she will see him, or her little girl, ever again.

She runs her fingers through her hair and tries to straighten it up a bit, removing some of the tangles and smoothing the frizziest parts. She turns from her reflection and looks at the door in front of her. "Now or never, Alicia," she tells herself. She walks forward and knocks on the door. "I'm ready," she announces.

She waits for a response from her captor. Instead of an answer, though, music begins to play beyond the door. She recognizes the song immediately. It was the song playing when she told Colin she was pregnant, the same song they used as their wedding song.

An uneasy feeling begins to set in. *Why this song?* she wonders.

The door in front of her unlocks and slowly swings open, once again revealing her captor, who's not only standing in the doorway and smiling at her but wearing a tuxedo. Behind him, multicolored dots of light follow a set path, dancing from the floor to the wall and then out of her sight.

Her uneasy feeling is now coupled with a weird feeling of déjà vu.

This time, her captor's left hand holds a familiar-looking device. A metal leg clamp, connected to a thick chain that disappears out of her view and into the large room.

"Please sit down on the bench so I can switch these," he says as he slightly raises the clamp and nods at the one attached to her right leg. "Keep in mind what will happen if you try anything."

She nods and obeys, sitting down on the bench and presenting her right leg to him. He kneels down and unlocks her leg clamp, unwrapping the cloth around it. The metal of the clamp, after the first few weeks, was cutting into her skin until he wrapped it with a cut-up towel. Alicia notices that this new clamp already has a cloth cushion on it.

A brief urge to try to escape now rushes through her body—but her captor has his left hand latched on to her leg and hasn't let go. He's also watching her closely, as if expecting her to try something. Anything she tries to do now would most likely end in another lost finger. Or worse.

After he secures the new clamp on her leg and makes sure it's locked, he stands up and presents his arm to her.

"My love, if you would kindly allow me to escort you, it would be my honor to show you what I have been working on."

Alicia stands up and reaches out her left arm, hesitantly taking her captor's arm. *Be patient and wait for the right opportunity*, she thinks. *Just play along for now.*

He leads her out of her prison and into the large room, where a mix of shock and confusion causes her to come to a complete stop.

The large room has been transformed into a gymnasium. But not just any gymnasium—an exact look-alike of the gymnasium from her high school, complete with the school flag on the wall. Multiple tables and chairs are positioned all around the floor, each with their own candle centerpiece. Along the wall to her right is a table with cups and a punch bowl. Streamers and balloons hang from the ceiling and all over the walls. The multicolored disco ball lights continue their dance around the room, and the smell of lavender reaches her nose. The whole experience is dizzying, making Alicia feel like she's back at her senior prom.

To her far left is a stage, and for a second she almost expects to see a band setting up. Instead of a band, though, there's a large metal cage in the center of the stage.

She feels her left arm being lightly tugged, and she's pulled away from the overwhelming sense of déjà vu. She focuses her eyes on her captor's as he speaks to her.

"Come on, beautiful, let me show you to your table. Now we can have the prom we were supposed to have before Colin ruined it all. The one where I tell you how much I care about you and how much you mean to me. The one where you tell me you love me as well and only want me in your life. The one where we end up together and have our happily-ever-after."

That's when it all finally sinks in and the puzzle pieces fall into place. The nagging feeling she's had from day one finally makes sense. Still looking into his eyes, she says one word. One word that is a realization, a confirmation, and a question all at the same time.

"Nick?"

CHAPTER 13

THE FAST-FORWARD

He slides open the large metal door and steps outside, taking a deep breath and looking around the clearing. Empty as expected. The beautiful full moon is providing plenty of light for him tonight. He steps through the doorway of his home and slides the door closed behind him, making sure to lock it.

Can never be too careful, he thinks, smiling.

He heads down the steps and off across the clearing, easily maneuvering around the various large dead tree stumps. He reminds himself, again, to remove those one day so his one can have the yard she dreams about. He reminds himself almost every day about those stumps but still has yet to take care of them. *One day soon, I promise, my love*, he thinks. Once he reaches the end of the clearing, he plunges into the forest. A path he's taken hundreds of times greets him, welcoming his footsteps back. He exits the forest in no time at all and enters the old logging camp road. He walks down it, enjoying the sounds of the night. When he's about forty feet from where the old road meets the highway, he turns to his left and heads back into the woods. He follows another trail this time, one he made nine or so years ago once he had no need for a vehicle anymore. A trail that's just far enough off the highway that anyone passing by wouldn't see him walking on it, day or night. He's still smart about it, though, and walks the trail only at night.

The smile still on his face, he thinks about his perfect life waiting for him back at home. His beautiful wife, keeping herself busy with chores while waiting for her man to come back home with dinner. He picks up the pace a little bit, anxious to get back to her. To see her face and her smile, to hold her in his arms and put little kisses on her forehead. To tell her how much he loves her and how happy she has made him all these years they have been together.

Of course, the first several years they were together had some difficult spots. The toxic grip her ex-husband had on her was extremely strong and resulted in some unpleasant fights that he's happy to finally have behind him. His smile disappears at the thought of her ex. They haven't had a fight about him in years. She does still ask about the child from her previous marriage, though. He avoids that conversation, not wanting to bring up her past. Her past when she wasn't by his side. She doesn't need to be reminded of how bad her life was before he was a part of it again.

A set of headlights abruptly cuts through the forest darkness a short distance ahead and breaks through his thoughts, and he pauses before taking another step. The headlights continue on their route, and soon he sees a set of taillights through the trees. *The parking lot must be close*, he surmises. He made better time than expected.

That's what missing your one and only can do to you, he thinks as his smile finds its way back onto his face. As he approaches the edge of the parking lot, he makes sure it's clear and no additional cars are around. The headlights he saw must've been the last employee heading home. He steps from the trees and quickly traverses the parking lot, walking around the side of the building and to the back door. He opens it and steps into the building, slowly walking down the hallway to the kitchen. His mother is standing in the kitchen finishing up wrapping a couple of sandwiches in cellophane. She glances over at him and nods. Nick waits until she's done placing the sandwiches in the paper bag next to her before he steps forward to grab it.

"Make sure no one sees you," she reminds him while handing him the bag, as she does every time he shows up for food. "Tomorrow night I'll have a couple burgers for you both. Tell Alicia I love her and I miss her and will come out to see her as soon as I can."

He nods in agreement and turns toward the back door, making his way down the hallway and into the parking lot. A few minutes later and he's on his way back down the path, headed back to have dinner with his girl.

The trip home is uneventful and quiet, and before he knows

it he's walking down the hallway toward the main room of the home he shares with Alicia, the paper bag with dinner in it safely secured in his right arm. He reaches the wooden door and opens it, allowing the welcoming sight of his happiness to overtake him. "Honey, I'm home!" he announces, as though he's in some cheesy TV sitcom.

Alicia is sitting in her chair next to the stage, reading one of the many novels stacked on the floor around the chair. She doesn't respond or look up from the page she's currently on. *Must be a good part of the book*, he thinks. He walks over to the table against the wall and sets the bag down. He pauses before he unpacks the contents and takes a look around their home, marveling at how many amazing memories they've made here since she first returned to him. She has taught him a lot of lessons over the last nine years about what it takes for him to be the man she deserves, and with each lesson he has adapted and in turn has shown her he is the strong, resilient man she always dreamed of.

Their home looks a little different now than it did the night he was able to finally bring his plan to fruition. All but two of the tables have been folded up and stacked in the far corner. One of those tables is against the wall behind him, and another is over near the front of the stage. Several books and water bottles are scattered around the surface of that table. Two of the folding chairs are pushed in against the table next to him, and the rest of the chairs are neatly stacked against the tables in the corner. The disco balls, streamers, candle centerpieces, and school flag have all been packed away in containers, joining all the supply boxes he moved to the main room above them.

Can't have another incident like we did with the hammer, can we? he asks himself, smiling, raising his right hand and rubbing the left side of his jaw. That lesson he learned took quite a few months to heal. For her, that lesson took much longer to heal.

He looks over at Alicia, who is still intently focused on reading. The chair she's sitting in, as well as all the books, was a request from her several years back. Nick thought the two of them sitting together and enjoying a good book was an excellent idea, so he indulged her by bringing home two comfy reading chairs and several large boxes filled with all genres of novels. Over the years, both of them have read every one of the books several times over, but she never seems to tire of reading them.

On the stage is Alicia's room, the door currently open. In her room is a cot with two pillows and a blanket on it, and a plastic bucket is placed against the bars in the far back corner. Outside her room, several feet away, is Nick's own cot. He would prefer to sleep with his wife by his side; however, that was another lesson learned the first time he tried it. He may still be learning how to be the perfect husband, but he's pretty sure no husband likes to be woken up by a chain being wrapped around his neck. That was about the last time he had to show his wife that, although he loves her and will do absolutely anything for her, he's also still the man of this house and should be treated as such. That night was a painful lesson for both of them. For her, because he had to take one of her last remaining fingers. And for him, because it revealed that no matter how much he'd done for her or tried to show her up until that night, she still did not love him like he loved her.

Learn and adapt. He thinks he has done both of those things perfectly.

Nick looks over at his beauty sitting in the chair and sighs. She looks just as perfect now as the first day he saw her. If anything, she looks even more perfect, because she belongs to him. His smile widens and he turns back to the table, unpacking the contents. Four sandwiches, four waters, four colas, several napkins and a couple of straws. He glances over at Alicia and asks, "Do you want a cola or water with dinner, my love?"

"Cola, please," she responds, her eyes still absorbing the story scrawled across the pages in her hands.

He puts a couple of the napkins and a straw in his back pocket, grabs two sandwiches and two colas, then walks over to his girl. He sets the sandwiches and colas down on the floor between the two chairs and kneels down in front of Alicia. Her left leg is tucked underneath her on the chair and her right leg is hanging down, the clamp and chain securely fastened as always. He reaches out and caresses her right calf a moment.

"I love you, beautiful," he tells her.

She nods at him. "I know you do."

Nick smiles. Although she has never told him she loves him, he knows the response she has given him for the last several years is the same thing as her telling him she loves him. It's her own cute roundabout way of telling him how much she cares.

He lets go of her calf and picks up one of the colas, opening it up. He retrieves the straw from his back pocket and, after removing the wrapper, places it in the cola. He offers the cola to his wife, who pulls her eyes away from the book and leans forward, placing her lips on the straw and taking a few drinks. She releases the straw and nods, returning her attention to the open pages. He sets the cola down on the floor and picks up one of the sandwiches, removing the cellophane wrapper and setting it next to the discarded straw wrapper. He offers her the sandwich and she repeats the motion of leaning forward and taking a couple bites, then returning to the book. The overall process with the cola and sandwich is repeated until Alicia indicates she is full. He gathers up the trash and stands up, walks over to the trash bin next to the table under the clock, and disposes of the garbage. He returns to Alicia and grabs his own sandwich and drink, sitting down into his chair next to hers.

He proceeds to eat his own dinner in silence while Alicia continues to read. He doesn't mind feeding her every day. Just another one of those husbandly duties he does to show her he cares, and he knows she appreciates it. It has been hard for her to feed herself for the last four years, and it was his job to step up and be there for her.

Nick finishes his dinner and gets up, walks over to the table, and places his own trash in the garbage bin. He glances up at the clock. Midnight. Almost time to go to sleep.

"Hey there, beautiful, you ready for bed?" he asks.

She nods again, still focused on the book.

"Need to go to the bathroom or need any help getting to bed?"

She shakes her head no and uses her right index finger to fold over a small part of the page she's reading to mark her place. She closes the book and sets it on the chair and slides her left leg out from under her. "I am going to go brush my teeth," she tells him as she gets up from the chair.

"Great idea. I'll join you," he tells her.

He watches as she slowly makes her way into the bathroom and then joins her. They brush their teeth in silence with their fingers, and once that's done, Alicia exits the room and heads toward her bed, the chain faithfully following behind her. He thought about getting her a toothbrush a long time ago but then decided, after careful consideration, that it might not be the best choice. She's never complained about using her finger, so there has never been a need for the actual brush.

Nick rinses the last of the toothpaste from his mouth and looks at his reflection in the mirror, taking a moment to fix his hair a bit. The noise of the chain behind him stops, and the familiar creaking noise of the cot echoes though the large room. He turns from the mirror and exits the bathroom, turning the light off behind him. He crosses the room to the wooden door and fishes the keys from his right pocket, locking the door. He then turns and flips the overhead light switches down, plunging the large room into almost complete darkness. The only light in the room now is from a small lamp on the stage near Nick's cot. Although he prefers the darkness, Alicia finds that the small amount of light from the lamp keeps away the nightmares that she started having a couple years ago. He was more than happy to learn to sleep with the light as long as it meant his wife was happy as well.

He crosses the room and walks up the stairs of the stage, stopping at the door to Alicia's room. She's lying on her back on her cot, arms resting on her stomach. He sighs and smiles at her. "You OK tonight?" he asks her.

She nods, not saying anything. He steps into her room and walks over to her, stopping at the side of her cot. He bends down and kisses her, his hand caressing the side of her face. As he pulls his lips away from hers, he runs his fingers down the line of her jaw to her chin, then down her neck and over her right breast, pausing a moment to trace around her nipple. His hand then continues down her stomach and to the waistband of her sweatpants, where his hand stops. Using both hands, he slides her sweatpants down to her ankles, carefully freeing her left leg from the cloth. He stands up and unbuttons his pants, pushing them down to the floor. He was already hard before he pulled her sweatpants down, and now it's time his wife satisfies her husband's need.

"I love you, baby," he tells her before he starts to crawl on top of her. Before he is pushing her legs apart. Before he is inside her.

≈

Alicia stares at the ceiling through the bars of her cage, past Nick's head, escaping her current reality by daydreaming of a world from long ago. As he repeatedly thrusts himself inside her, grunting and panting as he always does, she lets her mind drift off to her prior life. A life where she had love and happiness. A life where she had a daughter and a husband. A prior life that is just a dream now. An escape that she turns to for these moments.

She feels Nick tense up on top of her and feels him pulsating inside her, a sudden warmth and wetness spreading out within her. She fakes a moan, knowing the consequences if she does not pretend to enjoy it. Once he's done, he pushes himself off her and pulls his pants back up, buttoning them closed. He leans forward and carefully puts her sweatpants back on, sliding them up her legs and back to her waist. "Thank you, beautiful. That was amazing, as always," he tells her, placing another kiss on her lips and then a kiss on her forehead. He smiles at her and walks out of her prison cell, closing and locking the cage door behind him. She continues to stare at the ceiling until he reaches his cot and lies down.

Alicia lies there, still not moving. She feels some of his semen leak out of her and soak into her sweatpants. She stopped caring about him taking advantage of her a long time ago. Now it's just another chore with absolutely no feeling. Thankfully, she is unable to get pregnant due to complications from when she had her daughter.

Her beautiful daughter Penny, who was only a little girl when she saw her last.

Alicia wonders how her little girl is doing now, as a young woman. Is she thinking about college? Has she found love? Is she just as smart and beautiful as she was when she was a little girl? These questions dance through her mind, as they often do. Her thoughts also turn to Colin. She wonders how he's doing and if he's moved on. If he still thinks about her and loves her. If he is raising their little girl to be a strong and independent woman.

She breaks her gaze from the ceiling and blinks her eyes, allowing the tears that have built up to fall down her face and get lost in her hair.

Alicia isn't sure if she will ever see her family again. There is almost no way she can escape now, and she has paid for each and every time she has tried.

Ten times in total. Each one a failure. Each one costing her. She raises her hands to her face and wipes away the tears. All of her fingers, with the exception of her right index finger, have been cut off. Each missing finger a reminder of a failed escape attempt or something she did that Nick did not like. She was close to freedom a couple times, but each time Nick was there and stopped her. Kept her from that freedom.

And made her pay each time.

She gave up hope of ever making it free after the day with the hammer. Nick had just lengthened her chain, giving her more freedom to move around in the large room. A box of supplies was still sitting in the corner, and she had seen the handle of the hammer sticking out several weeks before. With the additional length of chain now attached to her metal leash, she had enough slack to be able to reach that hammer. She played it coy, of course, and tried to distract him with conversation while she slowly worked her way toward the hammer. Nick caught on to what she was doing just a moment too late, and before he could stop her she had the hammer in both hands, holding on as tight as she could with her last couple remaining fingers. She swung the hammer at him with all her might. If her swing had been better that day, if she had been able to grip the handle harder, she might've made it free. Instead of hitting Nick somewhere that would've knocked him out or killed him, the hammer caught his jaw, near his chin. The impact barely slowed him before he was on top of her, tearing the hammer away from her weak grip. She tried to fight him off, tried to gouge out his eyes, but all her attempts were in vain. Nick was able to subdue her once again, and after roughly dragging her down the long hallway, he bound her once more to the wooden chair in the small room with the metal chest. The punishment room.

Although this time, the penalty she had to pay wasn't another finger.

Nick, with blood pouring out of his mouth and a large gash on his face from where the hammer connected, was pacing back and forth in front of her. He explained his disappointment in her actions. Explained how she needed to appreciate the things he did for her. Explained how what he did was for her and only her and she needed to understand he was doing everything he could to make her happy. To be the perfect husband to her.

The entire time he was pacing in front of her, he was holding the hammer in his right hand.

Alicia was sure she was going to die that day. That Nick was going to finally snap and kill her.

Alicia pauses in her memories and pulls herself back to the present, where she's still staring at the ceiling and listening to Nick's deep breathing, indicating to her that he has fallen asleep. Maybe, in her mind that day, she was hoping he would kill her. Hoping he would release her from the hell he was keeping her captive in. Now, years later, she doesn't have that hope anymore.

Because Nick didn't kill her. No, what he did that day made sure her chances of escape were slim from that day forward.

Once he finished talking, he knelt down in front of her and looked her in the eyes and calmly told her he loved her. The dead look in his eyes showed no emotion and definitely not any love. Alicia closed her eyes and braced for the pain of another finger being removed when an explosion of pain erupted from her left foot. The location and shock of the pain caused her eyes to open wide, and she unwillingly watched as Nick repeatedly raised the hammer and slammed it down on her foot. The sound of bones breaking with each hammer strike was the last thing she heard before she passed out.

When she finally came to, she was lying on the cot in her cell. Her left leg, from the knee down, was tightly bandaged up and her left foot was completely gone. The pain was almost unbearable, even with whatever pills Nick was feeding to her. She wasn't able to walk for months after that day, and as time went on, the pain finally started to subside. When she did start walking again, or at least when she tried to start walking again, it was difficult and slow. Putting any weight on the nub of her left leg resulted in shooting pain all the way up to her ears.

It took a couple years and a lot of painful attempts before she was finally able to somewhat walk again. Even now, it's very slow going, and if she's not careful as to what part of the leg she puts weight on, it can cause a lightning jolt of pain to remind her that there's no foot there anymore.

She did try to escape one last time after what happened to her foot. She knew her only option now was to kill Nick. That was the only way she would ever be completely free.

One night, her captor, now confident that she wouldn't be running for the exits anymore, had decided to fall asleep next to her after he had his way with her. It took her a couple of hours, but she slowly and quietly pulled the slack of her metal leash toward her and onto her stomach, taking care not to wake Nick. Once she had gathered enough of the chain, she carefully looped as many of the links around Nick's neck as she could, constantly checking his face and his eyes in case he woke up. When his eyes did finally open, alert and full of confusion, she pulled with all her strength. But it wasn't enough. Nick struggled against the chain for a brief moment until he was able to pull it away and get out of the noose. After that night, she was left with only one finger on her right hand and none on her left.

Alicia sighs, trying to force the memories from her head

and replace them with thoughts of Penny and Colin and what her life would be like if Nick had never abducted her. Nick refuses to talk about either of them, convinced it was Colin's fault she wasn't interested in him when they were younger. She has tried, over the years, to convince Nick it wasn't because of Colin, but even the mention of Colin's name makes Nick's tone change from the soft voice to the much harder, darker one. The one she hears before she's about to feel pain.

Thankfully, Mrs. Ellie occasionally shows up and Alicia is able to, in brief and hushed whispers, confirm that her Penny is alive and doing well. Like Nick, Karen completely refuses to talk about Colin, and she says very little about Penny. When Alicia asks her why she did what she did to her, or why she allows this to go on, the woman only shushes her and tells her it's for her own good and she is where she belongs.

Alicia will never forgive Mrs. Ellie for her part and still doesn't understand why a woman who was practically her second mother would allow all this to happen to her, but she is thankful for the information she can get about her little girl. Although, now, her little girl is a young woman. Of course, the information Karen gives her is extremely limited and doesn't tell her anything about the young woman's life or how she's doing. But even hearing that Penny is alive and full of smiles is heartening.

She smiles weakly as her thoughts become filled with Penny, and she sighs, trying to push the remaining chaos from her mind. She closes her eyes, hoping to drift off to sleep, but tonight is like most nights and she doesn't find the sleep she's looking for. In no time at all, she hears Nick getting up and crossing the stage, signaling that the morning has arrived. She keeps her eyes closed, hoping he doesn't open her prison to come wake her up. Luckily, he doesn't stop at the door to the cage and instead continues on down the steps and into the bathroom. She hears one of the showers turn on and she opens her eyes. She knows that if she's not awake by the time he finishes his shower and comes back out of the bathroom, he will make sure he wakes her up.

She sits up and yawns, wondering if she did sleep or not. She swings her legs off the cot and carefully sets them on the floor. If she did sleep, it didn't do anything to help her exhaustion. This last year she has been tired all the time. The recurring nightmares of Nick taking a hammer to her foot don't help make her any less tired, nor does her insomnia.

The sound of the shower stops, and the urge to pee hits Alicia. Not willing to wait to see how long it will take for Nick to finish up and come unlock her prison door, she carefully makes her way to the bucket in the back corner of her cage. She lowers her sweatpants and leans forward against the bars, hovering the best she can over the plastic bucket, relieving herself. Once finished, she carefully raises herself back up and slowly pulls her sweatpants back on. She can clean the bucket later when Nick lets her out.

As she is slowly making her way back to her cot, Nick comes out of the bathroom and crosses the room to the light switches by the wooden door. He flips them on, and one by one the large overhead lights turn on, chasing all the shadows in the room away.

As he turns from the door, he calls over to her. "Well good morning, beautiful. Did you sleep well?"

She nods, not caring to tell him no. Not caring to tell him she hasn't slept well since the day he took her away from her life.

"Aw, good, I'm glad to hear that. Do you have any exciting plans for today?"

Alicia hesitates before giving him an answer, watching him walk across the room toward her cage. Normally she'd just tell him she's going to do a few chores and then plans on reading a new book. She then spends as much of the day as possible lost in the words of a different world, her only other escape from the hell she's currently living in besides her thoughts at night of the family she once had.

But today a new answer comes to her mind. Well, not so much an answer as a request. It's been several years since the last time she asked Nick for a favor. She wonders if he will entertain what she's about to ask for. She waits until he's standing at the cage door before she speaks.

"Actually, Nick, I have a request, if that's OK?"

He hesitates as he's putting the key into the lock and looks up at her, his left hand holding one of the bars on the door and his right the key. "For you, anything, my love," he responds, smiling.

She forces a smile on her face. "While I'm cleaning the house, would you be willing to go take a few photos of Penny for me? I don't have any, and I think I'd sleep a lot better if I was able to see she is OK."

She waits and watches for his reaction. His smile falters a bit, and she sees his eyes harden. Before he has a chance to speak, she steps forward a couple of steps, reaching out with her right hand to place it on his left, which is still holding one of the bars of the cage door.

"Please, Nick. For me."

CHAPTER 14

THE REQUEST

Colin sets his beer down on the table next to him, grabs the remote on the arm of his chair, and turns the volume down a little bit on the television. He will never understand why the sound of the commercials is always broadcasted thirty decibels higher than the sound of the movies they interrupt. He waits until the commercials end and the movie resumes before he turns the volume back up.

After he returns the remote to its place on the chair arm, he grabs his beer and takes a drink. Penny is staying the night at a friend's house tonight, so the house is all his until tomorrow.

The movie continues, and Colin watches as a zombie horde overruns a military base, eating everyone they can get their hands on while chanting the word *brains*. He smiles and shakes his head at the cheesiness of it. He takes another drink of his beer and sighs.

Alicia would've told him to change the channel no less than ten times by now.

He wonders what happened to her and why she left. All his attempts to reach her, to find her, were futile. It's as though she just disappeared. The GPS of her phone never showed up again after her shift at the restaurant. Her car was never reregistered or its tags renewed. Colin knows because he has checked multiple times over the years with the Department of Motor Vehicles. Even her driver's license expired and was never renewed. Her credit cards were never used again. The police never found anything that indicated foul play and ultimately decided that she just left him, which never made any sense to Colin. Sure, they would have the occasional fight, but never one that resulted in Alicia telling him she didn't want to be with him anymore.

He just didn't understand. Alicia was happy here. She loved Penny more than anything else in the world. She loved their little life. She never gave any indication at all that she wanted to leave it.

He finishes his beer and pushes himself out of the chair, stretching as he stands up. He walks into the kitchen and tosses the empty bottle into the trash. He walks over to the fridge and opens it, grabbing another bottle and twisting the top off, letting the door of the fridge close on its own. He drops the cap on the table and walks back to his chair. He sits down, allowing himself to sink into the cushions and sink back into his thoughts.

A lot happened in the first couple years following Alicia's disappearance.

Colin ended up losing his construction job in Shelton within a year after she went missing. His foreman was understanding for the first few months when he'd miss multiple days, but he wasn't so understanding several months later when Colin was still missing multiple days and the crew he was in charge of wasn't getting their contracts done in time.

After he burned through the savings he and Alicia had in the bank while trying to find her, he had to take a job here in Orchard Lake at the local car wash because it offered flexible hours and he still had little Penny to take care of. With the savings depleted, he couldn't afford after-school care anymore and needed to be home to take care of his little hummingbird. Alicia's disappearance was hard on her as well. She didn't understand why Mommy had left and never come back home, and for a while she thought it was because of her.

It took Colin a long time to convince Penny it wasn't her fault that Alicia had left and that sometimes mommies just left for no reason at all but that didn't mean they didn't still love their little girls. He can't remember how many nights she spent crying.

He can't remember how many nights he spent crying.

As time went on and no trace of Alicia was found, her parents stopped communicating with him. They, like the police, believed Alicia had left him and that it was his fault she was gone. Shortly after Alicia's parents stopped talking to him, many of the people in town started doing the same.

Ostracizing him. Looking at him sideways at the gas station or the supermarket. As though he were behind her disappearance. Thankfully for Penny, Alicia's parents and the locals didn't treat her the way they treated him and still showed her the support and love she needed.

He stopped caring what people thought about him as time went on, and over the years people began to acknowledge his existence again. Although, even after all this time, Alicia's parents still refuse to speak with him and communicate only with Penny. Colin learned a few years back that it was because they think he's the cause of their daughter's disappearance, since she never reached out to them again either after she disappeared.

His little hummingbird didn't understand what was happening for the longest time. Even now she rarely brings up her mother or any memories she has of her. Colin doesn't know if she just doesn't remember Alicia or has somehow blocked the memories, but he hopes she's aware how much Alicia loved her. How Alicia would look at her while she slept. How Alicia would stop what she was doing, no matter what it was, to pay attention to her little girl.

Multiple screams on the television pull him from his thoughts, and he focuses back on the movie. The zombie horde is now eating its way through a small town. He takes a sip of his beer and wonders what he's going to do for dinner, since Penny won't be home tonight. *Maybe I'll head down to Ellie's and get something to eat*, he contemplates. It's been a few weeks since the last time he was there, and it would be good to see Mrs. Ellie again. Of all the people in town, she's the only one who never wavered in her support when everyone else was beginning to look at him like he did something to Alicia. Colin could see she missed Alicia as much as he did. Karen loved her like a daughter. First she lost Nick; then she lost Alicia. Colin can't imagine how tough it has been for her, but he is thankful she never let it show and instead was always there for him and Penny.

To this day, the artwork Alicia painted is still hanging up on the walls of the restaurant. Even one of the missing-person fliers Colin made after Alicia first disappeared is still hanging near the restaurant's front door, now faded and weathered from time.

Colin decides against finishing his beer and grabs the remote, turning the television off. He gets up from the chair and heads toward his bedroom, briefly stopping in the kitchen to dump the rest of the beer down the sink and toss the bottle in the trash. He walks into his bathroom and checks his reflection in the mirror. The face looking back at him is a bit haggard but still presentable. A quick splash of cologne and he's ready to go. He heads toward the front door, turning off the lights as he goes. Grabbing his keys from the table next to the door and putting on his boots, he heads outside and onto the front porch. The sun is just beginning to set, casting competing shades of pink and orange across the sky and painting the vibrant hues on a few clouds lazily drifting their way to the north.

Colin forces a smile as he admires the sunset. For those in town not tormented by a past like he is, Orchard Lake is that postcard-perfect town you see showcased all over the country.

He pulls himself away from the sky and heads down the steps of the porch to the driver's side door of his truck, feeling the gravel of the driveway crunch underneath his boots. He gets in the truck and starts it up, the latest top-forty song filling the cab with an auto-tuned voice. Penny didn't change the station back to his oldies channel the last time she used the truck. He reaches forward and changes it, the sound of Sinatra replacing the upbeat female voice that was singing about heartbreak. *Much better*, he thinks.

He puts the truck in reverse and backs out of the driveway and onto the street, the crooner's voice filling the cab of the truck. The short trip to Ellie's is quiet, and Colin passes only a couple cars as he drives through the main part of town. Out of habit he waves as the cars pass, not paying enough attention to see if the other drivers wave back. As he passes Bell's Supermarket, he makes a mental note that he'll need to do a grocery trip soon, as they're running low on milk and bread, or at least ask Penny if she will after school or after her shift at the local health clinic where she works as the secretary on occasion. Colin smiles a moment as he hears Penny correcting him in his head. *Dad, it's medical receptionist, not secretary.*

The parking lot of Ellie's is almost empty, with only a couple of cars parked in random spots. Colin pulls into a spot near the front of the building and turns off the ignition. Either he just missed the evening dinner rush or he's slightly early for it. A quick glance at the clock on the dash confirms that he's early.

He exits the truck and heads into the restaurant, the chime above announcing his presence as he steps through the front door. The server on shift looks up from his order pad, nods at Colin with a smile, and continues talking about tonight's special with the table he's waiting on. Colin makes his way through the dining room, nodding and arbitrarily smiling at the people he recognizes. He reaches the bar and sits down, listening to the sounds of the kitchen beyond the mirrored shelves full of liquor bottles. Mrs. Ellie is explaining how to make the perfect roux for her locally famous gravy.

Colin smiles. He lost his parents quite some time back, and Karen has been like his adopted mother most of his life. Partly because he was best friends with her son, Nick. Partly because that's the type of person Mrs. Ellie is. Always caring about everyone around her.

The server makes his way over to Colin and asks what he'd like tonight. As usual, he asks for the Colin special—a double bacon burger with pepper jack cheese and jalapeños and an ice-cold draft to wash it all down. The server laughs and nods, scribbling down the order and taking it over to the order wheel. Although Colin's favorite burger isn't a menu item, he's ordered it regularly for years, and all the serving staff and cooks know exactly what he means when he does. The server returns with the beer, setting it down on the bar in front of

Colin, and excuses himself to head back to the occupied tables in the dining room.

Colin takes a sip of the beer and sets it back down, forcing his thoughts away and allowing his eyes to wander across the various bottles of liquor on the shelves in front of him. The bell on the pass-through dings, and Karen's voice echoes through the restaurant. "Order up!"

He looks over at the pass-through and watches as the order wheel turns and the ticket with his order disappears into the kitchen. The next thing he hears puts a smile on his face.

"Colin, young man, how dare you come into my restaurant without stopping to give me a hug first!"

Mrs. Ellie's large frame appears from the kitchen, a big smile on her face, and she walks over to him on his side of the bar.

"Sorry, ma'am, but I was hungry and thirsty and you always tell me I never eat enough," he responds as she approaches. He gets down off the bar stool and gives her a big hug.

"How have you been, honey? Feels like I haven't see you in weeks. How's little Penny doing? She still thinking about going out of state for college to one of those fancy medical schools?" she asks him, sitting down on the stool next to him. Before he can respond, she turns to the kitchen and yells to her current line cook, "Don't let that roux burn! You best keep stirring it until I get back in there."

Colin laughs as he sits back down on his stool. "Yes, ma'am, we are doing well. Penny has submitted applications to quite a few out-of-state schools. She hasn't heard anything yet, though.

How I ended up with a little girl who wants to be a doctor is beyond me."

Mrs. Ellie smiles at him and raises her hand, letting it come to a rest on his shoulder.

"Because you're a good father," she tells him. "Alicia would be proud of what you've done with Penny."

He nods, trying not to let the emotion inside him tied to Alicia surface on his face. A voice from the kitchen interrupts their conversation.

"Mrs. Ellie, I think the roux is burning."

Karen sighs and gets up off the stool. "Let me go see what that fool boy is doing," she tells him. "I'll have your dinner made up right quick, before the rush gets here." She winks at him and turns toward the kitchen.

Colin smiles and grabs his beer from the bar, taking another sip as Mrs. Ellie heads back into the kitchen. The noises in the dining room behind him grow louder as more and more of the residents of Orchard Lake show up for dinner. He gets lost in the sounds of the restaurant, reminiscing about all the times he's sat at this bar while waiting for Alicia to finish her shift. Every sound, every scent, every feeling here has a memory associated with it. And in almost every one of those memories is Alicia, her beautiful smiling face and light-filled eyes looking at him every chance they could. Stealing kisses between tables and quickly whispering *I love you*s between tickets.

As Penny's high school graduation nears, the thought of leaving this town when Penny leaves for college becomes more and more prevalent. Of finding somewhere new to start over again. Some new town where every single thing in town doesn't remind him of Alicia. Remind him of what he lost so many years ago.

Before he knows it, the server is setting a plate down in front of him, the large burger and a healthy helping of crispy steak fries gracing the ceramic surface. Colin thanks the young man and digs into his dinner, allowing the constant companion of Alicia's memories to keep him company while he eats.

≈

Nick looks at the table in front of him and takes a deep breath. He wants to do right by her, make sure she's happy in every way possible. That's what a loving husband is supposed to do. That's what you're supposed to do for the love of your life. Make them happy and fulfill their wishes.

But what she asked him to do? What she requested? This would only bring up a past she should've forgotten by now. Her past life that has nothing to do with her current life. She knows how much he despises her past life. Her life without him in it.

Nick's eyebrows furrow as he contemplates the possible outcomes of her request. If he does what she asks, the possibility exists that she'll love him even more for doing something he doesn't want to just to show her how much he loves her. Then again, the possibility exists that if she sees photos of Penny, it might reignite the toxic control Colin had over her and Nick might lose all the love he's become used to having in his life.

He shakes his head in frustration. *And if I refuse to do this for her, will her disappointment that I didn't do what she asked cause her to grow cold toward me?* he wonders. *Will she think I failed her as her husband? As her lover? As her one?*

He slams his right fist down on the table, the lone empty water bottle there jumping from the impact. Nick grits his teeth and forces himself to take another deep breath.

Another scenario plays across his mind. If he does this, he may run into Colin. Even the thought of seeing that bastard's loathsome face starts to turn Nick's frustration into rage. He knows Colin works in town now but doesn't know his schedule like he used to before Alicia decided her life was better with Nick than it was with Colin. He doesn't even really know what Penny looks like anymore, as he hasn't seen her since she was just a little girl. His mother has told him that she looks a lot like Alicia did when she was younger.

His mother. She never did give up hope that one day Alicia would fully come around and that Penny would be calling him Daddy versus Colin. Of course, Nick learned over time that Colin's toxic hold on Alicia also included Penny. Penny would forever represent and remind Alicia of Colin's hold on her, and over the years he's had to punish Alicia more times than he's wanted to in an effort to break that hold.

This knowledge leads to Nick's current dilemma. If he does what his love asks and takes pictures of Penny for her, will those photographs be enough to renew what Nick has worked so hard to break? Will he have to start the process all over again?

It's been a few years since the last time Alicia tried to get away, tried to run back to Colin. Maybe that control Colin had over her is finally broken. Maybe now, at last, Alicia fully belongs to him. If that's the case, the photographs will have no hold on her and will merely be photographs.

The furrow in his brow eases a bit, and he unclenches his fists. A new rationale forms in his thoughts.

Penny is a part of Alicia, and he loves all of Alicia with every atom in his body. If Penny does look like Alicia like his mother says she does, then maybe Penny is more Alicia than she is Colin. If that's the case, then, as a loving husband and Alicia's soul mate, he's obligated to love that part of her in Penny.

He sighs and nods his head. He knows what he should do.

He turns from the table in the small room and heads through the metal doorway and down the long hallway to the home he shares with his love. He opens the wooden door and steps through. Alicia is sitting in her chair, once again reading one of the many novels stacked around where she's sitting. She doesn't look up from her book when he enters the room. *I wonder if she's mad at me for not giving her an answer earlier this morning when she asked me to take the photos*, he wonders.

He crosses the large room and stops in front of her, his head held down. She still doesn't look up at him.

"I'm sorry I didn't answer you earlier this morning. I had to think about it a bit," he tells her. She gives no acknowledgment of his apology.

"I just wanted to tell you that I will do it. I will get you some photos of her like you asked me to, because I love you and want to do everything I can to make sure you are happy," he continues, waiting for her reaction after telling her he will do it.

He watches as she slowly looks up at him, her eyes locking onto his. A flush of warmth races through his body as he looks into her eyes, as though he can see into her soul. As though he can see her love for him shining back at him.

She smiles at him. "Thank you, Nick. It means a lot to me."

She lowers her gaze and returns to her book, the smile still on her face.

Her smile reassures Nick that he made the right decision. He made her happy with his choice, just as he's supposed to do for his one. A smile of his own forms on his face, and he reaches out and runs his fingers through her hair, starting at the hairline on her forehead and ending at the back of her head. "I love you, beautiful," he tells her. Before he turns to leave, he leans forward and kisses the top of her head. "I'll be back shortly, my love."

He quickly crosses the large room, heading toward the hallway. As he does, he glances at the clock on the wall. Almost eleven in the morning. Nick tries to remember what time school gets out, unsure if it's three or four when classes are let free. He'll need to move quickly. He knows, thanks to his mother, that the young woman works the evening shift at the medical clinic, but he isn't sure what days. If he can't catch her at school, he may be able to find her there.

His mother will know for sure, although she will not be happy he's visiting her in the daytime. As he reaches the doorway to the stairwell, after making sure he closed and locked the wooden door to their home behind him, he pauses. It would be smarter to do this later tonight and then try to get the photos of the girl tomorrow. He looks back toward the door separating him from his world and thinks back to her smile, to the look in her eyes when he told her he would do it. *No, I have to do it today for her*, he tells himself. *I can't disappoint her now. I am the perfect husband.* He nods, agreeing with himself, and opens the door to the stairwell, heading toward his next destination.

The few miles between the home he shares with Alicia and the restaurant pass relatively quickly, with Nick taking additional care not to be seen by anyone as well as planning out how he'll get the photographs. He'll need to get his mother's camera from her; then he'll need to have her print out the photos on the color printer she keeps upstairs where he used to live once he's done.

As the restaurant and parking lot come into view, Nick veers off the path and slowly follows the tree line along the parking lot and around the building to the back lot where his mother parks, avoiding catching the attention of any of the restaurant patrons getting in and out of their cars as they come and go for lunch.

Once in the back of the restaurant, he quickly crosses the gravel lot to his mother's truck and opens the door. He hits the horn twice, the loud beeps coming in rapid succession. He quickly closes the door and heads around the truck to the front, crouching down out of sight, making sure no one is out on the lake who might be able to see where he is. Confident he has not been seen, he waits.

A couple moments later he hears the back door of the restaurant open and the gravel crunching under slow but heavy steps. The sound continues to grow closer until it reaches the driver's side door of the truck, where her steps come to a stop. His mother's voice, low but just loud enough for him to hear where he's crouched, replaces the sound of the gravel.

"Why the hell are you here at this time of the day? Don't tell me she's gotten out again."

He responds, making sure he matches her volume, "No. She asked me for photos of Penny. I told her I would get her some."

The sound of the gravel where his mother is standing crunches a bit, as though she's shifting her weight. While he waits for her response, he hears the various birds down at the lake and the multitude of noises coming from inside the building. He remembers the long weekend days when he was younger, when he was alone, and he would come out here and sit at the edge of the parking lot, watching the lake and listening to the sounds all around. He shakes the feeling of familiarity away. That was his old life. His life without Alicia. That life is long gone and will never come back.

His mother finally speaks, breaking through his reminiscing. "Well, you picked a fine time to need a camera, because I don't have one anymore. Nor do I have any recent photos of her. But you know very well who would have some recent photos of her," she tells him. "It's tourist season and it's busy. I need to get back to work. You need to figure this out on your own."

Once she's done talking, he hears her turn and head back inside the restaurant.

Nick waits a few moments to ensure that no one else is nearby, then he exits his position at the front of the truck. He crosses the small parking lot and retreats back into the safety of the forest. His mother was right though. He does know who would have recent photos of the girl.

Colin.

Without a vehicle, Nick won't be able to just go buy a camera somewhere far out of town where no one will wonder who he is. It's too risky to even think about buying one here in town. His only other option now is to pay a certain home a visit for the photos. It's not like he hasn't been there before. It's not like he hasn't been inside the house before. It may have been quite a few years, but he doubts much has changed since he was last there. It will take him a couple hours to get there on foot from where he is, though. He points himself in the direction he needs to go and quickly makes his way toward his next destination.

The time goes by quickly, with Nick lost in his thoughts of Alicia and how happy what he's doing will make her. As he makes his way through the trees behind Colin's house, getting closer with each carefully placed step, the setting sun behind him colors the tops of the trees above with reds and oranges and casts long, dark shadows all around him where the dying light is unable to reach ground. He moves within these shadows, keeping himself low and as hidden as he can. Ahead, through the trees, he can see the back side of the house, the light in the kitchen visible from the window, and he can see the front of Colin's truck parked in the driveway. A few more steps closer and the light in the kitchen suddenly goes out, causing Nick to pause, wondering if he may have been seen. He waits, looking to see if there's any indication he was detected. The light doesn't turn back on, and instead Nick sees Colin appear from the side of the house and get in the truck.

His eyes harden at the sight of Colin, and for a brief moment Nick considers whether killing Colin might be the only way to ever truly free Alicia from his grasp.

No, you deserve to suffer for eternity, he thinks as he watches Colin start the truck up, back out of the driveway, and drive off down the road.

He waits a bit longer, allowing the shadows from the sun to dip even farther below the horizon to deepen before he exits the tree line and crosses the backyard. He pauses under the kitchen window when he reaches the back of the house, listening for any sound that might indicate the young woman is home. The interior of the house is silent and the lights remain off.

He quickly makes his way to the front of the house and up the steps of the porch. The front door is unlocked, as most normally are when you live in a small town, and Nick hastily makes his way inside, quietly closing the door behind him. It wouldn't have mattered if the door was locked, though, since

Nick has a key that he obtained a long time ago during one of his late-night visits.

The house smells different now, without Alicia here. He remembers how it used to smell when she still lived here, before she left Colin for him. Now the house smells foreign. Alien. *Good*, he thinks. *Colin didn't deserve it anyway.* He deftly makes his way to Penny's room in the darkness of the house, letting the last few rays of the setting sun give him the light he needs. Once inside her room, he pauses as a brief sense of confusion ripples across his skin. For one moment, on very brief moment, he can smell Alicia. He can feel her presence against him.

He regains his composure and looks around the young woman's room. Finding photos of her is easier than he expected, as she has quite a few stuck all around the edges of the mirror on her desk. He looks over the photos in the failing light, grabbing three he hopes she doesn't notice are gone. He repositions the remaining photos to fill the now open spots. Content with his work, he looks at the photos he selected. *She really does look like Alicia*, he thinks. No wonder he felt Alicia's presence when he first entered the room. In a different life, maybe she could've been his, along with Alicia. A perfect family.

He puts the photos of the young woman into his pocket and steps out of her room, pulling the door closed behind him. As he's passing Colin's room on his left and stepping into the kitchen, a new sound in the house makes him stop in his tracks.

The sound of the front door opening.

CHAPTER 15

THE REUNION

Karen steps back into the restaurant and lets the rear door close behind her. She pauses a moment in the hallway before she continues into the kitchen. She takes a deep breath, trying to regain her composure.

Why her fool son had to visit her during the lunch rush hour, she just doesn't understand. And about a silly request for photos of Penny. If Alicia would quit being so difficult, she would've had Penny by her side years ago.

That boy knows damn well I got rid of that camera years ago, she thinks. *I swear he is going to be the death of me one day.*

She forces a smile back on her face, steps from the hallway, and heads into the kitchen. Her line cook is finishing up a couple burgers and beginning to plate them. She walks over and checks his work. Content with what she sees, she leaves him be and heads into the dining room to visit with her patrons.

Tourist season always brings a large boom in business

during the five months that Orchard Lake has beautiful weather. During those months she usually has to staff an additional cook as well as a couple of additional servers. Once the tourist season is over, though, she can easily manage the restaurant by herself with just a couple of the local kids as servers on the weekends.

This year's tourist season is coming to an end, and she's glad it is. It's been exceptionally busy and she's looking forward to the slow season, when only a few regulars show up and she has time to just sit back and enjoy what she has spent her life building. She doesn't want for money, since her husband, as vicious as he was, was also very business savvy, very frugal, and the logging camp was actually very profitable until it was permanently shut down. And during the tourist season the restaurant turns enough profit to make up for the months when she ends up in the red. Between her savings and the tourist season, she has a very comfortable life.

Of course, she prefers to live simply, and that simple life has saved her from spending money on fancy things like a big house or expensive cars. The most expensive thing in her life has been her boy and all the stuff he needed to buy to build that silly gym in the logging camp. Of course, he finished that years ago, and he hasn't asked for much since beyond some furniture.

Karen finishes checking on all the diners to make sure they're happy with their meals and heads behind the bar, assuming her normal place on the stool located there.

Minutes slowly pass while she watches the customers finish their meals, one after another. She smiles and waves while they pay their bills and head out the door, inviting them to come back anytime. Soon the restaurant is almost empty. She looks at the clock in the bar. Almost five in the evening. Dinner rush will kick up in about an hour or two. She is getting up to go help the line cook prep for the dinner crowd when the bar phone rings. She stops and turns toward the phone, picking it up and answering it. A nice gentleman on the other line inquires if they need a reservation for a party of ten. Karen assures him no reservation is needed and they can put two tables together for the group. After confirming what time the party will arrive, she hangs up the phone.

"We're gonna have a party of ten coming in at seven. Let's get tables two and three pushed together and grab some extra chairs from under the stairwell," she announces. Her server on duty, a polite young high school student, is standing at the pass-through talking to the cook. He looks over at her and nods before heading off to move the tables. Karen looks over at the storage area under the stairwell that leads up to her apartment. Eight extra chairs are stacked up there, with two additional folding tables stored behind the chairs. She rarely has to pull out the extra tables, but the chairs come in handy more often than not. She continues on her way into the kitchen and sends the line cook to help set up the tables and chairs for the large party. She begins the evening prep and is soon joined by her cook.

Just as they complete prep, the door chime begins to go off. Orders start coming in on a regular basis and Karen gets to work, cooking and plating food as quick as she can. She makes sure to double-check everything before it leaves the kitchen and verifies, when she can, that her young server is checking each ticket for completion prior to taking the food out to the dining room.

The clock hits six thirty in no time, and while waiting for an order to finish cooking, she explains to her line cook how to properly make the roux for the gravy. A timer on the deep fryer goes off, and Karen leaves the line cook to stir the roux while she plates another order. Once that's done, she drops off the two plates now loaded with hot food in the pass-through, hitting the bell and announcing an order up for her young server. He hangs another ticket on the wheel as he grabs the current ticket and then picks up the completed order to take out to the customers. "Make sure you always check the ticket," she reminds him as he heads off into the dining room with the loaded serving tray. She grabs the next ticket and is getting ready to call out the order when she sees what's written on it. She laughs a bit, knowing there's only one person who's ever ordered the Colin special. She calls out to him, knowing he's sitting at the bar and waiting on her reaction.

"Colin, young man, how dare you come into my restaurant without stopping to give me a hug first!"

She turns to the line cook and makes sure he's still stirring the roux before she steps out into the bar and walks over to give Colin a big hug.

As they chat a bit about how everyone is doing and Penny's

career ambitions, she finds a smug happiness in seeing just how sad Colin is. She makes sure to work a comment about Alicia into the conversation, just to see his reaction. The loss in his eyes when she mentions Alicia satisfies her, knowing he's suffering like he made her boy suffer for all those years. Her enjoyment from Colin's pain is cut short, though, as her line cook lets her know he may have burned the roux. She excuses herself and heads back into the kitchen, checking what the line cook has done.

"You didn't burn it, young man; it's supposed to look like that. Take it off the heat and add it to the gravy. Make sure to stir it until it's nice and thick." The line cook follows her directions, and Karen turns her attention to making Colin his hamburger. As she does, the party of ten shows up and the order wheel quickly fills up with tickets waiting to be completed.

She loses track of time again, churning out order after order with her young line cook by her side. As they finally get to the last ticket, she leaves the line cook on his own to complete the order and heads back out into the bar to see if Colin is still there. As she expected, Colin is sitting on the bar stool, a half-empty mug of beer in front of him on the bar. He appears to be staring at the mug, possibly contemplating whether he wants to drink any more of it. Karen knows exactly what he's thinking about, and knowing those thoughts are about his loss of Alicia makes her smile.

"Young man, no camping at my bar," she calls over to him, watching as he pulls himself away from staring at his beer. He smiles and nods at her, taking a sip. He grimaces slightly.

"Well now, we can't be letting folks drink warm beer here at my establishment, can we?" she tells him as she walks over. She grabs his mug and dumps the contents into the bar sink, quickly giving the glass a rinse. She refills the mug with cold beer from the tap and sets it back down in front of Colin. "On the house," she tells him.

Colin laughs and nods, taking a sip. "Thank you, Mrs. Ellie, that's much better," he tells her.

Karen looks at the bar clock. Almost nine in the evening. She wonders if her boy has made it to Colin's house yet for those photographs he's getting for Alicia. *Best I keep Colin occupied for a bit longer*, she surmises. *Just in case.*

She grabs one of the lowball glasses from the bar and pulls a bottle of Jack down from its spot on the shelf. She pours a bit into the glass and returns the bottle to its prior location.

"What's Penny doing tonight?" she asks, partially to determine if she'll have to help her boy cover up two disappearances from Colin's life instead of just one.

Colin takes another sip and sets the mug down. "She's staying the night at a friend's house, so I decided I'd come see you and get some dinner, since I'm a bad cook and Penny normally does the cooking for us." He laughs at his last sentence and Karen joins him, shaking her head.

"You're not a bad cook. You're a terrible cook. There is a difference," she tells him.

They both laugh openly at her observation.

"You're probably right, Karen. I was never the cook of the house. Alicia loved to cook as much as you do, and Penny must have inherited that skill from her."

She watches as Colin lowers his head a bit, as though remembering what it was like when he had his perfect little life.

"I can always teach you how to cook, ya know," she tells him. "Not like I haven't offered before."

He nods in response and takes another sip of his beer. "I know, Mrs. Ellie, and I appreciate it. Maybe one day I will take you up on that."

She raises her glass and clinks it against Colin's mug. "To learning, then," she toasts, and takes a sip of her whiskey. Colin nods and follows suit, taking another drink.

She smiles and watches as her server wraps up busing the last table in the dining room. She's about to speak again when Colin says something that makes her pause.

"Do you miss them?"

Karen hesitates. The first thought that comes to her mind is not one she can share. *No, Colin, because I know where they are and that they're happy without you in their lives.* She takes a deep breath and looks at him. "I think about them both every single day. I know that wherever they are now, they are happy. And that knowledge gives me peace."

She watches Colin look down at the bar as she waits for his response. The sounds of the line cook cleaning and prepping for tomorrow as well as the server putting the tables back in their original positions fill the room.

Colin continues to stare at the bar in front of him and sighs. "I think you're right, Karen. And it's a beautiful way to look at it," he finally tells her.

He finishes his beer and sets the mug down on the bar. "I think I'm going to head on home now. Thank you for the company and, of course, the delicious food."

She smiles and nods, taking another sip of her whiskey. "You let me know if you need anything, OK?" she tells him as he gets up from the bar stool and heads toward the front door.

He pauses as he reaches the dining room and turns back around to face her. "Thank you for being the one other person besides Penny in this town who never gave up on me."

He heads out the front door, the door chime announcing his exit. She watches as he leaves, waiting to smile until he's gone.

Karen drinks up her whiskey and pours another while her staff finishes up for the evening. Although the restaurant doesn't officially close for another twenty minutes or so, she doubts anyone else will come in. She watches and nods as her staff each clock out and say good night. As the door chime sings its song for the last time this evening, she gets up from the bar stool and walks over to the front door, locking it. She changes the lights on the open sign to closed and heads back to her perch at the bar, turning off the dining room lights as she goes. She sits down and takes another sip of her whiskey. Her boy should be on his way back by now, and she expects to see him tonight. The sandwiches she made a couple days ago will have run out already, and she knows he'll want to tell her if he was able to get some photos. Or he'll tell her he didn't get any photos and needs her help to get them.

The latter wouldn't surprise her. If it hadn't been for her, her boy would never have gotten as far as he has. He would never have accomplished as much. If it hadn't been for his momma, he wouldn't have everything he wanted like he does now.

Karen wonders if he'll ever appreciate everything she's done for him. She finishes off the last little bit of her whiskey and pours herself another glass. She gets up off the bar stool and heads into the kitchen, taking her glass with her. Once in the kitchen, she begins to double-check that everything has been prepped properly for tomorrow, starting with the ingredients bins. *Poor boy doesn't know what a roux is, but he has pretty good knife skills*, she thinks as she inspects the bins.

≈

A momentary jolt of panic freezes Nick as the sound reaches his ears. A voice joins the sound of the door opening.

"Give me five minutes to grab some clothes, and I'll be right out!"

Not Colin, Nick thinks the moment he hears the feminine voice from around the corner, in the living room. The lights from the ceiling fan in the living room turn on, bathing the room in front of him as well as a good portion of the kitchen with the glow from its four bulbs. Nick swiftly takes a couple steps backward and ducks left into Colin's room. He steps back from the doorframe and into the darkness, out of view of anyone passing by the door.

Footsteps pass, and he hears the door to Penny's room open. He listens as drawers open and close, accompanied by a rummaging sound.

He slowly takes a step forward toward the door, curious to see the pretty young brunette in person instead of just from the pictures in his pocket. Another step forward and he's at the border of the doorframe, on the edge of darkness where it meets the fading light from the living room. He reaches into his left pocket and pulls out his pocketknife, slowly opening it and muffling the click as the blade locks into place. *I could take her away from you right now, Colin*, he thinks. *Would you like that, having no one left at all? No one left, like I did for all those years?*

A horn outside honks, and the rummaging sound stops. He hears the door to Penny's room close and footsteps hurry down the hall and past the door where Nick is waiting in the shadows. He catches a brief glance of the young woman as she passes. Her long, flowing brunette hair is trailing behind her, and a black backpack is slung over her right shoulder. Her tight jean shorts are cut off just a few inches down her thighs and her long bare legs end in a pair of white sneakers.

Nick fights the urge to go after her, to stop her from leaving this house and permanently take her away from Colin.

The glow of light fighting to push back the darkness in Colin's room abruptly goes out, plunging the room back into almost complete black.

He hears the front door open again at the same time the horn outside blares once more. The soft feminine voice from a moment ago once again fills the house. "Holy shit, Laura, relax. I'm coming!"

The horn repeats its call one last time just as the front door closes. Nick waits in the darkness. He listens, almost expecting to hear the door open again.

Five minutes turns into ten minutes. He continues to wait.

The house is silent beyond the tick of the wall clock in the kitchen. Nick finally moves from his position next to the wall of the bedroom and steps into the hallway. He takes a deep breath. The young woman's perfume still lingers in the air, almost the same scent as Alicia used to wear. He pauses a moment, wondering if a bottle of Alicia's perfume is still on the bathroom shelf where it used to be. He almost turns to go check but decides against it. The photos of Penny will be enough. If he gives Alicia too many reminders of her past life, she may fall under Colin's spell again. It took too many years for Nick to break that spell the first time.

He maneuvers down the hall and through the living room to the front door. He looks out the window, confirming that the driveway is empty and there's no one in the street. A breath later and he's down the steps of the porch, hurriedly making his way around the corner of the house and across the backyard to the tree line.

As he proceeds back to his love, his one, he wonders if he should stop by the restaurant on the way to let his mother know that once again he handled it and he didn't need her to fix anything—to save him from his own mistakes, as she likes to tell him all the time. He knows she's probably expecting him to show up tonight, at least to get food.

He decides not to visit the restaurant immediately, as he's too excited to see Alicia's reaction to the good deed he's done for her, and instead continues his trek through the trees and underbrush toward the home he shares with his love. The trip is uneventful, and Nick enjoys the sounds of the forest in the dark until the old logging camp finally comes into view, its dark shape outlined by the faint light of the rising moon as it flows down upon the clearing from above. As usual, he pauses at the edge of the clearing, making sure there's no one around, and then he proceeds home. Three doors later and he's walking down the hallway with the wooden door ahead. Beyond that door is his one and only, anxiously waiting his return. He wonders if she's already eaten dinner, as he knows he's getting home fairly late. He hopes she isn't mad at him. Instead, he hopes she's excited about what he might have brought her. Excited that he will show her once again how much he loves her by making another one of her wishes come true.

He reaches the wooden door between him and his world and he unlocks it, pushing the door open before stepping through. Alicia is nowhere to be seen in the large room.

Panic fills Nick. A myriad thoughts race through his mind. What if she's somehow gotten free again and he's too late to rescue her? What if Colin found out she was here and came and took her away from him and that's why Colin wasn't home tonight? What if his mother decided he wasn't good enough for

Alicia anymore and came and took her away from him?

His eyes dart around the room as these thoughts come at him, one after another, filling him with dread and allowing the panic inside him to grow. As his eyes scour through the room for any sign of his one, he sees her chain on the floor. He follows the chain, hoping he won't see an open clamp at the end of it.

The chain, still secured to the wall, winds along the floor until it disappears into the bathroom. The door, from Nick's viewpoint, looks completely closed, but as he looks closer it's still open a bit due to the chain. As he's looking at the door, seconds away from racing over and ripping it open to see if she's there, it opens and Alicia appears, slowly hobbling her way toward her chair.

A sense of relief floods through his system and he nervously laughs at himself. He's so accustomed to seeing her in her chair when he comes home that the one time she's not there almost causes him to have a panic attack. He sighs and smiles, happy to see his love again. He glances at the clock on the wall. Almost eight thirty. He isn't as late as he thought he was going to be.

As Alicia sits down, she notices him standing in the doorway. "When are we going to have dinner?" she asks him. "I'm hungry."

He nods and steps into the room, pulling the wooden door closed behind him and locking it. He instantly regrets not stopping by the restaurant first in his rush to get back here with the photographs.

"I'm sorry I'm late, beautiful. It took me a bit longer to get home than I expected," he tells her as he walks over to the table against the wall. He opens the top of the small cooler sitting on the table and looks inside. The sandwiches ran out yesterday, but a few water bottles and colas remain. "I'll get us dinner in just a bit. Are you thirsty, my love?"

She nods. He puts the lid back on the cooler after pulling out one of the colas, grabs one of the straws on the table, and walks over to Alicia. As he has done for the last several years, he kneels down in front of her and opens the cola and the straw. He puts the straw in the cola and offers it to her. She takes several sips and then shakes her head, indicating she's done. Nick gets up from the floor and sits down in his own chair. He finishes the remainder of the cola and then gets up to throw it away.

While he's walking back to the table and the trash bin underneath, he thinks about how he'll tell Alicia he has the photos of Penny that she requested. *Do I just hand them to her?* he wonders, *or should I wrap them and give them to her like a present?* He decides against the latter. They're not exactly a present, since she requested them. If he makes a big deal of the photographs, then she might ask him for something more from her past life.

She might ask him for photographs of her ex-husband.

He stops at the table and throws the empty cola can and straw in the bin. His smile falters a bit.

Colin. The name feels like poison in his mind. *No, just give them to her and let her know you only got those for her because of how much you love her and how much her happiness means to you*, he tells himself. Satisfied with his choice, he turns from the table and walks back to his chair. He sits down and looks over at his love. His one. Her dark hair is hanging down on either side of her face while she reads, partially concealing the delicate features that make her so beautiful. Those same features grace the face of the young woman in the photos in his back pocket, with only a few differences between the two. Nick smiles as he looks at Alicia, happy that she belongs to him. Every minute he's been with her since she left her ex-husband for him has been worth all the years he spent alone, wishing she was by his side. He keeps watching her read. She has her left hand supporting the bottom of the book in her lap to hold the book open while she uses her right index finger to turn the pages. He looks at the scar tissue where her fingers used to be. He feels bad that she had to learn so many lessons, but he felt her pain as well for each one. *She is still perfect. Still my one*, he thinks. He continues to watch her as she slowly flips through a few more pages before he breaks the silence and speaks.

"I have the photos you requested."

She raises her head from the book and looks at him with wide eyes. Nick's smile gets even bigger as he sees a light in her eyes that he doesn't see very often anymore. Sometimes, when he tells her he loves her, he thinks he sees it. And sometimes, when they are making love and she is moaning underneath him, he thinks he sees that same light. That light from when she was younger that just drew everyone around her in. That same light that made Nick fall in love with her the moment he met her. She continues to look at him and forgets about the book in her lap, letting it fall to the floor in front of her. "May I see them, please?" she asks.

He nods and reaches into his back pocket. He pulls the three photographs out and reaches over, setting them on the arm of her chair. She looks down at the top photo, not moving. Minute after minute passes before she finally moves, her right hand cautiously reaching forward, shaking as it moves toward the arm of the chair. As her hand reaches the photographs, she uses her one remaining finger to slowly slide the top photo to the right, along the arm of the chair, uncovering the second photo. He watches as she repeats the process with the last photo until she's uncovered them all, spreading them out along the arm of the chair so she can look at them. She puts her hand back in her lap and sits there, silent.

"I got those for you because I love you and your happiness means the world to me," he finally says.

Alicia remains motionless, her head hanging down and her attention focused on the photos strewn out along the arm of her chair. Her hair is once again hanging down around the sides of her face, hiding most of her features from Nick.

He wonders what she's thinking about. He wonders if she's looking at the photos and slowly realizing she's looking at a stranger from a past life she no longer needs or wants. Or is she looking at the photos and imaging herself when she was younger? Maybe she's imagining Nick as the father to the young woman in the photos. Imagining the three of them as a happy family. Or is she imagining Colin?

He forces Colin from his mind and reminds himself that she's with him now and not her ex-husband. He waits for Alicia's reaction. He doesn't have to wait much longer before she speaks.

"She looks like me," she says, her voice cracking. "My little girl is a woman now." She looks up at Nick, and he finally sees her face. Tears have left streaks down her cheeks and are still building in her eyes. She sniffs and blinks, causing another set of tears to race each other down to her chin. She looks back down at the photographs spread out on the arm of the chair. She raises her right hand once again, still shaking, and reaches out for one of the photographs. It looks as though it may have been Penny's school photo for this year. She traces the face of the girl in the photo, her finger shaking the entire time. Her tears continue as her sobs grow louder and louder.

Nick isn't sure what to do next. He wasn't expecting this reaction from her. He wonders if he should collect the photographs and destroy them before her mind turns to Colin and the control that bastard had over her returns.

He doesn't have to wait long for his answer. The next words out of her mouth hit Nick like a speeding truck, and a rage explodes inside his body as though his beating heart had just been ripped out of his chest.

"Please let me go, Nick. Please let me go home to my daughter and my husband. Please let me go home to my family."

CHAPTER 16

THE RELEASE

Alicia sits in the chair and watches the wooden door across the room, waiting for what will happen when it opens back up.

Seeing the photos of Penny rekindled a fire inside her that she thought had died years ago. That fire quickly grew into a raging inferno the more she looked at those photographs. Her little girl, who was still playing with dolls and having fake tea parties when she last saw her, is now a grown young woman who looks almost like Alicia did at that age. That little girl has grown up only miles away from where Alicia is a prisoner and has grown up without her mother being there for her. Without her mother being there to give her love and support and to celebrate her achievements. Without her mother being there to dry the tears and kiss away the bruises when she hurt herself. Without her mother being there to help her through her disappointments and heartbreaks.

And it was all Nick's fault.

The tears she was crying when looking at the photos of her daughter weren't of sadness. They weren't of loss.

They were of anger. Anger toward this bastard who used to be her best friend, who has locked her away from the world because he thinks he loves her, who has permanently disfigured her because he wanted to break her will. And he did break her will, ultimately. For years she had lost all hope of ever being free and accepted this hell as her new normal.

But seeing the photos of her little girl all grown woke up something long dormant. An anger, a fire inside her, that she thought was gone for good. Seeing Penny now as a young woman reminded Alicia of just how long she has been here. Of just how much she has missed.

And Colin. Her poor Colin, who has had to bear the responsibility of raising Penny on his own, all while not knowing what happened to her. When Alicia figured out that Karen was a part of all this, she couldn't help but wonder if her husband was as well. But through hushed conversations with Karen over the years, Alicia learned that Colin had no idea where she was or what had happened. Nor did her little girl.

Alicia takes a deep breath, allowing the oxygen to feed the fire inside her. After she asked Nick to let her go back to her life, he grabbed the photos of Penny off the arm of the chair and stormed out of the room, slamming the wooden door behind him. The look on his face just before he left told her everything she needed to know about what might happen next. She only wonders when and what the punishment will be. She knew what she said would upset him, and she said it intentionally to hurt him. She wants him to feel the anger she feels. To loathe what he has become, like she does. She was complacent because she gave up. She will never allow that to happen again.

The wooden door begins to open and Alicia waits. Bracing herself for what will happen. As the door swings open, Nick comes into view. In his left hand is a small wooden box.

He steps into the room and closes the door behind him. He slowly walks toward her, his face expressionless. Alicia watches as he approaches. As he gets closer, she looks into his eyes. She has seen the occasional light in his dead eyes over the years, making her wonder if her best friend is still in there. Now his eyes are not just dead. They are cold. Hollow. The Nick of her childhood is long gone. A slight wave of fear washes over her inferno of anger. *Maybe he is going to kill me this time*, she thinks.

He stops in front of her and kneels down. He sets the small wooden box down in her lap and then stands up, stepping back a few paces. He waits and stares at her.

Alicia hesitates before moving, not sure if she wants to know what's in the box now sitting on her lap. He speaks while she hesitates, his voice sharp as it cuts through the air between them.

"Open it."

Her thoughts bring back the pictures of her Penny. The anger inside her resurfaces, chasing the fear away, and she shoves the box off her lap and onto the floor, the wood-on-wood impact echoing throughout the room. A strength she forgot was inside her speaks up. "I'm not your fucking toy anymore, Nick. You want to cut off my last finger so you can feel powerful, then just fucking do it already."

She watches his face as it contorts with rage and then suddenly softens. His eyes remain emotionless. He nods and steps forward, bending down and picking up the box. Instead of setting the box back on her lap, he turns the box so it faces her and unlatches it. Alicia fights the habitual urge to look away from his eyes, to retreat into her thoughts as she has done for so long. He opens the box and holds the lid up, to allow her to see the contents. He waits, silent, staring into her eyes and waiting to see them look down at the box in his hands.

Seconds turn to minutes, and Alicia finally pulls her stare, laced with hate and anger, away from Nick's eyes, and she looks into the box. A pile of ash is in the box, with burn marks all over the inside walls. Not sure what he is showing her, she looks back up at Nick. Only now he's smiling.

"I know seeing the photos of someone from your past life caused you a lot of pain earlier and you have said some things you didn't mean. I love you and will do anything I can to make you happy. So I put those photos in this box for you, so you can keep them and look at them whenever you want."

He closes the box and latches the lid, setting the box down on the arm of her chair.

"Enjoy them, because that is the last you will ever see from your other life. The life I saved you from. You will never have to suffer the pain from your life before me again, and I am sorry I reminded you of how bad it used to be."

Still smiling, he turns away from her and heads back toward the hallway. Alicia watches as he leaves, the angry tears forming in her eyes once again.

Nick pauses before he goes through the wooden door and looks back at her. "I am your husband, your love, and your one. I am only going to say this one last time. If you ever bring up Colin or Penny again, I will bring you their dead bodies, one piece at a time. Enjoy your present, my love. I am going to go get us some dinner. I love you."

The wooden door closes and Alicia hears the lock engage, echoing through the room.

She blinks her eyes and feels the first of her tears fall. She looks at the box on the arm of the chair. Reaching forward with her right index finger, she unlatches the small metal latch, the click uncharacteristically loud in the quiet room. She reaches forward with her left hand and steadies the box while she uses her right hand to open it. A faint heat is radiating from the wooden sides and from the pile of ash they contain.

Alicia runs her index finger through the ash. Near the bottom of the pile, a small, charred corner of a photograph remains. More angry tears spill from her eyes as she fights back a sob. Nick really did put the photos of Penny in this box and then burn them all.

She closes the lid of the box and cleans the ash from her

right index finger by wiping it on the chair arm, watching the black of the ash mark the cloth of the chair.

Another flow of tears escapes her eyes, racing each other down her cheeks to her chin. She reaches forward with her left hand and pushes the box off the arm of the chair. The box slams onto the floor on its side. The impact causes the lid to open, and the ash spills out across the polished floor. Alicia doesn't hear the sound of the box hitting the floor, as she's lost in the sudden realization of what she has to do so she can escape this hell. So she can protect her family. The anger boiling inside her quiets, allowing new feelings to take over. A sense of calm. A sense of purpose.

She looks up at the clock on the wall. A few minutes after nine at night. She will have about an hour and a half before Nick returns from Ellie's with dinner. It shouldn't take her long for what she has to do, but she will have to move quickly.

Pushing herself out of the chair, she kneels next to the overturned box and the ashes spilled on the floor. Using the heel of her right hand, she tries to scoop as much of the ash back into the box as she can. She carefully sets the box upright and closes the lid. She slowly stands up, taking care not to drop the box and once again spill the contents. She steps back from the chair and slowly makes her way up the stairs and into her prison cell, carefully setting the box down on the floor, near the back of the cage.

Alicia steps back from the box and walks over to her cot, stripping the bedding from it. She leaves one of the sheets bundled up on the cot after throwing the blanket and pillows into the corner of the cell. She drags the cot along the stage floor to where the box sits, the metal legs of the cot gouging the polished lacquer of the wood. Satisfied with the position of the cot, Alicia grabs the sheet and slowly crawls onto the cot, very carefully standing up.

With the added height of the cot, she is now able to reach the bars at the top of her cage. Alicia meticulously pushes one end of the sheet over the second-to-last bar, smoothing and straightening the sheet out until it's hanging evenly over the bar. The upper bars of her prison cell run from side to side on the stage versus front to back. With the white sheet hanging over the upper cage bar, it gives her exactly what she needs.

A large canvas to write on.

She carefully gets down off the cot and once again begins to drag it, moving it toward the front of the cage this time, near the door, once again cutting marks into the lacquer. She checks the position of the cot, ensuring there is still adequate room between it and the front of the cage.

She glances at the clock. Almost thirty minutes after nine. She's going to have to hurry.

Returning to the small wooden box and her newly erected white canvas, she opens the box and wets the tip of her right index finger. She dips her finger in the ash inside the box and then begins to write on the canvas. One word after another quickly appears on the sheet, each one requiring her to rewet her finger and dip it in the ash again. Once she's done, she steps back and admires her handiwork. The words are large and very legible, and the near black of the ash stands out in glaring contrast to the white of the sheet.

For the first time in a long time, Alicia smiles. Not one of the fake smiles she puts on out of habit for her captor, but a true smile.

She glances at the clock again. A quarter until ten. Her sense of calm is joined by a sense of urgency. She has to do this before Nick gets back. *This has to work*, she tells herself. *There is no other way.*

Alicia walks to the doorway of the steel-bar-encased cage that Nick calls her bedroom and kneels down, only a couple feet away from the cot. She begins to gather all the slack in her metal leash until she has several of the silver oval-shaped coils next to her. She continues to pull the slack until the chain is almost taut from its anchor point in the wall near the bathroom. After carefully piling the chain onto the cot, Alicia reaches over and pulls the door of her cage closed, trapping the part of the chain coming from the wall under the cage door to prevent it from moving. She repeats the process of climbing onto the cot and bends down, picking up the part of the chain that she estimates is the midpoint between where the chain connects to her leg and where the chain comes into her prison cell. She carefully balances the oval links between her hands and slowly pushes the links over an upper bar of the cage, one that's just past the edge of the cot, toward the now closed door.

Just as she gets the first couple links slightly hanging over the bar and is trying to reposition her hands to push more of the slack over, the weight of the chain pulls the first few links back down and the chain slips away from her grip, the thick metal rings slamming down against the hard wooden floor below and pulling the slack from the cot to the floor as well. The sound is almost like an explosion in the large room and echoes off the walls. The sudden shift of the gathered slack from cot to floor almost causes her to lose her balance and fall over. She quickly puts her right hand between the steel bars overhead and steadies herself.

She looks at the clock through the bars of the cage. Ten fifteen. Time is running out. He could be back any minute. She has to do this now. If Nick catches her, she may never have this opportunity again. She grits her teeth and tries to ignore the pain now coming from the stubs where her fingers used to be.

Alicia renews her efforts and again gets the slack from the chain piled up on the cot. This time she hangs some of the slack over her right shoulder. She carefully stands up and slowly gets the first few links of her leash over the steel bar once more. This time, she uses her only remaining finger to quickly hook one of the links already over the bar and she pulls downward, feeding the chain over the bar until the chain is taut between the bar and the bottom of her cage door. She eyes how much of the chain is hanging down and loops it around the bar one more time, making sure to twist the loop a couple times in the process. The second wrap around the upper cage bar removes the last of the excess slack, leaving the loop of the chain at the perfect height.

Alicia stands on the tiptoes of her right foot to get herself to the height she needs to be, her left hand between two of the overhead bars to maintain her balance. With her right index finger, she carefully works the loop of the chain fully around her neck. The metal is hard and cold against her skin. The two twists in the chain should stop it from coming off her neck once her body weight is hanging from it. It should also stop the chain from pulling her right leg up and causing her to just flip over and hit the floor.

Fresh tears begin to fall down her face as her thoughts turn to her family.

I love you Penny, so very much. I am sorry I wasn't there for you. I'm sorry I won't be there for you. Just know your mother loves you and misses you. Colin, you have always been and always will be my one and only. Take care of our little girl, and I will see you again one day. I will always be with you both, and I hope you can forgive me.

Alicia squeezes her eyes shut and takes a deep breath. In one fluid motion she leans slightly forward and with her right foot kicks away from the cot as hard as she can, pushing it backward and causing it to flip over onto its side. For a split second she feels as though she's floating in midair, until the chain abruptly tightens its cold grip around her neck, causing bright light to explode under her eyelids.

A searing heat fills her chest and her head and continues

growing until it's all she can feel. She thinks of Penny and Colin through the all-encompassing pain until it finally begins to subside.

The bright white light turns to hues of oranges and yellows and reds, until all the colors slowly fade into nothing.

A few minutes later, the room is silent once again.

≈

Nick's smile remains as he makes his way through the woods to the restaurant. He should have known giving those photographs to Alicia would have immediately reminded her of the brainwashing she suffered from her ex-husband. What she said to him after she looked at those photos angered him and made him want to punish her, to drive those thoughts from her mind once again. To drive Colin's poisonous control away once more.

But he forced himself to remain calm. This was his fault. He should have never agreed to get the pictures for her. After he left the main room of their home, trying to calm the sudden rage within, he grabbed one of the smaller wooden storage boxes from upstairs. One with a lid and a latch. In the dark of the warehouse, accompanied by various dust-covered logging equipment, he placed the photos inside the box and lit them on fire with some matches he retrieved from a nearby drawer. The blue-and-orange flames cast large shadows that danced on the walls around him as the pictures burned down to nothing.

Alicia's punishment this time was the box, filled with the ashes of her prior life. The act was a form of symbolism that didn't escape Nick as he gave her the box. Even when she tried to hurt him once more with what she said, he remained calm. He remained the strong, confident man she needs.

The dark outline of the restaurant comes into view as Nick draws closer. He hopes that while he's getting their dinner, his love can look at those ashes and maybe finally be free from her past. Be born again like a phoenix rising from the ashes of her horrible prior life. *Those ashes will set you free, my love*, he thinks, as the parking lot comes into view. *You will rise from those ashes as my phoenix. Reborn back into my dedicated one and only.*

As Nick gets closer, he pauses. There are three vehicles still in the parking lot.

One of them is Colin's truck.

Nick's smile disappears, and he feels a heat begin to radiate from him. His calm is quickly replaced by rage. He kneels down and waits, watching for Colin to leave the restaurant.

He doesn't have to wait long before he sees Colin emerge and walk to the truck. He fights the urge to follow Colin to his next destination and plunge a knife into his throat. Into his heart. It's his fault Alicia is upset with Nick. It's his fault she can't let go of her terrible past. The truck's taillights glow and soon disappear as the vehicle pulls out of the parking lot and turns onto the highway toward the main part of town. He will have to ask his mother why Colin is here this late. Nick keeps waiting for the last two vehicles in the parking lot to drive away before he makes his way to the back door of the restaurant.

Nick makes sure no one is around, as usual, before he enters. He walks down the short hallway, and as the kitchen comes into view on his right, he sees his mother at the prep tables, checking all the condiment bins. He stops at the entrance to the kitchen and waits until his mother sees him.

"Well, don't just stand there and stare at me. Did you get the photos?" she asks him as she looks over in his direction. He nods. "Did you show them to her yet?" she asks. He nods again.

His mother shakes her head and smiles. "And was her reaction what you thought it was going to be? Did she appreciate what you did for her?"

He hesitates before he answers. If he tells her no, she will just lecture him about how it was a foolish idea and he should have known better and how his mother is always right.

He smiles, nods in response, and watches her expression. A surprised look graces her features and then disappears. "I would've expected her to raise quite a fuss, but maybe she really has started to come around. Might be time to consider reuniting Penny with her momma."

Nick doesn't respond. Alicia's reaction tonight was proof that he will never be able to allow her to see Penny. He can't risk losing her or losing the progress they've made over all these years, like he almost did tonight. His mother is convinced they will all be one happy family and living back here at the restaurant one day. The home he shares with his love is not the apartment above this restaurant and can never be. Nick knows this now, since it only took a few photographs to almost change

Alicia back to how she was when she first left her ex for him.

Karen opens the door to the walk-in and grabs a paper bag from a shelf close to the door, speaking to him as she walks back out. "I figured Alicia would've been pretty upset after the photos, so I made you both some burgers for dinner tonight, just the way she likes them. Looks like it might be more of a celebration, though."

She hands him the bag and smiles. "There are also a couple sandwiches for tomorrow in there. And you can thank me later for keeping Colin busy while you were getting those pictures."

Nick nods, still quiet, then turns and leaves. *I didn't need you to keep Colin busy*, he thinks as he steps through the back door and onto the gravel of the parking lot. He swiftly heads back into the forest and makes his way home, the bag of food tucked under his right arm. He walks briskly, anxious to get back to Alicia. To get back to his home. His happiness. His one. He wonders if she is missing him and if she feels bad for saying those hurtful things to him. He wonders if she is anxiously waiting for him to get back as much as he is. It has been a couple months since she had her favorite burger, and Nick will have to thank his mother for thinking of making them tonight. He wonders how his mother knew that Alicia would've been upset by the pictures instead of being happy. *Does she know something I don't?* he wonders. *And if she does, why didn't she say anything when I told her I was going to get them for Alicia?*

Lost in his thoughts, he suddenly sees the dark outline of the logging camp looming and then he's inside the main warehouse, closing and locking the large sliding metal door behind him. His happiness growing, he rushes down the steps two at a time to get back to his love. One door and one hallway later and he's standing in front of the wooden door that separates him from his world. He quickly unlocks the door and swings it open, announcing his return to his beautiful wife.

"Hey, beautiful, I'm home, and I have a special treat for . . ."

His eyes try to comprehend what he's seeing. The bag of food drops from under his right arm and hits the floor, spilling its contents all around Nick's feet. It takes several moments for what he is seeing to register in his mind.

Alicia, his beautiful and perfect Alicia, is hanging by her neck in her room, slightly swaying back and forth in the air. Her arms hang limply at her sides.

"No!" he screams, and takes off toward the stage. "I'm coming, my love! Hold on!"

Nick sprints across the room and up the stairs of the stage, grabbing at the bars of her bedroom door. The tension of the chain under the door makes it difficult to open, but he frantically tugs and pulls until the door's free of the chain.

The sudden slack in the chain causes Alicia's body to drop a couple feet and then stop as the chain is once again pulled tight from the wall anchor. Her right foot and the stump of her left leg are now touching the floor. The chain's grip around her neck continues to hold firm and not let go.

Nick steps into her room and wraps his left arm around her waist, lifting her as high as he can while trying to remove the loop of the chain from around her neck with one hand. Seconds later he has her free from the metal noose. He kicks the overturned cot toward the back of the room, out of the way, and quickly lays her down on the shiny wooden floor.

"Stay with me, my love," he tells her while he checks for her pulse. Nothing. Her skin is still slightly warm to the touch. Her lips are a pale blue. Nick doesn't remember much about CPR, but he puts his hands together and begins chest compressions on her.

One. Two. Three. Four. He keeps counting in his head, unsure when he's supposed to breathe into her mouth. Once he reaches twenty, he guesses he's close and stops compressions. He leans forward and breathes into Alicia's mouth, holding her nose closed like they taught him in school. He resumes compressions until he gets to twenty once again and breathes for her one more time.

He checks her pulse. Still nothing.

Nick leans back and sits down, his back against the cold bars of Alicia's room, slowly realizing there is nothing he can do to bring her back, and looks at the lifeless woman lying on the floor in front of him. Tears well up in his eyes and he begins to cry, his sobs echoing throughout the large room as though laughing at him. Laughing at him for losing her once again. Laughing at him for not being smart enough to save her. Laughing at him for not being enough to keep her happy.

Little by little, Nick regains his composure, and the tears slowly abate. He raises his head from his chest and looks around, noticing something he didn't see before because his focus was on Alicia. One of her sheets is hanging over the bars in the back of her room, with a single sentence written on it, in two lines, in all capital letters.

He reads the sentence and hesitates, blinking his eyes several times as though he doesn't believe what he just read.

He reads it again, feeling the familiar rage inside him spark back into life.

IF I HAVE TO LIVE WITHOUT MY DAUGHTER
AND HUSBAND
THEN YOU HAVE TO LIVE WITHOUT ME

Nick reads the sentence several more times, focusing on one specific word. The more he reads it, the more the inferno of rage within him grows. Husband. She didn't mean him. She meant Colin.

Colin. He rereads the sentence over and over, the anger inside him growing larger and hotter. It's Colin's fault she is dead.

Colin killed his love. His world. His one.

Colin couldn't have her, so he found a way to kill her and take her away from Nick once again.

He stands up and walks over to the hanging sheet, reaches out, and rips it down from the bar. He turns and exits Alicia's room, stepping over the dead body of his wife and walking down the stairs to the chairs they spent countless hours sitting in, enjoying each other's time, love, and company. He tosses the sheet on Alicia's chair, pulls the matches from his pocket, and lights the sheet on fire.

Nick backs up a few steps and sits down on the edge of the stage. He watches as the flames slowly consuming the sheet start spreading to Alicia's chair.

He watches as the fire gets bigger. As it spreads to the various books on the floor and then finally to his own chair. The heat forces him back onto the stage, and he sits down at the front of Alicia's room, his back against the bars.

He watches as the flames leap higher and higher, the smoke overwhelming the ventilation system and slowly forming a thick fog along the ceiling above him.

He watches as the glossy wooden floor beneath the chairs clouds over, the thick layer of wax begins to melt, and the wood underneath begins to burn.

Nick continues to sit there until the flames reach their peak, begin to die down, and then finally extinguish. The smoke makes his eyes water and it hard for his lungs to find air. He ignores the discomforts, the burning in his eyes and his chest a fitting feeling for the fury inside him. He sits there until the smoke fully clears from the room through the struggling air vents. He sits there and lets the rage inside him grow until it's all he can feel.

He looks at the clock on the wall, the clear plastic surface now smudged by smoke. Four in the morning.

Nick wonders what Colin is doing. If he's going to be waking up with a smile, knowing he took Alicia back. If he's laughing at Nick, as though all this was just a game to him. As if Nick's pain is the prize and Colin just won.

The fire within Nick starts to seep out of his skin. He can feel the heat radiating off his body.

If it's games he wants, I have a game for him, he thinks. *Maybe my plan wasn't meant for Alicia after all. Maybe it was meant for Colin.*

He looks back over his left shoulder at the body of his love. His one.

"Don't worry, beautiful, I will make them both pay for what they did to you," he tells her. "I promise."

His gaze moves to the spot where the two chairs used to be. A large section of charred and damaged wood floor encompasses two piles of ash with metal springs exposed. *OK, Colin. You want to take away my world, I will take away yours.*

He stands up and walks across the stage and down the steps. He continues until he's standing in the middle of the charred, ash-covered section of the floor. He ignores the still-smoldering coals of heat burning their way through his shoes to his feet.

He raises his arms, his palms facing upward, until they're even with his shoulders.

He tilts his head back and closes his eyes, raising his face toward the smoke-stained ceiling as though he is now the phoenix reborn.

With a rage-filled voice that fills every inch of the room, he screams.

ABOUT THE AUTHOR

RJ Sundean was born in upstate New York but currently resides in central Florida with his spoiled teenage cat. He has bachelor degrees in both clinical psychology and business administration, as well as served two enlistment terms in the Army as a paratrooper. In his spare time, RJ enjoys working on his Jeep Wrangler, partaking of a nice cigar with a glass of bourbon, and spending time in his kitchen cooking.

To stay up to date with RJ, please visit his website:

rjsundean.com

www.ingramcontent.com/pod-product-compliance
Lightning Source LLC
Chambersburg PA
CBHW031648100726
47898CB00006B/2023